THE PALE HORSE

ALSO BY AGATHA CHRISTIE

* novelized by Charles Osborne   † contributor

Agatha Christie®

The Pale Horse

HarperCollins*Publishers*

HarperCollins*Publishers* Ltd
1 London Bridge Street
London SE1 9GF
www.harpercollins.co.uk

This paperback edition 2017
6

First published in Great Britain by
Collins, The Crime Club 1961

The Pale Horse™ is a trade mark of Agatha Christie Limited
and Agatha Christie® and the Agatha Christie Signature are
registered trade marks of Agatha Christie Limited in the UK and elsewhere.
Copyright © 1961 Agatha Christie Limited. All rights reserved.
www.agathachristie.com

A catalogue record for this book is available from the British Library

ISBN 978-0-00-819638-7 (PB)
ISBN 978-0-00-825611-1 (POD PB)

Set in Sabon LT Std by Palimpsest Book Production Limited, Falkirk, Stirlingshire
Printed and bound in Great Britain by
CPI Group (UK) Ltd, Croydon, CR0 4YY

MIX
Paper from
responsible sources
FSC® C007454

FSC™ is a non-profit international organisation established to promote
the responsible management of the world's forests. Products carrying the
FSC label are independently certified to assure consumers that they come
from forests that are managed to meet the social, economic and
ecological needs of present and future generations,
and other controlled sources.

Find out more about HarperCollins and the environment at
www.harpercollins.co.uk/green

To John and Helen Mildmay White
with many thanks for the opportunity
given me to see justice done

FOREWORD

by Mark Easterbrook

There are two methods, it seems to me, of approaching this strange business of the Pale Horse. In spite of the dictum of the White King, it is difficult to achieve simplicity. One cannot, that is to say, 'Begin at the beginning, go on to the end, and then stop.' For where is the beginning?

To a historian, that always is the difficulty. At what point in history does one particular portion of history begin?

In this case, you can begin at the moment when Father Gorman set forth from his presbytery to visit a dying woman. Or you can start before that, on a certain evening in Chelsea.

Perhaps, since I am writing the greater part of this narrative myself, it is there that I should begin.

CHAPTER 1

Mark Easterbrook's Narrative

The Espresso machine behind my shoulder hissed like an angry snake. The noise it made had a sinister, not to say devilish, suggestion about it. Perhaps, I reflected, most of our contemporary noises carry that implication. The intimidating angry scream of jet planes as they flash across the sky; the slow menacing rumble of a tube train approaching through its tunnel; the heavy road transport that shakes the very foundations of your house . . . Even the minor domestic noises of today, beneficial in action though they may be, yet carry a kind of alert. The dish-washers, the refrigerators, the pressure cookers, the whining vacuum cleaners—'Be careful,' they all seem to say. 'I am a genie harnessed to your service, but if your control of me fails . . .'

A dangerous world—that was it, a dangerous world.

I stirred the foaming cup placed in front of me. It smelt pleasant.

'What else will you have? Nice banana and bacon sandwich?'

It seemed an odd juxtaposition to me. Bananas I connected with my childhood—or occasionally *flambé* with sugar and rum. Bacon, in my mind, was firmly associated with eggs. However, when in Chelsea, eat as Chelsea does. I agreed to a nice banana and bacon sandwich.

Although I lived in Chelsea—that is to say, I had had a furnished flat there for the last three months—I was in every other way a stranger in these parts. I was writing a book on certain aspects of Mogul architecture, but for that purpose I could have lived in Hampstead or Bloomsbury or Streatham or Chelsea and it would have been all the same to me. I was oblivious of my surroundings except for the tools of my trade, and the neighbourhood in which I lived was completely indifferent to me, I existed in a world of my own.

On this particular evening, however, I had suffered from one of those sudden revulsions that all writers know.

Mogul architecture, Mogul Emperors, the Mogul way of life—and all the fascinating problems it raised, became suddenly as dust and ashes. What did they matter? Why did I want to write about them?

I flicked back various pages, rereading what I had written. It all seemed to me uniformly bad—poorly written and singularly devoid of interest. Whoever had said 'History is bunk' (Henry Ford?) had been absolutely right.

I pushed back my manuscript with loathing, got up and looked at my watch. The time was close on eleven p.m. I tried to remember if I had had dinner . . . From my inner sensations I thought not. Lunch, yes, at the Athenaeum. That was a long time ago.

I went and looked into the refrigerator. There was a small remnant of desiccated tongue. I looked at it without favour. So it was that I wandered out into the King's Road, and eventually turned into an Espresso Coffee Bar with the name Luigi written in red neon light across its window, and was now contemplating a bacon and banana sandwich whilst I reflected on the sinister implications of present-day noises and their atmospheric effects.

All of them, I thought, had something in common with my early memories of pantomime. Davy Jones arriving from his locker in clouds of smoke! Trap doors and windows that exuded the infernal powers of evil, challenging and defying a Good Fairy Diamond, or some such name, who in turn waved an inadequate-looking wand and recited hopeful platitudes as to the ultimate triumph of good in a flat voice, thus prefacing the inevitable 'song of the moment' which never had anything to do with the story of that particular pantomime.

It came to me suddenly that evil was, perhaps, necessarily always more impressive than good. It *had* to make a show! It had to startle and challenge! It was instability attacking stability. And in the end, I thought, stability will always win. Stability can survive the triteness of Good Fairy Diamond; the flat voice, the rhymed couplet, even the irrelevant vocal statement of 'There's a Winding Road runs down the Hill, To the Olde World Town I love.' All very poor weapons it would seem, and yet those weapons would inevitably prevail. The pantomime would end in the way it always ended. The staircase, and the descending cast in order of seniority, with Good Fairy Diamond, practising the Christian virtue of humility and not seeking to be first (or, in this case, last) but arriving about half-way through the procession, side by side with her late opponent, now seen to be no longer the snarling Demon King breathing fire and brimstone, but just a man dressed up in red tights.

The Espresso hissed again in my ear. I signalled for another cup of coffee and looked around me. A sister of mine was always accusing me of not being observant, not noticing what was going on. 'You live in a world of your own,' she would say accusingly. Now, with a feeling of conscious virtue, I took note of what was going on. It was almost impossible not to read about the coffee bars of Chelsea and their patrons every day in the newspapers; this was my chance to make my own appraisal of contemporary life.

It was rather dark in the Espresso, so you could not see very clearly. The clientele were almost all young people. They were, I supposed vaguely, what was called the off-beat generation. The girls looked, as girls always did look to me nowadays, dirty. They also seemed to be much too warmly dressed. I had noticed that when I had gone out a few weeks ago to dine with some friends. The girl who had sat next to me had been about twenty. The restaurant was hot, but she had worn a yellow wool pullover, a black skirt and black woollen stockings, and the perspiration poured down her face all through the meal. She smelt of perspiration-soaked wool and also, strongly, of unwashed hair. She was said, according to my friends, to be very attractive. Not to me! My only reaction was a yearning to throw her into a hot bath, give her a cake of soap and urge her to get on with it! Which just showed, I suppose, how out of touch with the times I was. Perhaps it came of having lived abroad so much. I recalled with pleasure Indian women with their beautifully-coiled black hair, and their saris of pure bright colours hanging in graceful folds, and the rhythmic sway of their bodies as they walked . . .

I was recalled from these pleasant thoughts by a sudden accentuation of noise. Two young women at the table next to me had started a quarrel. The young men who were with them tried to adjust things, but without avail.

Suddenly they were screaming at each other. One girl slapped the other's face, the second dragged the first from her chair. They fought each other like fishwives, screaming abuse hysterically. One was a tousled red-head, the other a lank-haired blonde.

What the quarrel was about, apart from terms of abuse, I did not gather. Cries and catcalls arose from other tables.

'Attagirl! Sock her, Lou!'

The proprietor behind the bar, a slim Italian-looking fellow with sideburns, whom I had taken to be Luigi, came to intervene in a voice that was pure cockney London.

'Nah then—break it up—break it up—You'll 'ave the whole street in in a minute. You'll 'ave the coppers here. Stop it, I say.'

But the lank blonde had the red-head by the hair and was tugging furiously as she screamed:

'You're nothing but a man-stealing bitch!'

'Bitch yourself.'

Luigi and the two embarrassed escorts forced the girls apart. In the blonde's fingers were large tufts of red hair.

She held them aloft gleefully, then dropped them on the floor.

The door from the street was pushed open and Authority, dressed in blue, stood on the threshold and uttered the regulation words majestically.

'What's going on here?'

Immediately a common front was presented to the enemy.

'Just a bit of fun,' said one of the young men.

'That's all,' said Luigi. 'Just a bit of fun among friends.'

With his foot he kicked the tufts of hair adroitly under the nearest table. The contestants smiled at each other in false amnesty.

The policeman looked at everybody suspiciously.

'We're just going now,' said the blonde sweetly. 'Come on, Doug.'

By a coincidence several other people were just going. Authority watched them go grimly. His eye said that he was overlooking it *this* time, but he'd got his eye on them. He withdrew slowly.

The red-head's escort paid the check.

'You all right?' said Luigi to the girl who was adjusting a headscarf. 'Lou served you pretty bad, tearing out your hair by the roots like that.'

'It didn't hurt,' said the girl nonchalantly. She smiled at him. 'Sorry for the row, Luigi.'

The party went out. The bar was now practically empty. I felt in my pocket for change.

'She's a sport all right,' said Luigi approvingly, watching the door close. He seized a floor brush and swept the tufts of red hair behind the counter.

'It must have been agony,' I said.

'*I'd* have hollered if it had been me,' admitted Luigi. 'But she's a real sport, Tommy is.'

'You know her well?'

'Oh, she's in here most evenings. Tuckerton, that's her name, Thomasina Tuckerton, if you want the whole set out. But Tommy Tucker's what she's called round here. Stinking rich, too. Her old man left her a fortune, and what does she go and do? Comes to Chelsea, lives in a slummy room half-way to Wandsworth Bridge, and mooches around with a gang all doing the same thing. Beats me, half of that crowd's got money. Could have any mortal thing they want; stay at the Ritz if they liked. But they seem to get a kick out of living the way they do. Yes—it beats me.'

'It wouldn't be your choice?'

'Ar, I've got sense!' said Luigi. 'As it is, I just cash in.'

I rose to go and asked what the quarrel was about.

'Oh, Tommy's got hold of the other girl's boy friend. He's not worth fighting about, believe me!'

'The other girl seemed to think he was,' I observed.

'Oh, Lou's very romantic,' said Luigi tolerantly.

It was not my idea of romance, but I did not say so.

It must have been about a week later that my eye was caught by a name in the Deaths column of *The Times*.

TUCKERTON. On October 2nd at Fallowfield Nursing Home, Amberley, Thomasina Ann, aged twenty, only daughter of the late Thomas Tuckerton, Esq., of Carrington Park, Amberley, Surrey. Funeral private. No flowers.

No flowers for poor Tommy Tucker; and no more 'kicks' out of life in Chelsea. I felt a sudden fleeting compassion for the Tommy Tuckers of today. Yet after all, I reminded myself, how did I know that my view was the right one? Who was I to pronounce it a wasted life? Perhaps it was *my* life, my quiet scholarly life, immersed in books, shut off from the world, that was the wasted one. Life at second hand. Be honest now, was *I* getting kicks out of life? A very unfamiliar idea! The truth was, of course, that I didn't want kicks. But there again, perhaps I ought to? An unfamiliar and not very welcome thought.

I dismissed Tommy Tucker from my thoughts, and turned to my correspondence.

The principal item was a letter from my cousin Rhoda Despard, asking me to do her a favour. I grasped at this, since I was not feeling in the mood for work this morning, and it made a splendid excuse for postponing it.

I went out into King's Road, hailed a taxi, and was driven to the residence of a friend of mine, a Mrs Ariadne Oliver.

Mrs Oliver was a well-known writer of detective stories. Her maid, Milly, was an efficient dragon who guarded her mistress from the onslaughts of the outside world.

I raised my eyebrows inquiringly, in an unspoken question. Milly nodded a vehement head.

'You'd better go right up, Mr Mark,' she said. 'She's in

a mood this morning. You may be able to help her snap out of it.'

I mounted two flights of stairs, tapped lightly on a door, and walked in without waiting for encouragement. Mrs Oliver's workroom was a good-sized room, the walls papered with exotic birds nesting in tropical foliage. Mrs Oliver herself, in a state apparently bordering on insanity, was prowling round the room, muttering to herself. She threw me a brief uninterested glance and continued to prowl. Her eyes, unfocused, swept round the walls, glanced out of the window, and occasionally closed in what appeared to be a spasm of agony.

'But why,' demanded Mrs Oliver of the universe, 'why doesn't the idiot say at once that he *saw* the cockatoo? Why shouldn't he? He couldn't have helped seeing it! But if he *does* mention it, it ruins everything. There must be a way . . . there must be . . .'

She groaned, ran her fingers through her short grey hair and clutched it in a frenzied hand. Then, looking at me with suddenly focused eyes, she said, 'Hallo, Mark. I'm going mad,' and resumed her complaint.

'And then there's Monica. The nicer I try to make her, the more irritating she gets . . . Such a stupid girl . . . Smug, too! Monica . . . Monica? I believe the name's wrong. Nancy? Would that be better? Joan? Everybody is always Joan. Anne is the same. Susan? I've had a Susan. Lucia? *Lucia?* Lucia? I believe I can *see* a Lucia. Red-haired. Polo-necked jumper . . . Black tights? Black stockings, anyway.'

This momentary gleam of good cheer was eclipsed by the memory of the cockatoo problem, and Mrs Oliver

11

resumed her unhappy prowling, picking up things off tables unseeingly and putting them down again somewhere else. She fitted with some care her spectacle case into a lacquered box which already contained a Chinese fan and then gave a deep sigh and said:

'I'm glad it's you.'

'That's very nice of you.'

'It might have been anybody. Some silly woman who wanted me to open a bazaar, or the man about Milly's insurance card which Milly absolutely refuses to have—or the plumber (but that would be too much good fortune, wouldn't it?). Or, it might be someone wanting an interview—asking me all those embarrassing questions which are always the same every time. What made you first think of taking up writing? How many books have you written? How much money do you make? Etc. etc. I never know the answers to any of them and it makes me look such a fool. Not that any of that matters because I think I am going mad, over this cockatoo business.'

'Something that won't jell?' I said sympathetically. 'Perhaps I'd better go away.'

'No, don't. At any rate you're a distraction.'

I accepted this doubtful compliment.

'Do you want a cigarette?' Mrs Oliver asked with vague hospitality. 'There are some somewhere. Look in the typewriter lid.'

'I've got my own, thanks. Have one. Oh no, you don't smoke.'

'Or drink,' said Mrs Oliver. 'I wish I did. Like those American detectives that always have pints of rye conveniently in their collar drawers. It seems to solve all their problems. You know, Mark, I really can't think how anyone ever gets away with a murder in real life. It seems to me that the moment you've done a murder the whole thing is so terribly obvious.'

'Nonsense. You've done lots of them.'

'Fifty-five at least,' said Mrs Oliver. 'The murder part is quite easy and simple. It's the covering up that's so difficult. I mean, why *should* it be anyone else but you? You stick out a mile.'

'Not in the finished article,' I said.

'Ah, but what it costs me,' said Mrs Oliver darkly. 'Say what you like, it's not *natural* for five or six people to be on the spot when B is murdered and all have a motive for killing B—unless, that is, B is absolutely madly unpleasant and in that case nobody will mind whether he's been killed or not, and doesn't care in the least who's done it.'

'I see your problem,' I said. 'But if you've dealt with it successfully fifty-five times, you will manage to deal with it once again.'

'That's what I tell myself,' said Mrs Oliver, 'over and over again, but every single time I can't believe it, and so I'm in agony.'

She seized her hair again and tugged it violently.

'Don't,' I cried. 'You'll have it out by the roots.'

'Nonsense,' said Mrs Oliver. 'Hair's tough. Though when I had measles at fourteen with a very high temperature, it did come out—all round the front. Most shaming. And it was six whole months before it grew properly again. Awful for a girl—girls mind so. I thought of it yesterday

13

when I was visiting Mary Delafontaine in that nursing home. Her hair was coming out just like mine did. She said she'd have to get a false front when she was better. If you're sixty it doesn't always grow again, I believe.'

'I saw a girl pull out another girl's hair by the roots the other night,' I said. I was conscious of a slight note of pride in my voice as one who has seen life.

'What extraordinary places have you been going to?' asked Mrs Oliver.

'This was in a coffee bar in Chelsea.'

'Oh *Chelsea!*' said Mrs Oliver. 'Everything happens there, I believe. Beatniks and sputniks and squares and the beat generation. I don't write about them much because I'm so afraid of getting the terms wrong. It's safer, I think, to stick to what you know.'

'Such as?'

'People on cruises, and in hotels, and what goes on in hospitals, and on parish councils—and sales of work—and music festivals, and girls in shops, and committees and daily women, and young men and girls who hike round the world in the interests of science, and shop assistants—'

She paused, out of breath.

'That seems fairly comprehensive to be getting on with,' I said.

'All the same, you might take me out to a coffee bar in Chelsea some time—just to widen my experience,' said Mrs Oliver wistfully.

'Any time you say. Tonight?'

'Not tonight. I'm too busy writing or rather worrying because I can't write. That's really the most tiresome thing about writing—though everything is tiresome really, except the one moment when you get what you think is going to be a wonderful idea, and can hardly wait to begin. Tell me, Mark, do you think it is possible to kill someone by remote control?'

'What do you mean by remote control? Press a button and set off a radioactive death ray?'

'No, no, not science fiction. I suppose,' she paused doubt-fully, 'I really mean black magic.'

'Wax figures and pins in them?'

'Oh, wax figures are right out,' said Mrs Oliver scorn-fully. 'But queer things do happen—in Africa or the West Indies. People are always telling you so. How natives just curl up and die. Voodoo—or ju-ju . . . Anyway, you know what I mean.'

I said that much of that was attributed nowadays to the power of suggestion. Word is always conveyed to the victim that his death has been decreed by the medicine-man—and his subconscious does the rest.

Mrs Oliver snorted.

'If anyone hinted to me that I had been doomed to lie down and die, I'd take a pleasure in thwarting their expec-tations!'

I laughed.

'You've got centuries of good Occidental sceptical blood in your veins. No predispositions.'

'Then you think it *can* happen?'

'I don't know enough about the subject to judge. What put it into your head? Is your new masterpiece to be Murder by Suggestion?'

'No, indeed. Good old-fashioned rat poison or arsenic is good enough for me. Or the reliable blunt instrument. *Not* firearms if possible. Firearms are so tricky. But you didn't come here to talk to me about my books.'

'Frankly no—The fact is that my cousin Rhoda Despard has got a church fête and—'

'Never again!' said Mrs Oliver. 'You know what happened last time? I arranged a Murder Hunt, and the first thing that happened was a *real corpse*. I've never quite got over it!'

'It's not a Murder Hunt. All you'd have to do would be to sit in a tent and sign your own books—at five bob a time.'

'We-e-l-l-l,' said Mrs Oliver doubtfully. 'That might be all right. I shouldn't have to open the fête? Or say silly things? Or have to wear a hat?'

None of these things, I assured her, would be required of her.

'And it would only be for an hour or two,' I said coaxingly. 'After that, there'll be a cricket match—no, I suppose not this time of year. Children dancing, perhaps. Or a fancy dress competition—'

Mrs Oliver interrupted me with a wild scream.

'That's it,' she cried. '*A cricket ball!* Of course! He sees it from the window . . . rising up in the air . . . and it distracts him—and so he never mentions the cockatoo! What a good thing you came, Mark. You've been wonderful.'

'I don't quite see—'

'Perhaps not, but I do,' said Mrs Oliver. 'It's all rather complicated, and I don't want to waste time explaining.

Nice as it's been to see you, what I'd really like you to do now is to go away. At once.'

'Certainly. About the fête—'

'I'll think about it. Don't worry me now. Now where on earth did I put my spectacles? Really, the way things just disappear . . .'

CHAPTER 2

Mrs Gerahty opened the door of the presbytery in her usual sharp pouncing style. It was less like answering a bell, than a triumphant manoeuvre expressing the sentiment 'I've caught you this time!'

'Well now, and what would you be wanting?' she demanded belligerently.

There was a boy on the doorstep, a very negligible looking boy—a boy not easily noticeable nor easily remembered—a boy like a lot of other boys. He sniffed because he had a cold in his head.

'Is this the priest's place?'

'Is it Father Gorman you're wanting?'

'He's wanted,' said the boy.

'Who wants him and where and what for?'

'Benthall Street. Twenty-three. Woman as says she's dying. Mrs Coppins sent me. This is a Carthlick place all right, isn't it? Woman says the vicar won't do.'

Mrs Gerahty reassured him on this essential point, told him to stop where he was and retired into the presbytery.

Some three minutes later a tall elderly priest came out carrying a small leather case in his hand.

'I'm Father Gorman,' he said. 'Benthall Street? That's round by the railway yards, isn't it?'

''Sright. Not more than a step, it isn't.'

They set out together, the priest walking with a free striding step.

'Mrs—Coppins, did you say? Is that the name?'

'She's the one what owns the house. Lets rooms, she does. It's one of the lodgers wants you. Name of Davis, I think.'

'Davis. I wonder now. I don't remember—'

'She's one of you all right. Carthlick, I mean. Said as no vicar would do.'

The priest nodded. They came to Benthall Street in a very short time. The boy indicated a tall dingy house in a row of other tall dingy houses.

'That's it.'

'Aren't you coming in?'

'I don't belong. Mrs C. give me a bob to take the message.'

'I see. What's your name?'

'Mike Potter.'

'Thank you, Mike.'

'You're welcome,' said Mike, and went off whistling. The imminence of death for someone else did not affect him.

The door of No. 23 opened and Mrs Coppins, a large red-faced woman, stood on the threshold and welcomed the visitor with enthusiasm.

'Come in, come in. She's bad, I'd say. Ought to be in hospital, not here. I've rung up, but goodness knows when anybody will come nowadays. Six hours my sister's husband had to wait when he broke his leg. Disgraceful, I call it. Health Service, indeed! Take your money and when you want them where are they?'

She was preceding the priest up the narrow stairs as she talked.

'What's the matter with her?'

''Flu's what she's had. Seemed better. Went out too soon I'd say. Anyway she comes in last night looking like death. Took to her bed. Wouldn't eat anything. Didn't want a doctor. This morning I could see she was in a raging fever. Gone to her lungs.'

'Pneumonia?'

Mrs Coppins, out of breath by now, made a noise like a steam engine, which seemed to signify assent. She flung open a door, stood aside to let Father Gorman go in, said over his shoulder: 'Here's the Reverend for you. *Now* you'll be all right!' in a spuriously cheerful way, and retired.

Father Gorman advanced. The room, furnished with old-fashioned Victorian furniture, was clean and neat. In the bed near the window a woman turned her head feebly. That she was very ill, the priest saw at once.

'You've come . . . There isn't much time—' she spoke between panting breaths.'. . . Wickedness . . . such wickedness . . . I must . . . I must . . . I can't die like this . . . Confess—confess—my sin—grievous—grievous . . .' the eyes wandered . . . half closed . . .

A rambling monotone of words came from her lips.

Father Gorman came to the bed. He spoke as he had spoken so often—so very often. Words of authority—of

20

reassurance . . . the words of his calling and of his belief. Peace came into the room . . . The agony went out of the tortured eyes . . .

Then, as the priest ended his ministry, the dying woman spoke again.

'Stopped . . . It must be stopped . . . You will . . .'

The priest spoke with reassuring authority.

'I will do what is necessary. You can trust me . . .'

A doctor and an ambulance arrived simultaneously a little later. Mrs Coppins received them with gloomy triumph.

'Too late as usual!' she said. 'She's gone . . .'

Father Gorman walked back through the gathering twilight. There would be fog tonight, it was growing denser rapidly. He paused for a moment, frowning. Such a fantastic extraordinary story . . . How much of it was born of delirium and high fever? *Some* of it was true, of course—but how much? Anyway it was important to make a note of certain names whilst they were fresh in his memory. The St Francis Guild would be assembled when he got back. He turned abruptly into a small café, ordered a cup of coffee and sat down. He felt in the pocket of his cassock. Ah, Mrs Gerahty—he'd asked her to mend the lining. As usual, she hadn't! His notebook and a loose pencil and the few coins he carried about him, had gone through to the lining. He prised up a coin or two and the pencil, but the notebook was too difficult. The coffee came, and he asked if he could have a piece of paper.

'This do you?'

It was a torn paper bag. Father Gorman nodded and took it. He began to write—the *names*—it was important not to forget the names. Names were the sort of thing he did forget . . .

The café door opened and three young lads in Edwardian dress came in and sat down noisily.

Father Gorman finished his memorandum. He folded up the scrap of paper and was about to shove it into his pocket when he remembered the hole. He did what he had often done before, pressed the folded scrap down into his shoe.

A man came in quietly and sat down in a far corner. Father Gorman took a sip or two of the weak coffee for politeness' sake, called for his bill, and paid. Then he got up and went out.

The man who had just come in seemed to change his mind. He looked at his watch as though he had mistaken the time, got up, and hurried out.

The fog was coming on fast. Father Gorman quickened his steps. He knew his district very well. He took a short-cut by turning down the small street which ran close by the railway. He may have been conscious of steps behind him but he thought nothing of them. Why should he?

The blow from the cosh caught him completely unaware. He heeled forward and fell . . .

Dr Corrigan, whistling 'Father O'Flynn', walked into the D.D.I.'s room and addressed Divisional Detective Inspector Lejeune in a chatty manner.

'I've done your padre for you,' he said.

'And the result?'

'We'll save the technical terms for the coroner. Well and truly coshed. First blow probably killed him, but whoever it was made sure. Quite a nasty business.'

'Yes,' said Lejeune.

He was a sturdy man, dark haired and grey eyed. He had a misleadingly quiet manner, but his gestures were sometimes surprisingly graphic and betrayed his French Huguenot ancestry.

He said thoughtfully:

'Nastier than would be necessary for robbery?'

'Was it robbery?' asked the doctor.

'One supposes so. His pockets were turned out and the lining of his cassock ripped.'

'They couldn't have hoped for much,' said Corrigan. 'Poor as a rat, most of these parish priests.'

'They battered his head in—to make sure,' mused Lejeune. 'One would like to know *why*.'

'Two possible answers,' said Corrigan. 'One, it was done by a vicious-minded young thug, who likes violence for violence's sake—there are plenty of them about these days, more's the pity.'

'And the other answer?'

The doctor shrugged his shoulders.

'Somebody had it in for your Father Gorman. Was that likely?'

Lejeune shook his head.

'Most unlikely. He was a popular man, well loved in the district. No enemies, as far as one can hear. And robbery's unlikely. Unless—'

'Unless what?' asked Corrigan. 'The police have a clue! Am I right?'

'He did have something on him that wasn't taken away. It was in his shoe, as a matter of fact.'

Corrigan whistled.

'Sounds like a spy story.'

Lejeune smiled.

'It's much simpler than that. He had a hole in his pocket. Sergeant Pine talked to his housekeeper. She's a bit of a slattern, it seems. Didn't keep his clothes mended in the way she might have done. She admitted that, now and again, Father Gorman would thrust a paper or a letter down the inside of his shoe—to prevent it from going down into the lining of his cassock.'

'And the killer didn't know that?'

'The killer never thought of that! Assuming, that is, that this piece of paper is what he may have been wanting—rather than a miserly amount of small change.'

'What was on the paper?'

Lejeune reached into a drawer and took out a flimsy piece of creased paper.

'Just a list of names,' he said.

Corrigan looked at it curiously.

Ormerod
Sandford
Parkinson
Hesketh-Dubois
Shaw
Harmondsworth

Tuckerton
Corrigan?
Delafontaine?

His eyebrows rose.

'I see *I'm* on the list!'

'Do any of the names mean anything to you?' asked the inspector.

'None of them.'

'And you've never met Father Gorman?'

'Never.'

'Then you won't be able to help us much.'

'Any ideas as to what this list means—if anything?'

Lejeune did not reply directly.

'A boy called at Father Gorman's about seven o'clock in the evening. Said a woman was dying and wanted the priest. Father Gorman went with him.'

'Where to? If you know?'

'We know. It didn't take long to check up. Twenty-three Benthall Street. House owned by a woman named Coppins. The sick woman was a Mrs Davis. The priest got there at a quarter past seven and was with her for about half an hour. Mrs Davis died just before the ambulance arrived to take her to hospital.'

'I see.'

'The next we hear of Father Gorman is at Tony's Place, a small down-at-heel café. Quite decent, nothing criminal about it, serves refreshment of poor quality and isn't much patronised. Father Gorman asked for a cup of coffee. Then apparently he felt in his pocket, couldn't find what he wanted and asked the proprietor, Tony, for a piece of paper. This—' he gestured with his finger, 'is the piece of paper.'

'And then?'

'When Tony brought the coffee, the priest was writing on the paper. Shortly afterwards he left, leaving his coffee practically untasted (for which I don't blame him), having completed this list and shoved it into his shoe.'

'Anybody else in the place?'

'Three boys of the Teddy boy type came in and sat at one table and an elderly man came in and sat at another. The latter went away without ordering.'

'He followed the priest?'

'Could be. Tony didn't notice when he went. Didn't notice what he looked like, either. Described him as an inconspicuous type of man. Respectable. The kind of man that looks like everybody else. Medium height, he thinks, dark blue overcoat—or could be brown. Not very dark and not very fair. No reason he should have had anything to do with it. One just doesn't know. He hasn't come forward to say he saw the priest in Tony's place—but it's early days yet. We're asking for anyone who saw Father Gorman between a quarter to eight and eight-fifteen to communicate with us. Only two people so far have responded: a woman and a chemist who had a shop nearby. I'll be going to see them presently. His body was found at eight-fifteen by two small boys in West Street—you know it? Practically an alleyway, bounded by the railway on one side. The rest—you know.'

Corrigan nodded. He tapped the paper.

'What's your feeling about this?'

'I think it's important,' said Lejeune.

'The dying woman told him something and he got these names down on paper as soon as he could before he forgot them? The only thing is—would he have done that if he'd been told under seal of the confessional?'

'It needn't have been under a seal of secrecy,' said Lejeune. 'Suppose, for instance, these names have a connection of—say, blackmail—'

'That's your idea, is it?'

'I haven't any ideas yet. This is just a working hypothesis. These people were being blackmailed. The dying woman was either the blackmailer, or she knew about the blackmail. I'd say that the general idea was, repentance, confession, and a wish to make reparation as far as possible. Father Gorman assumed the responsibility.'

'And then?'

'Everything else is conjectural,' said Lejeune. 'Say it was a paying racket, and someone didn't want it to stop paying. Someone knew Mrs Davis was dying and that she'd sent for the priest. The rest follows.'

'I wonder now,' said Corrigan, studying the paper again. 'Why do you think there's an interrogation mark after the last two names?'

'It could be that Father Gorman wasn't sure he'd remembered those two names correctly.'

'It might have been Mulligan instead of Corrigan,' agreed the doctor with a grin. 'That's likely enough. But I'd say that with a name like Delafontaine, either you'd remember it or you wouldn't—if you know what I mean. It's odd

27

that there isn't a single address—' He read down the list again.

'Parkinson—lots of Parkinsons. Sandford, not uncommon—Hesketh-Dubois—that's a bit of a mouthful. Can't be many of them.'

On a sudden impulse he leaned forward and took the telephone directory from the desk.

'E to L. Let's see. Hesketh, Mrs A . . . John and Co., Plumbers . . . Sir Isidore. Ah! here we are! Hesketh-Dubois, Lady, Forty-nine, Ellesmere Square, S.W.1. What say we just ring her up?'

'Saying what?'

'Inspiration will come,' said Doctor Corrigan airily.

'Go ahead,' said Lejeune.

'What?' Corrigan stared at him.

'I said go ahead,' Lejeune spoke airily. 'Don't look so taken aback.' He himself picked up the receiver. 'Give me an outside line.' He looked at Corrigan. 'Number?'

'Grosvenor 64578.'

Lejeune repeated it, then handed the receiver over to Corrigan.

'Enjoy yourself,' he said.

Faintly puzzled, Corrigan looked at him as he waited. The ringing tone continued for some time before anyone answered. Then, interspersed with heavy breathing, a woman's voice said:

'Grosvenor 64578.'

'Is that Lady Hesketh-Dubois's house?'

'Well—well, yes—I mean—'

Doctor Corrigan ignored these uncertainties.

28

'Can I speak to her, please?'

'No, that you can't do! Lady Hesketh-Dubois died last April.'

'Oh!' Startled, Dr Corrigan ignored the 'Who is it speaking, please?' and gently replaced the receiver.

He looked coldly at Inspector Lejeune.

'So that's why you were so ready to let me ring up.'

Lejeune smiled maliciously.

'We don't really neglect the obvious,' he pointed out.

'Last April,' said Corrigan thoughtfully. 'Five months ago. Five months since blackmail or whatever it was has failed to worry her. She didn't commit suicide, or anything like that?'

'No. She died of a tumour on the brain.'

'So now we start again,' said Corrigan, looking down at the list.

Lejeune sighed.

'We don't really know that list had anything to do with it,' he pointed out. 'It may have been just an ordinary coshing on a foggy night—and precious little hope of finding who did it unless we have a piece of luck . . .'

Dr Corrigan said:

'Do you mind if I continue to concentrate on this list?'

'Go ahead. I wish you all the luck in the world.'

'Meaning *I'm* not likely to get anywhere if *you* haven't! Don't be too sure. I shall concentrate on Corrigan. Mr or Mrs or Miss Corrigan—with a big interrogation mark.'

CHAPTER 3

'Well, really, Mr Lejeune, I don't see what more I can tell you! I told it all before to your sergeant. *I* don't know who Mrs Davis was, or where she came from. She'd been with me about six months. She paid her rent regular, and she seemed a nice quiet respectable person, and what more you expect me to say I'm sure I don't know.'

Mrs Coppins paused for breath and looked at Lejeune with some displeasure. He gave her the gentle melancholy smile which he knew by experience was not without its effect.

'Not that I wouldn't be willing to help if I could,' she amended.

'Thank you. That's what we need—help. Women know— they feel instinctively—so much more than a man can know.'

It was a good gambit, and it worked.

'Ah,' said Mrs Coppins. 'I wish Coppins could hear you. So hoity-toity and off-hand he always was. "Saying you know things when you haven't got anything to go on!" he'd say and snort. And nine times out of ten I was right.'

30

'That's why I'd like to hear what ideas you have about Mrs Davis. Was she—an unhappy woman, do you think?'

'Now as to that—no, I wouldn't say so. Businesslike. That's what she always seemed. Methodical. As though she'd got her life planned and was acting accordingly. She had a job, I understand, with one of these consumer research associations. Going around and asking people what soap powder they used, or flour, and what they spend on their weekly budget and how it's divided up. Of course I've always felt that sort of thing is snooping really—and why the Government or anyone else wants to know beats me! All you hear at the end of it is only what everybody has known perfectly well all along—but there, there's a craze for that sort of thing nowadays. And if you've got to have it, I should say that poor Mrs Davis would do the job very nicely. A pleasant manner, not nosy, just businesslike and matter-of-fact.'

'You don't know the actual name of the firm or association that employed her?'

'No, I don't, I'm afraid.'

'Did she ever mention relatives—?'

'No. I gathered she was a widow and had lost her husband many years ago. A bit of an invalid he'd been, but she never talked much about him.'

'She didn't mention where she came from—what part of the country?'

'I don't think she was a Londoner. Came from somewhere up north, I should say.'

'You didn't feel there was anything—well, mysterious about her?'

Lejeune felt a doubt as he spoke. If she was a suggestible

woman—But Mrs Coppins did not take advantage of the opportunity offered to her.

'Well, I can't say really that I did. Certainly not from anything she ever *said*. The only thing that perhaps might have made me wonder was her suitcase. Good quality it was, but not new. And the initials on it had been painted over. J.D.—Jessie Davis. But originally it had been J. something else. H., I think. But it might have been an A. Still, I didn't think anything of that at the time. You can often pick up a good piece of luggage second-hand ever so cheap, and then it's natural to get the initials altered. She hadn't a lot of stuff—only the one case.'

Lejeune knew that. The dead woman had had curiously few personal possessions. No letters had been kept, no photographs. She had had apparently no insurance card, no bank book, no cheque book. Her clothes were of good everyday serviceable quality, nearly new.

'She seemed quite happy?' he asked.

'I suppose so.'

He pounced on the faint doubtful tone in her voice.

'You only *suppose* so?'

'Well, it's not the kind of thing you think about, is it? I should say she was nicely off, with a good job, and quite satisfied with her life. She wasn't the bubbling over sort. But of course, when she got ill—'

'Yes, when she got ill?' he prompted her.

'Vexed, she was at first. When she went down with 'flu, I mean. It would put all her schedule out, she said. Missing appointments and all that. But 'flu's 'flu, and you can't ignore it when it's there. So she stopped in bed, and made

32

herself tea on the gas ring, and took aspirin. I said why not have the doctor and she said no point in it. Nothing to do for 'flu but stay in bed and keep warm and I'd better not come near her to catch it. I did a bit of cooking for her when she got better. Hot soup and toast. And a rice pudding now and again. It got her down, of course, 'flu does—but not more than what's usual, I'd say. It's after the fever goes down that you get the depression—and she got that like everyone does. She sat there, by the gas fire, I remember, and said to me, "I wish one didn't have so much time to *think*. I don't like having time to think. It gets me down."'

Lejeune continued to look deeply attentive and Mrs Coppins warmed to her theme.

'Lent her some magazines, I did. But she didn't seem able to keep her mind on reading. Said once, I remember, "If things aren't all they should be, it's better not to know about it, don't you agree?" and I said, "That's right, dearie." And she said, "I don't know—I've never really been *sure*." And I said that was all right, then. And she said, 'Everything *I*'ve done has always been perfectly straightforward and above board. I've nothing to reproach *myself* with." And I said, "Of course you haven't, dear." But I did just wonder in my own mind whether in the firm that employed her there mightn't have been some funny business with the accounts maybe, and she'd got wind of it—but had felt it wasn't really her business.'

'Possible,' agreed Lejeune.

'Anyway, she got well again—or nearly so, and went back to work. I told her it was too soon. Give yourself another day or two, I said. And there, how right I was!

Come back the second evening, she did, and I could see at once she'd got a high fever. Couldn't hardly climb the stairs. You must have the doctor, I says, but no, she wouldn't. Worse and worse she got, all that day, her eyes glassy, and her cheeks like fire, and her breathing terrible. And the next day in the evening she said to me, hardly able to get the words out: "A priest. I must have a priest. And quickly . . . or it will be too late." But it wasn't our vicar she wanted. It had to be a Roman Catholic priest. I never knew she was a Roman, never any crucifix about or anything like that.'

But there had been a crucifix, tucked away at the bottom of the suitcase. Lejeune did not mention it. He sat listening.

'I saw young Mike in the street and I sent him for that Father Gorman at St Dominic's. And I rang for the doctor, and the hospital on my own account, not saying nothing to her.'

'You took the priest up to her when he came?'

'Yes, I did. And left them together.'

'Did either of them say anything?'

'Well now, I can't exactly remember. I was talking myself, saying here was the priest and now she'd be all right, trying to cheer her up, but I do call to mind now as I closed the door I heard her say something about wickedness. Yes—and something, too, about a horse—horse-racing, maybe. I like a half-crown on myself occasionally—but there's a lot of crookedness goes on in racing, so they say.'

'Wickedness,' said Lejeune. He was struck by the word.

'Have to confess their sins, don't they, Romans, before they die? So I suppose that was it.'

Lejeune did not doubt that that was it, but his imagination was stirred by the word used. Wickedness . . .

Something rather special in wickedness, he thought, if the priest who knew about it was followed and clubbed to death . . .

There was nothing to be learnt from the other three lodgers in the house. Two of them, a bank clerk and an elderly man who worked in a shoe shop, had been there for some years. The third was a girl of twenty-two who had come there recently and had a job in a nearby department store. All three of them barely knew Mrs Davis by sight.

The woman who had reported having seen Father Gorman in the street that evening had no useful information to give. She was a Catholic who attended St Dominic's and she knew Father Gorman by sight. She had seen him turn out of Benthall Street and go into Tony's Place about ten minutes to eight. That was all.

Mr Osborne, the proprietor of the chemist's shop on the corner of Barton Street, had a better contribution to make.

He was a small, middle-aged man, with a bald domed head, a round ingenuous face, and glasses.

'Good evening, Chief Inspector. Come behind, will you?' He held up the flap of an old-fashioned counter. Lejeune passed behind and through a dispensing alcove where a young man in a white overall was making up bottles of medicine with the swiftness of a professional conjurer, and so through an archway into a tiny room with a couple of easy-chairs, a table and a desk. Mr Osborne pulled the curtain of the archway behind him in a secretive manner and sat down in one chair, motioning to Lejeune to take the other. He leaned forward, his eyes glinting in pleasurable excitement.

'It just happens that I *may* be able to assist you. It wasn't a busy evening—nothing much to do, the weather being unfavourable. My young lady was behind the counter. We keep open until eight on Thursdays always. The fog was coming on and there weren't many people about. I'd gone to the door to look at the weather, thinking to myself that the fog was coming up fast. The weather forecast had said it would. I stood there for a bit—nothing going on inside that my young lady couldn't deal with—face creams and bath salts and all that. Then I saw Father Gorman coming along on the other side of the street. I know him quite well by sight, of course. A shocking thing, this murder, attacking a man so well thought of as he is. "There's Father Gorman," I said to myself. He was going in the direction of West Street, it's the next turn on the left before the railway, as you know. A little way behind him there was another man. It wouldn't have entered my head to notice or think anything of that, but quite suddenly this second man came to a stop—quite abruptly, just when he was level with my door. I wondered why he'd stopped— and then I noticed that Father Gorman, a little way ahead, was slowing down. He didn't quite stop. It was as though he was thinking of something so hard that he almost forgot he was walking. Then he started on again, and this other man started to walk, too—rather fast. I thought— inasmuch as I thought at all, that perhaps it was someone who knew Father Gorman and wanted to catch him up and speak to him.'

'But in actual fact he could simply have been following him?'

'That's what I'm sure he was doing now—not that I thought anything of it at the time. What with the fog coming up, I lost sight of them both almost at once.'

'Can you describe this man at all?'

Lejeune's voice was not confident. He was prepared for the usual nondescript characteristics. But Mr Osborne was made of different mettle to Tony of Tony's Place.

'Well, yes, I think so,' he said with complacency. 'He was a tall man—'

'Tall? How tall?'

'Well—five eleven to six feet, at least, I'd say. Though he might have seemed taller than he was because he was very thin. Sloping shoulders he had, and a definite Adam's apple. Grew his hair rather long under his Homburg. A great beak of a nose. *Very* noticeable. Naturally I couldn't say as to the colour of his eyes. I saw him in profile as you'll appreciate. Perhaps fifty as to age. I'm going by the walk. A youngish man moves quite differently.'

Lejeune made a mental survey of the distance across the street, then back again to Mr Osborne, and wondered. He wondered very much . . .

A description such as that given by the chemist could mean one of two things. It could spring from an unusually vivid imagination—he had known many examples of that kind, mostly from women. They built up a fancy portrait of what they thought a murderer ought to look like. Such fancy portraits, however, usually contained some decidedly spurious details—such as rolling eyes, beetle brows, ape-like jaws, snarling ferocity. The description given by Mr Osborne sounded like the description of a real person. In that case it was possible that here was the witness in a million—a man who observed accurately and in detail—and who would be quite unshakable as to what he had seen.

Again Lejeune considered the distance across the street. His eyes rested thoughtfully on the chemist.

He asked: 'Do you think you would recognise this man if you saw him again?'

'Oh, yes.' Mr Osborne was supremely confident. 'I never forget a face. It's one of my hobbies. I've always said that if one of these wife murderers came into my place and bought a nice little package of arsenic, I'd be able to swear to him at the trial. I've always had my hopes that something like that would happen one day.'

'But it hasn't happened yet?'

Mr Osborne admitted sadly that it hadn't.

'And not likely to now,' he added wistfully. 'I'm selling this business. Getting a very nice price for it, and retiring to Bournemouth.'

'It looks a nice place you've got here.'

'It's got class,' said Mr Osborne, a note of pride in his voice. 'Nearly a hundred years we've been established here. My grandfather and my father before me. A good old-fashioned family business. Not that I saw it that way as a boy. Stuffy, I thought it. Like many a lad, I was bitten by the stage. Felt sure I could act. My father didn't try to stop me. "See what you can make of it, my boy," he said. "You'll find you're no Sir Henry Irving." And how right he was! Very wise man, my father. Eighteen months or so in repertory and back I came into the business. Took a pride in it, I did. We've always kept good solid stuff. Old-fashioned. But quality. But nowadays'—he shook his head sadly—'disappointing for a pharmaceutist. All this toilet stuff. You've got to keep it. Half the profits come from all that muck. Powder and lipstick and face creams; and hair shampoos and fancy sponge bags. I don't touch the stuff myself. I have a young lady behind the counter who attends to all that. No, it's not what it used to be, having a chemist's establishment. However, I've a good sum put by, and I'm getting a very good price, and I've made a down payment on a very nice little bungalow near Bournemouth.'

He added:

'Retire whilst you can still enjoy life. That's my motto. I've got plenty of hobbies. Butterflies, for instance. And a bit of bird watching now and then. And gardening—plenty of good books on how to start a garden. And there's travel. I might go on one of these cruises—see foreign parts before it's too late.'

Lejeune rose.

'Well, I wish you the best of luck,' he said. 'And if, before you actually leave these parts, you *should* catch sight of that man—'

'I'll let you know at once, Mr Lejeune. Naturally. You can count on me. It will be a pleasure. As I've told you, I've a very good eye for a face. I shall be on the lookout. On the *qui vive*, as they say. Oh yes. You can rely on me. It will be a pleasure.'

CHAPTER 4

Mark Easterbrook's Narrative

I came out of the Old Vic, my friend Hermia Redcliffe beside me. We had been to see a performance of *Macbeth*. It was raining hard. As we ran across the street to the spot where I had parked the car, Hermia remarked unjustly that whenever one went to the Old Vic it always rained.

'It's just one of those things.'

I dissented from this view. I said that, unlike sundials, she remembered only the rainy hours.

'Now at Glyndebourne,' went on Hermia as I let in the clutch, 'I've always been lucky. I can't imagine it other than perfection: the music—the glorious flower borders—the white flower border in particular.'

We discussed Glyndebourne and its music for a while, and then Hermia remarked:

'We're not going to Dover for breakfast, are we?'

'Dover? What an extraordinary idea. I thought we'd go to the Fantasie. One needs some really good food and drink after all the magnificent blood and gloom of *Macbeth*, Shakespeare always makes me ravenous.'

'Yes. So does Wagner. Smoked salmon sandwiches at Covent Garden in the intervals are never enough to stay the pangs. As to why Dover, it's because you're driving in that direction.'

'One has to go round,' I explained.

'But you've overdone going round. You're well away on the Old (or is it the New?) Kent Road.'

I took stock of my surroundings and had to admit that Hermia, as usual, was quite right.

'I always get muddled here,' I said in apology.

'It is confusing,' Hermia agreed. 'Round and round Waterloo Station.'

Having at last successfully negotiated Westminster Bridge we resumed our conversation, discussing the production of *Macbeth* that we had just been viewing. My friend Hermia Redcliffe was a handsome young woman of twenty-eight. Cast in the heroic mould, she had an almost flawless Greek profile, and a mass of dark chestnut hair, coiled on the nape of her neck. My sister always referred to her as 'Mark's girl friend' with an intonation of inverted commas about the term that never failed to annoy me.

The Fantasie gave us a pleasant welcome and showed us to a small table against the crimson velvet wall. The Fantasie is deservedly popular, and the tables are close together. As we sat down, our neighbours at the next table greeted us cheerfully. David Ardingly was a lecturer in History at Oxford. He introduced his companion, a very pretty girl, with a fashionable hairdo, all ends, bits and pieces, sticking out at improbable angles on the crown of her head. Strange to say, it suited her. She had enormous blue eyes and a mouth that was usually half-open. She was, as all David's girls were known to be, extremely silly. David, who was a remarkably clever young man, could only find relaxation with girls who were practically half-witted.

'This is my particular pet, Poppy,' he explained. 'Meet Mark and Hermia. They're very serious and highbrow and you must try and live up to them. We've just come from *Do it for Kicks*. Lovely show! I bet you two are straight from Shakespeare or a revival of Ibsen.'

'*Macbeth* at the Old Vic,' said Hermia.

'Ah, what do you think of Batterson's production?'

'I liked it,' said Hermia. 'The lighting was very interesting. And I've never seen the banquet scene so well managed.'

'Ah, but what about the witches?'

'Awful!' said Hermia. 'They always are,' she added.

David agreed.

'A pantomime element seems bound to creep in,' he said. 'All of them capering about and behaving like a three-fold Demon King. You can't help expecting a Good Fairy to appear in white with spangles to say in a flat voice:

Your evil shall not triumph. In the end,
It is Macbeth who will be round the bend.'

We all laughed, but David, who was quick on the uptake, gave me a sharp glance.

'What gives with you?' he asked.

'Nothing. It was just that I was reflecting only the other day about Evil and Demon Kings in pantomime. Yes—and Good Fairies, too.'

'*À propos de* what?'

'Oh, in Chelsea at a coffee bar.'

'How smart and up to date you are, aren't you, Mark? All among the Chelsea set. Where heiresses in tights marry corner boys on the make. That's where Poppy ought to be, isn't it, duckie?'

Poppy opened her enormous eyes still wider.

'I hate Chelsea,' she protested. 'I like the Fantasie *much* better! Such lovely, lovely food.'

'Good for you, Poppy. Anyway, you're not really rich enough for Chelsea. Tell us more about *Macbeth*, Mark, and the awful witches. I know how I'd produce the witches if I were doing a production.'

David had been a prominent member of the O.U.D.S. in the past.

'Well, how?'

'I'd make them very ordinary. Just sly quiet old women. Like the witches in a country village.'

'But there aren't any witches nowadays?' said Poppy, staring at him.

'You say that because you're a London girl. There's still a witch in every village in rural England. Old Mrs Black, in the third cottage up the hill. Little boys are told not to annoy her, and she's given presents of eggs and a home-baked cake now and again. Because,' he wagged a finger impressively, 'if you get across her, your cows will stop giving milk, your potato crop will fail, or little Johnnie will twist his ankle. You must keep on the right side of old Mrs Black. Nobody says so outright—but they all *know*!'

'You're joking,' said Poppy, pouting.

'No, I'm not. I'm right, aren't I, Mark?'

'Surely all that kind of superstition has died out completely with education,' said Hermia sceptically.

'Not in the rural pockets of the land. What do you say, Mark?'

'I think perhaps you're right,' I said slowly. 'Though I wouldn't really know. I've never lived in the country much.'

'I don't see *how* you could produce the witches as ordinary old women,' said Hermia, reverting to David's earlier remark. 'They must have a supernatural atmosphere about them, surely.'

'Oh, but just think,' said David. 'It's rather like madness. If you have someone who raves and staggers about with straws in their hair and *looks* mad, it's not frightening at all! But I remember being sent once with a message to a doctor at a mental home and I was shown into a room to wait, and there was a nice elderly lady there, sipping a glass of milk. She made some conventional remark about the weather and then suddenly she leant forward and asked in a low voice:

'"*Is it your poor child who's buried there behind the fireplace?*" And then she nodded her head and said "*12.10 exactly. It's always at the same time every day. Pretend you don't notice the blood.*"

'It was the matter-of-fact way she said it that was so spine-chilling.'

'Was there *really* someone buried behind the fireplace?' Poppy wanted to know.

David ignored her and went on:

'Then take mediums. At one moment trances, darkened

rooms, knocks and raps. Afterwards the medium sits up, pats her hair and goes home to a meal of fish and chips, just an ordinary quite jolly woman.'

'So your idea of the witches,' I said, 'is three old Scottish crones with second sight—who practise their arts in secret, muttering their spells round a cauldron, conjuring up spirits, but remaining themselves just an ordinary trio of old women. Yes—it could be impressive.'

'If you could ever get any actors to play it that way,' said Hermia drily.

'You have something there,' admitted David. 'Any hint of madness in the script and an actor is immediately determined to go to town on it! The same with sudden deaths. No actor can just quietly collapse and fall down dead. He has to groan, stagger, roll his eyes, gasp, clutch his heart, clutch his head, and make a terrific performance of it. Talking of performances, what did you think of Fielding's *Macbeth*? Great division of opinion among the critics.'

'I thought it was terrific,' said Hermia. 'That scene with the doctor, after the sleep-walking scene. "*Canst thou not minister to a mind diseas'd*." He made clear what I'd never thought of before—that he was really ordering the doctor to kill her. And yet he loved his wife. He brought out the struggle between his fear and his love. That "*Thou shouldst have died hereafter*" was the most poignant thing I've ever known.'

'Shakespeare might get a few surprises if he saw his plays acted nowadays,' I said drily.

'Burbage and Co. had already quenched a good deal of his spirit, I suspect,' said David.

Hermia murmured:

'The eternal surprise of the author at what the producer has done to him.'

'Didn't somebody called Bacon really write Shakespeare?' asked Poppy.

'That theory is quite out of date nowadays,' said David kindly. 'And what do *you* know of Bacon?'

'He invented gunpowder,' said Poppy triumphantly.

'You see why I love this girl?' he said. 'The things she knows are always so unexpected. Francis, not Roger, my love.'

'I thought it interesting,' said Hermia, 'that Fielding played the part of Third Murderer. Is there a precedent for that?'

'I believe so,' said David. 'How convenient it must have been in those times,' he went on, 'to be able to call up a handy murderer whenever you wanted a little job done. Fun if one could do it nowadays.'

'But it is done,' protested Hermia. 'Gangsters. Hoods— or whatever you call them. Chicago and all that.'

'Ah,' said David. 'But what I meant was not gangsterdom, not racketeers or Crime Barons. Just ordinary everyday folk who want to get rid of someone. That business rival; Aunt Emily, so rich and so unfortunately long-lived; that awkward husband always in the way. How convenient if you could ring up Harrods and say "Please send along two good murderers, will you?"'

We all laughed.

'But one *can* do that in a way, can't one?' said Poppy.

We turned towards her.

46

'What way, poppet?' asked David.

'Well, I mean, people can do that if they want to . . . People like us, as you said. Only I believe it's very expensive.'

Poppy's eyes were wide and ingenuous, her lips were slightly parted.

'What *do* you mean?' asked David curiously.

Poppy looked confused.

'Oh—I expect—I've got it mixed. I meant the Pale Horse. All that sort of thing.'

'A pale *horse?* What kind of a pale horse?'

Poppy flushed and her eyes dropped.

'I'm being stupid. It's just something someone mentioned—but I must have got it all wrong.'

'Have some lovely Coupe Nesselrode,' said David kindly.

One of the oddest things in life, as we all know, is the way that when you have heard a thing mentioned, within twenty-four hours you nearly always come across it again. I had an instance of that the next morning.

My telephone rang and I answered it—

'Flaxman 73841.'

A kind of gasp came through the phone. Then a voice said breathlessly but defiantly:

'I've thought about it, and I'll come!'

I cast round wildly in my mind.

'Splendid,' I said, stalling for time. 'Er—is that—?'

'After all,' said the voice, 'lightning never strikes twice.'

'Are you sure you've got the right number?'

'Of course I have. You're Mark Easterbrook, aren't you?'

Agatha Christie

'Got it!' I said. 'Mrs Oliver.'

'Oh,' said the voice, surprised. 'Didn't you know who it was? I never thought of that. It's about that fête of Rhoda's. I'll come and sign books if she wants me to.'

'That's frightfully nice of you. They'll put you up, of course.'

'There won't be parties, will there?' asked Mrs Oliver apprehensively.

'You know the kind of thing,' she went on. 'People coming up to me and saying am I writing something just now—when you'd think they could see I'm drinking ginger ale or tomato juice and not writing at all. And saying they like my books—which of course is pleasing, but I've never found the right answer. If you say "I'm so glad" it sounds like "Pleased to meet you." A kind of stock phrase. Well, it is, of course. And you don't think they'll want me to go out to the Pink Horse and have drinks?'

'The Pink *Horse*?'

'Well, the Pale Horse. Pubs, I mean. I'm so bad in pubs. I can *just* drink beer at a pinch, but it makes me terribly gurgly.'

'Just what do you mean by the Pale Horse?'

'There's a pub called that down there, isn't there? Or perhaps I do mean the Pink Horse? Or perhaps that's somewhere else. I may have just imagined it. I do imagine quite a lot of things.'

'How's the Cockatoo getting on?' I asked.

'The Cockatoo?' Mrs Oliver sounded at sea.

'And the cricket ball?'

'Really,' said Mrs Oliver with dignity. 'I think you must be mad or have a hangover or something. Pink Horses and cockatoos and cricket balls.'

She rang off.

I was still considering this second mention of the Pale Horse when my telephone rang again.

This time, it was Mr Soames White, a distinguished solicitor who rang up to remind me that under the will of my godmother, Lady Hesketh-Dubois, I was entitled to choose three of her pictures.

'There is nothing outstandingly valuable, of course,' said Mr Soames White in his defeatist melancholy tones. 'But I understand that at some time you expressed admiration of some of the pictures to the deceased.'

'She had some very charming water colours of Indian scenes,' I said. 'I believe you already have written to me about this matter, but I'm afraid it slipped my memory.'

'Quite so,' said Mr Soames White. 'But probate has now been granted, and the executors, of whom I am one, are arranging for the sale of the effects of her London house. If you *could* go round to Ellesmere Square in the near future . . .'

'I'll go now,' I said.

It seemed an unfavourable morning for work.

Carrying the three water colours of my choice under my arm, I emerged from Forty-nine Ellesmere Square and immediately cannoned into someone coming up the steps to the front door. I apologised, received apologies in return, and was just about to hail a passing taxi when something clicked in my mind and I turned sharply to ask:

'Hallo—isn't it Corrigan?'

'It is—and—yes—you're Mark Easterbrook!'

Jim Corrigan and I had been friends in our Oxford days—but it must have been fifteen years or more since we had last met.

'Thought I knew you—but couldn't place you for the moment,' said Corrigan. 'I read your articles now and again—and enjoy them, I must say.'

'What about you? Have you gone in for research as you meant to do?'

Corrigan sighed.

'Hardly. It's an expensive job—if you want to strike out on your own. Unless you can find a tame millionaire, or a suggestible Trust.'

'Liver flukes, wasn't it?'

'What a memory! No, I went off liver flukes. The properties of the secretions of the Mandarian glands; that's my present-day interest. You wouldn't have heard of them! Connected with the spleen. Apparently serving no purpose whatever!'

He spoke with a scientist's enthusiasm.

'What's the big idea, then?'

'Well,' Corrigan sounded apologetic. 'I have a theory that they may influence behaviour. To put it very crudely, they may act rather as the fluid in your car brakes does. No fluid—the brakes don't act. In human beings, a deficiency in these secretions might—I only say *might*—make you a criminal.'

I whistled.

'And what happens to Original Sin?'

'What indeed?' said Dr Corrigan. 'The parsons wouldn't like it, would they? I haven't been able to interest anyone in my theory, unfortunately. So I'm a police surgeon, in N.W. division. Quite interesting. One sees a lot of criminal types. But I won't bore you with shop—unless you'll come and have some lunch with me?'

'I'd like to. But you were going in there,' I nodded towards the house behind Corrigan.

'Not really,' said Corrigan. 'I was just going to gatecrash.'

'There's nobody there but a caretaker.'

'So I imagined. But I wanted to find out something about the late Lady Hesketh-Dubois if I could.'

'I dare say I can tell you more than a caretaker could. She was my godmother.'

'Was she indeed? That's a bit of luck. Where shall we go to feed? There's a little place off Lowndes Square—not grand, but they do a special kind of sea food soup.'

We settled ourselves in the little restaurant—a cauldron of steaming soup was brought to us by a pale-faced lad in French sailor trousers.

'Delicious,' I said, sampling the soup. 'Now then, Corrigan, what do you want to know about the old lady? And incidentally, why?'

'Why's rather a long story,' said my friend. 'First tell me what kind of an old lady she was?'

I considered.

'She was an old-fashioned type,' I said. 'Victorian. Widow of an ex-Governor of some obscure island. She was rich and liked her comfort. Went abroad in the winters to Estoril and places like that. Her house is hideous, full of Victorian furniture and the worst and most ornate kind of Victorian silver. She had no children, but kept a couple of fairly well-behaved poodles whom she loved dearly. She was opinionated and a staunch Conservative. Kindly, but autocratic. Very set in her ways. What more do you want to know?'

'I'm not quite sure,' said Corrigan. 'Was she ever likely to have been blackmailed, would you say?'

'*Blackmailed?*' I asked in lively astonishment. 'I can imagine nothing more unlikely. What *is* this all about?'

It was then I heard for the first time of the circumstances of Father Gorman's murder.

I laid down my spoon and asked,

'This list of names? Have you got it?'

'Not the original. But I copied them out. Here you are.'

I took the paper he produced from his pocket and proceeded to study it.

'Parkinson? I know two Parkinsons. Arthur who went into the Navy. Then there's a Henry Parkinson in one of the Ministries. Ormerod—there's a Major Ormerod in the Blues—Sandford—our old Rector when I was a boy was Sandford. Harmondsworth? No—Tuckerton—' I paused. 'Tuckerton . . . Not Thomasina Tuckerton, I suppose?'

Corrigan looked at me curiously.

'Could be, for all I know. Who's she and what does she do?'

'Nothing now. Her death was in the paper about a week ago.'

'That's not much help, then.'

I continued with my reading. 'Shaw. I know a dentist called Shaw, and there's Jerome Shaw, Q.C. . . . Delafontaine—I've heard that name lately, but I can't remember where. Corrigan. Does that refer to you, by any chance?'

'I devoutly hope not. I've a feeling that it's unlucky to have your name on that list.'

'Maybe. What made you think of blackmail in connection with it?'

'It was Detective Inspector Lejeune's suggestion if I remember rightly. It seemed the most likely possibility—But there are plenty of others. This may be a list of dope smugglers or drug addicts or secret agents—it may be anything in fact. There's only one thing sure, it was important enough for murder to be committed in order to get hold of it.'

I asked curiously: 'Do you always take such an interest in the police side of your work?'

He shook his head.

'Can't say I do. My interest is in criminal *character*. Background, upbringing, and particularly glandular health—all that!'

'Then why the interest in this list of names?'

'Blessed if I know,' said Corrigan slowly. 'Seeing my own name on the list, perhaps. Up the Corrigans! One Corrigan to the rescue of another Corrigan.'

'Rescue? Then you definitely see this as a list of victims— *not* a list of malefactors. But surely it *could* be either?'

'You're entirely right. And it's certainly odd that I should be so positive. Perhaps it's just a feeling. Or perhaps it's something to do with Father Gorman. I didn't come across him very often, but he was a fine man, respected by everyone and loved by his own flock. He was the good tough militant kind. I can't get it out of my head that he considered this list a matter of life or death . . .'

'Aren't the police getting anywhere?'

'Oh yes, but it's a long business. Checking here, checking there. Checking the antecedents of the woman who called him out that night.'

'Who was she?'

'No mystery about her, apparently. Widow. We had an idea that her husband might have been connected with horse-racing, but that doesn't seem to be so. She worked for a small commercial firm that does consumer research. Nothing wrong there. They are a reputable firm in a small way. They don't know much about her. She came from the north of England—Lancashire. The only odd thing about her is that she had so few personal possessions.'

I shrugged my shoulders.

'I expect that's true for a lot more people than we ever imagine. It's a lonely world.'

'Yes, as you say.'

'Anyway, you decided to take a hand?'

'Just nosing around. Hesketh-Dubois is an uncommon name. I thought if I could find out a little about the lady—' He left the sentence unfinished. 'But from what you tell me, there doesn't seem to be any possible lead there.'

'Neither a dope addict nor a dope smuggler,' I assured him. 'Certainly not a secret agent. Has led far too blameless a life to have been blackmailed. I can't imagine what kind of a list she could possibly be on. Her jewellery she keeps at the bank so she wouldn't be a hopeful prospect for robbery.'

'Any other Hesketh-Duboises that you know about? Sons?'

'No children. She's got a nephew and a niece, I think, but not of that name. Her husband was an only child.'

Corrigan told me sourly that I'd been a lot of help. He looked at his watch, remarked cheerfully that he was due to cut somebody up, and we parted.

I went home thoughtful, found it impossible to concentrate on my work, and finally, on an impulse, rang up David Ardingly.

'David? Mark here. That girl I met with you the other evening. Poppy. What's her other name?'

'Going to pinch my girl, is that it?'

David sounded highly amused.

'You've got so many of them,' I retorted. 'You could surely spare one.'

'You've got a heavyweight of your own, old boy. I thought you were going steady with her.'

'Going steady.' A repulsive term. And yet, I thought, struck suddenly with its aptitude, how well it described my relationship with Hermia. And why should it make me feel depressed? I had always felt in the back of my mind that some day Hermia and I would marry . . . I liked her better than anyone I knew. We had so much in common . . .

For no conceivable reason, I felt a terrible desire to yawn . . . Our future stretched out before me. Hermia and I going to plays of significance—that mattered. Discussions of art—of music. No doubt about it, Hermia was the perfect companion.

But not much fun, said some derisive imp, popping up from my subconscious. I was shocked.

'Gone to sleep?' asked David.

'Of course not. To tell the truth, I found your friend Poppy very refreshing.'

'Good word. She is—taken in small doses. Her actual name is Pamela Stirling, and she works in one of those arty flower places in Mayfair. You know, three dead twigs, a tulip with its petals pinned back and a speckled laurel leaf. Price three guineas.'

He gave me the address.

'Take her out and enjoy yourself,' he said in a kindly avuncular fashion. 'You'll find it a great relaxation. That girl knows nothing—she's absolutely empty headed. She'll believe anything you tell her. She's virtuous by the way, so don't indulge in any false hopes.'

He rang off.

I invaded the portals of Flower Studies Ltd. with some trepidation. An overpowering smell of gardenia nearly knocked me backwards. A number of girls, dressed in pale green sheaths and all looking exactly like Poppy, confused me. Finally, I identified her. She was writing down an address with some difficulty, pausing doubtfully over the spelling of Fortescue Crescent. As soon as she was at liberty, after having further difficulties connected with producing the right change for a five-pound note, I claimed her attention.

'We met the other night—with David Ardingly,' I reminded her.

'Oh *yes!*' agreed Poppy warmly, her eyes passing vaguely over my head.

'I wanted to ask you something.' I felt sudden qualms. 'Perhaps I'd better buy some flowers?'

Like an automaton who has had the right button pressed, Poppy said:

'We've some lovely roses, fresh in today.'

'These yellow ones, perhaps?' There were roses everywhere. 'How much are they?'

'Vewy vewy cheap,' said Poppy in a honeyed persuasive voice. 'Only five shillings each.'

I swallowed and said I would have six of them.

'And some of these vewy special leaves with them?'

I looked dubiously at the special leaves which appeared to be in an advanced state of decay. Instead I chose some bright green asparagus fern, which choice obviously lowered me in Poppy's estimation.

'There was something I wanted to ask you,' I reiterated as Poppy was rather clumsily draping the asparagus fern round the roses. 'The other evening you mentioned something called the Pale Horse.'

With a violent start, Poppy dropped the roses and the asparagus fern on the floor.

'Can you tell me more about it?'

Poppy straightened herself after stooping.

'What did you say?' she asked.

'I was asking you about the Pale Horse.'

'A pale horse? What do you mean?'

'You mentioned it the other evening.'

'I'm sure I never did anything of the kind! I've never heard of any such thing.'

'Somebody told you about it. Who was it?'

Poppy drew a deep breath and spoke very fast.

'I don't in the least know what you mean! And we're not supposed to talk to customers.' . . . She slapped paper round my choice. 'That will be thirty-five shillings, please.'

I gave her two pound notes. She thrust six shillings into my hand and turned quickly to another customer.

Her hands, I noticed, were shaking slightly.

I went out slowly. When I had gone a little way, I realised she had quoted the wrong price (asparagus fern was seven and six) and had also given me too much change. Her mistakes in arithmetic had previously been in the other direction.

I saw again the rather lovely vacant face and the wide blue eyes. There had been something showing in those eyes . . .

'Scared,' I said to myself. 'Scared stiff . . . Now why? *Why?*'

CHAPTER 5

Mark Easterbrook's Narrative

'What a relief,' sighed Mrs Oliver. 'To think it's over and nothing has happened!'

It was a moment of relaxation. Rhoda's fête had passed off in the manner of fêtes. Violent anxiety about the weather which in the early morning appeared capricious in the extreme. Considerable argument as to whether any stalls should be set up in the open, or whether everything should take place in the long barn and the marquee. Various passionate local disputes regarding tea arrangements, produce stalls, et cetera. Tactful settlement of same by Rhoda. Periodical escapes of Rhoda's delightful but undisciplined dogs who were supposed to be incarcerated in the house, owing to doubts as to their behaviour on this great occasion. Doubts fully justified! Arrival of pleasant but vague starlet in a profusion of pale fur, to open the fête, which she did very charmingly, adding a few moving words about the plight of refugees which puzzled everybody, since the object of the fête was the restoration of the church tower. Enormous success of the bottle stall. The usual

Agatha Christie

difficulties about change. Pandemonium at tea-time when every patron wanted to invade the marquee and partake of it simultaneously.

Finally, blessed arrival of evening. Displays of local dancing in the long barn were still going on. Fireworks and a bonfire were scheduled, but the weary household had now retired to the house, and were partaking of a sketchy cold meal in the dining-room, indulging meanwhile in one of those desultory conversations where everyone utters their own thoughts, and pays little attention to those of other people. It was all disjointed and comfortable. The released dogs crunched bones happily under the table.

'We shall take more than we did for the Save the Children last year,' said Rhoda gleefully.

'It seems very extraordinary to me,' said Miss Macalister, the children's Scottish nursery governess, 'that Michael Brent should find the buried treasure three years in succession. I'm wondering if he gets some advance information?'

'Lady Brookbank won the pig,' said Rhoda. 'I don't think she wanted it. She looked terribly embarrassed.'

The party consisted of my cousin Rhoda, and her husband Colonel Despard, Miss Macalister, a young woman with red hair suitably called Ginger, Mrs Oliver, and the vicar, the Rev. Caleb Dane Calthrop and his wife. The vicar was a charming elderly scholar whose principal pleasure was finding some apposite comment from the classics. This, though often an embarrassment, and a cause of bringing the conversation to a close, was perfectly in order now. The vicar never required acknowledgement of his sonorous

Latin, his pleasure in having found an apt quotation was its own reward.

'As Horace says . . .' he observed, beaming round the table.

The usual pause happened and then:

'I think Mrs Horsefall cheated over the bottle of champagne,' said Ginger thoughtfully. 'Her nephew got it.'

Mrs Dane Calthrop, a disconcerting woman with fine eyes, was studying Mrs Oliver thoughtfully. She asked abruptly:

'What did you expect to happen at this fête?'

'Well, really, a murder or something like that?'

Mrs Dane Calthrop looked interested.

'But why should it?'

'No reason at all. Most unlikely, really. But there was one at the last fête I went to.'

'I see. And it upset you?'

'Very much.'

The vicar changed from Latin to Greek.

After the pause, Miss Macalister cast doubts on the honesty of the raffle for the live duck.

'Very sporting of old Lugg at the King's Arms to send us twelve dozen beer for the bottle stall,' said Despard.

'King's Arms?' I asked sharply.

'Our local, darling,' said Rhoda.

'Isn't there another pub round here? The—Pale Horse, didn't you say,' I asked, turning to Mrs Oliver.

There was no such reaction here as I had half expected. The faces turned towards me were vague and uninterested.

'The Pale Horse isn't a pub,' said Rhoda. 'I mean, not *now*.'

'It *was* an old inn,' said Despard. 'Mostly sixteenth-century I'd say. But it's just an ordinary house now. I always think they should have changed the name.'

'Oh, *no*,' exclaimed Ginger. 'It would have been awfully silly to call it Wayside, or Fairview. I think the Pale Horse is *much* nicer, and there's a lovely old inn sign. They've got it framed in the hall.'

'Who's they?' I asked.

'It belongs to Thyrza Grey,' said Rhoda. 'I don't know if you saw her today? Tall woman with short grey hair.'

'She's very occult,' said Despard. 'Goes in for spiritualism and trances, and magic. Not quite black masses, but that sort of thing.'

Ginger gave a sudden peal of laughter.

'I'm sorry,' she said apologetically. 'I was just thinking of Miss Grey as Madame de Montespan on a black velvet altar.'

'Ginger!' said Rhoda. 'Not in front of the vicar.'

'Sorry, Mr Dane Calthrop.'

'Not at all,' said the vicar, beaming. 'As the ancients put it—' he continued for some time in Greek.

After a respectful silence of appreciation, I returned to the attack.

'I still want to know who are "they"—Miss Grey and who else?'

'Oh, there's a friend who lives with her. Sybil Stamfordis. She acts as medium, I believe. You must have seen her about—Lots of scarabs and beads—and sometimes she puts on a sari—I can't think why—she's never been in India—'

'And then there's Bella,' said Mrs Dane Calthrop. 'She's

their cook,' she explained. 'And she's also a witch. She comes from the village of Little Dunning. She had quite a reputation for witchcraft there. It runs in the family. Her mother was a witch, too.'

She spoke in a matter-of-fact way.

'You sound as though you believe in witchcraft, Mrs Dane Calthrop,' I said.

'But of course! There's nothing mysterious or secretive about it. It's all quite matter-of-fact. It's a family asset that you inherit. Children are told not to tease your cat, and people give you a cottage cheese or a pot of home-made jam from time to time.'

I looked at her doubtfully. She appeared to be quite serious.

'Sybil helped us today by telling fortunes,' said Rhoda. 'She was in the green tent. She's quite good at it, I believe.'

'She gave me a lovely fortune,' said Ginger. 'Money in my hand. A handsome dark stranger from overseas, two husbands and six children. Really very generous.'

'I saw the Curtis girl come out giggling,' said Rhoda. 'And she was very coy with her young man afterwards. Told him not to think he was the only pebble on the beach.'

'Poor Tom,' said her husband. 'Did he make any comeback?'

'Oh, yes. "I'm not telling you what she promised *me*," he said. "Mebbe you wouldn't like it too well, my girl!"'

'Good for Tom.'

'Old Mrs Parker was quite sour,' said Ginger, laughing. '"'Tis all foolishness," that's what she said. "Don't you believe none of it, you two." But then Mrs Cripps piped up and said, "You know, Lizzie, as well as I do, that Miss Stamfordis sees things as others can't see, and Miss Grey knows to a day when there's going to be a death. Never wrong, she is! Fairly gives me the creeps sometimes." And Mrs Parker said: "Death—that's different. It's a gift." And Mrs Cripps said: "Anyway I wouldn't like to offend none of those three, that I wouldn't!"'

'It does all sound exciting. I'd love to meet them,' said Mrs Oliver wistfully.

'We'll take you over there tomorrow,' Colonel Despard promised. 'The old inn is really worth seeing. They've been very clever in making it comfortable without spoiling its character.'

'I'll ring up Thyrza tomorrow morning,' said Rhoda.

I must admit that I went to bed with a slight feeling of deflation.

The Pale Horse which had loomed in my mind as a symbol of something unknown and sinister had turned out to be nothing of the sort.

Unless, of course, there was another Pale Horse somewhere else?

I considered that idea until I fell asleep . . .

There was a feeling of relaxation next day, which was a Sunday. An after-the-party feeling. On the lawn the marquee and tents flapped limply in a damp breeze, awaiting removal by the caterer's men at early dawn on the morrow. On Monday we would all set to work to take stock of what damage had been done, and clear things up. Today, Rhoda had wisely decided, it would be better to go out as much as possible.

We all went to church, and listened respectfully to Mr Dane Calthrop's scholarly sermon on a text taken from Isaiah which seemed to deal less with religion than with Persian history.

'We're going to lunch with Mr Venables,' explained Rhoda afterwards. 'You'll like him, Mark. He's really a most interesting man. Been everywhere and done everything. Knows all sorts of out-of-the-way things. He bought Priors Court about three years ago. And the things he's done to it must have cost him a fortune. He had polio and is semi-crippled, so he has to go about in a wheeled chair. It's very sad for him because up to then he was a great traveller, I believe. Of course he's rolling in money, and, as I say, he's done up the house in a wonderful way—it was an absolute ruin, falling to pieces. It's full of the most gorgeous stuff. The sale rooms are his principal interest nowadays, I believe.'

Priors Court was only a few miles away. We drove there and our host came wheeling himself along the hall to meet us.

'Nice of you all to come,' he said heartily. 'You must be exhausted after yesterday. The whole thing was a great success, Rhoda.'

Mr Venables was a man of about fifty, with a thin hawk-like face and a beaked nose that stood out from it arrogantly. He wore an open-wing collar which gave him a faintly old-fashioned air.

Rhoda made introductions.

Venables smiled at Mrs Oliver.

'I met this lady yesterday in her professional capacity,' he said. 'Six of her books with signatures. Takes care of six presents for Christmas. Great stuff you write, Mrs Oliver. Give us more of it. Can't have too much of it.' He grinned at Ginger. '*You* nearly landed me with a live duck, young woman.' Then he turned to me. 'I enjoyed your article in the Review last month,' he said.

'It was awfully good of you to come to our fête, Mr Venables,' said Rhoda. 'After that generous cheque you sent us, I didn't really hope that you'd turn up in person.'

'Oh, I enjoy that kind of thing. Part of English rural life, isn't it? I came home clasping a most terrible Kewpie doll from the hoop-la, and had a splendid but unrealistic future prophesied me by Our Sybil, all dressed up in a tinsel turban with about a ton of fake Egyptian beads slung over her torso.'

'Good old Sybil,' said Colonel Despard. 'We're going there to tea with Thyrza this afternoon. It's an interesting old place.'

'The Pale Horse? Yes. I rather wish it had been left as an inn. I always feel that that place has had a mysterious and unusually wicked past history. It can't have been smuggling; we're not near enough to the sea for that. A resort for highwaymen, perhaps? Or rich travellers spent the night there and were never seen again. It seems, somehow, rather tame to have turned it into a desirable residence for three old maids.'

'Oh—I *never* think of them like that!' cried Rhoda. 'Sybil Stamfordis, perhaps—with her saris and her scarabs, and always seeing auras round people's heads—she *is* rather ridiculous. But there's something really awe-inspiring about Thyrza, don't you agree? You feel she knows just what you're thinking. She doesn't *talk* about having second sight—but everyone says that she has got it.'

'And Bella, far from being an old maid, has buried two husbands,' added Colonel Despard.

'I sincerely beg her pardon,' said Venables, laughing.

'With sinister interpretations of the deaths from the neighbours,' added Despard. 'It's said they displeased her, so she turned her eyes on them, and they slowly sickened and pined away!'

'Of course, I forgot, she is the local witch?'

'So Mrs Dane Calthrop says.'

'Interesting thing, witchcraft,' said Venables thoughtfully. 'All over the world you get variations of it—I remember when I was in East Africa—'

He talked easily, and entertainingly, on the subject. He spoke of medicine-men in Africa; of little-known cults in Borneo. He promised that, after lunch, he would show us some West African sorcerers' masks.

'There's everything in this house,' declared Rhoda with a laugh.

'Oh well—' he shrugged his shoulders—'if you can't go out to everything—then everything must be made to come to you.'

Just for a moment there was a sudden bitterness in his voice. He gave a swift glance downwards towards his paralysed legs.

'"*The world is so full of a number of things*,"' he quoted.

'I think that's always been my undoing. There's so much I want to know about—to see! Oh well I haven't done too badly in my time. And even now—life has its consolations.'

'Why *here?*' asked Mrs Oliver suddenly.

The others had been slightly ill at ease, as people become when a hint of tragedy looms in the air. Mrs Oliver alone had been unaffected. She asked because she wanted to know. And her frank curiosity restored the light-hearted atmosphere.

Venables looked towards her inquiringly.

'I mean,' said Mrs Oliver, 'why did you come to live here, in this neighbourhood? So far away from things that are going on. Was it because you had friends here?'

'No. I chose this part of the world, since you are interested, because I had *no* friends here.'

A faint ironical smile touched his lips.

How deeply, I wondered, had his disability affected him? Had the loss of unfettered movement, of liberty to explore the world, bitten deep into his soul? Or had he managed to adapt himself to altered circumstances with comparative equanimity—with a real greatness of spirit?

As though Venables had read my thoughts, he said: 'In your article you questioned the meaning of the term "greatness"—you compared the different meanings attached to it—in the East and the West. But what do we all mean nowadays, here in England, when we use the term "a great man"?—'

'Greatness of intellect, certainly,' I said, 'and surely moral strength as well?'

He looked at me, his eyes bright and shining.

'Is there no such thing as an evil man, then, who can be described as great?' he asked.

'Of course there is,' cried Rhoda. 'Napoleon and Hitler and oh, lots of people. They were all great men.'

'Because of the effect they produced?' said Despard. 'But if one had known them personally—I wonder if one would have been impressed.'

Ginger leaned forward and ran her fingers through her carroty mop of hair.

'That's an interesting thought,' she said. 'Mightn't they, perhaps, have seemed pathetic, undersized little figures? Strutting, posturing, feeling inadequate, determined to *be* someone, even if they pulled the world down round them?'

'Oh, *no*,' said Rhoda vehemently. 'They couldn't have produced the results they did if they had been like that.'

'I don't know,' said Mrs Oliver. 'After all, the stupidest child can set a house on fire quite easily.'

'Come, come,' said Venables. 'I really can't go along with this modern playing down of evil as something that doesn't really exist. There *is* evil. And evil is powerful. Sometimes more powerful than good. It's there. It has to be recognised—and fought. Otherwise—' he spread out his hands. 'We go down to darkness.'

'Of course I was brought up on the devil,' said Mrs Oliver, apologetically. 'Believing in him, I mean. But you know he always did seem to me so *silly*. With hoofs and a tail and all that. Capering about like a ham actor. Of course I often have a master criminal in my stories—people like it—but really he gets harder and harder to do. So long as one doesn't know who he is, I can keep him impressive—but when it all comes out—he seems, somehow, so *inadequate*. A kind of anti-climax. It's much easier if you just have a bank manager who's embezzled the funds, or a husband who wants to get rid of his wife and marry the children's governess. So much more *natural*—if you know what I mean.'

Everyone laughed and Mrs Oliver said apologetically:

'I know I haven't put it very well—but you do see what I mean?'

We all said that we knew exactly what she meant.

CHAPTER 6

Mark Easterbrook's Narrative

It was after four o'clock when we left Priors Court. After a particularly delicious lunch, Venables had taken us on a tour of the house. He had taken a real pleasure in showing us his various possessions—a veritable treasure house the place was.

'He must be rolling in money,' I said when we had finally departed. 'Those jades—and the African sculpture—to say nothing of all his Meissen and Bow. You're lucky to have such a neighbour.'

'Don't we know it?' said Rhoda. 'Most of the people down here are nice enough—but definitely on the dull side. Mr Venables is positively exotic by comparison.'

'How did he make his money?' asked Mrs Oliver. 'Or has he always had it?'

Despard remarked wryly that nobody nowadays could boast of such a thing as a large inherited income. Death duties and taxation had seen to that.

'Someone told me,' he added, 'that he started life as a stevedore but it seems most unlikely. He never talks about

71

his boyhood or his family—' He turned towards Mrs Oliver. 'A Mystery Man for you—'

Mrs Oliver said that people were always offering her things she didn't want—

The Pale Horse was a half-timbered building (genuine half-timbering not faked). It was set back a little way from the village street. A walled garden could be glimpsed behind it which gave it a pleasant old-world look.

I was disappointed in it, and said so.

'Not nearly sinister enough,' I complained. 'No atmosphere.'

'Wait till you get inside,' said Ginger.

We got out of the car and went up to the door, which opened as we approached.

Miss Thyrza Grey stood on the threshold, a tall, slightly masculine figure in a tweed coat and skirt. She had rough grey hair springing up from a high forehead, a large beak of a nose, and very penetrating light blue eyes.

'Here you are at last,' she said in a hearty bass voice. 'Thought you'd all got lost.'

Behind her tweed-clad shoulders I became aware of a face peering out from the shadows of the dark hall. A queer, rather formless face, like something made in putty by a child who had strayed in to play in a sculptor's studio. It was the kind of face, I thought, that you sometimes see amongst a crowd in an Italian or Flemish primitive painting.

Rhoda introduced us and explained that we had been lunching with Mr Venables at Priors Court.

'Ah!' said Miss Grey. 'That explains it! Fleshpots. That Italian cook of his! And all the treasures of the treasure house as well. Oh well, poor fellow—got to have something to cheer him up. But come in—come in. We're rather proud of our own little place. Fifteenth-century—and some of it fourteenth.'

The hall was low and dark with a twisting staircase leading up from it. There was a wide fireplace and over it a framed picture.

'The old inn sign,' said Miss Grey, noting my glance. 'Can't see much of it in this light. The Pale Horse.'

'I'm going to clean it for you,' said Ginger. 'I said I would. You let me have it and you'll be surprised.'

'I'm a bit doubtful,' said Thyrza Grey, and added bluntly, 'Suppose you ruin it?'

'Of course I shan't ruin it,' said Ginger indignantly. 'It's my job.

'I work for the London Galleries,' she explained to me. 'Great fun.'

'Modern picture restoring takes a bit of getting used to,' said Thyrza. 'I gasp every time I go into the National Gallery nowadays. All the pictures look as though they'd had a bath in the latest detergent.'

'You can't really prefer them all dark and mustard coloured,' protested Ginger. She peered at the inn sign. 'A lot more would come up. The horse *may* even have a rider.'

I joined her to stare into the picture. It was a crude painting with little merit except the doubtful one of old age and dirt. The pale figure of a stallion gleamed against a dark indeterminate background.

'Hi, Sybil,' cried Thyrza. 'The visitors are crabbing our Horse, damn their impertinence!'

Miss Sybil Stamfordis came through a door to join us.

She was a tall willowy woman with dark, rather greasy hair, a simpering expression, and a fish-like mouth.

She was wearing a bright emerald green sari which did nothing to enhance her appearance. Her voice was faint and fluttery.

'Our dear, dear Horse,' she said. 'We fell in love with that old inn sign the moment we saw it. I really think it influenced us to buy the house. Don't you, Thyrza? But come in—come in.'

The room into which she led us was small and square and had probably been the bar in its time. It was furnished now with chintz and Chippendale and was definitely a lady's sitting-room, country style. There were bowls of chrysanthemums.

Then we were taken out to see the garden which I could see would be charming in summer, and then came back into the house to find tea had been laid. There were sandwiches and home-made cakes and as we sat down, the old woman whose face I had glimpsed for a moment in the hall came in bearing a silver teapot. She wore a plain dark green overall. The impression of a head made crudely from Plasticine by a child was borne out on closer inspection. It had a witless primitive face but I could not imagine why I had thought it sinister.

Suddenly I felt angry with myself. All this nonsense about a converted inn and three middle-aged women!

'Thank you, Bella,' said Thyrza.

'Got all you want?'

It came out almost as a mumble.

'Yes, thanks.'

Bella withdrew to the door. She had looked at nobody, but just before she went out, she raised her eyes and took a speedy glance at me. There was something in that look that startled me—though it was difficult to describe why. There was malice in it, and a curious intimate knowledge. I felt that without effort, and almost without curiosity, she had known exactly what thoughts were in my mind.

Thyrza Grey had noticed my reaction.

'Bella is disconcerting, isn't she, Mr Easterbrook?' she said softly. 'I noticed her look at you.'

'She's a local woman, isn't she?' I strove to appear merely politely interested.

'Yes. I dare say someone will have told you she's the local witch.'

Sybil Stamfordis clanked her beads.

'Now do confess, Mr—Mr—'

'Easterbrook.'

'Easterbrook. I'm sure you've heard that we all practise witchcraft. Confess now. We've got quite a reputation, you know—'

'Not undeserved, perhaps,' said Thyrza. She seemed amused. 'Sybil here has great gifts.'

Sybil sighed pleasurably.

'I was always attracted by the occult,' she murmured. 'Even as a child I realised that I had unusual powers. Automatic writing came to me quite naturally. I didn't even know what it *was*! I'd just sit there with a pencil in my hand—and not know a thing about what was happening. And of course I was always ultra-sensitive. I fainted once when taken to tea in a friend's house. Something awful had happened in that very room . . . I knew it! We got the explanation later. There had been a murder there—-twenty-five years ago. In that very room!'

She nodded her head and looked round at us with great satisfaction.

'Very remarkable,' said Colonel Despard with polite distaste.

'Sinister things have happened in *this* house,' said Sybil darkly. 'But we have taken the necessary steps. The earthbound spirits have been freed.'

'A kind of spiritual spring cleaning?' I suggested.

Sybil looked at me rather doubtfully.

'What a lovely coloured sari you are wearing,' said Rhoda.

Sybil brightened.

'Yes, I got it when I was in India. I had an interesting time there. I explored yoga, you know, and all that. But I could not help feeling that it was all too sophisticated—not near enough to the natural and the primitive. One must go back, I feel, to the beginnings, to the early primitive powers. I am one of the few women who have visited Haiti. Now there you really *do* touch the original springs of the occult. Overlaid, of course, by a certain amount of corruption and distortion. But the root of the matter is there.

'I was shown a great deal, especially when they learnt that I had twin sisters a little older than myself. The child who is born next after twins has special powers, so they told me. Interesting, wasn't it? Their death dances are wonderful. All the panoply of death, skulls and cross bones, and the tools of a gravedigger, spade, pick and hoe. They dress up as undertakers' mutes, top hats, black clothes—

'The Grand Master is Baron Samedi, and the Legba is the god he invokes, the god who "removes the barrier". You send the dead forth—to cause death. Weird idea, isn't it?

'Now this,' Sybil rose and fetched an object from the window sill. 'This is my Asson. It's a dried gourd with a network of beads and—you see these bits?—dried snake vertebrae.'

We looked politely, though without enthusiasm.

Sybil rattled her horrid toy affectionately.

'Very interesting,' said Despard courteously.

'I could tell you lots more—'

At this point my attention wandered. Words came to me hazily as Sybil continued to air her knowledge of sorcery and voodoo—Maître Carrefour, the *Coa*, the Guidé family—

I turned my head to find Thyrza looking at me quizzically.

'You don't believe any of it, do you?' she murmured. 'But you're wrong, you know. You can't explain away *everything* as superstition, or fear, or religious bigotry. There *are* elemental truths and elemental powers. There always have been. There always will be.'

'I don't think I would dispute that,' I said.

'Wise man. Come and see my library.'

I followed her out through the french windows into the garden and along the side of the house.

'We made it out of the old stables,' she explained.

The stables and outbuildings had been reconstituted as

one large room. The whole of one long wall was lined with books. I went across to them and was presently exclaiming.

'You've got some very rare works here, Miss Grey. Is this an original *Malleus Maleficorum*? My word, you have some treasures.'

'I have, haven't I?'

'That Grimoire—very rare indeed.' I took down volume after volume from the shelves. Thyrza watched me—there was an air of quiet satisfaction about her which I did not understand.

I put back *Sadducismus Triumphatus* as Thyrza said:

'It's nice to meet someone who can appreciate one's treasures. Most people just yawn or gape.'

'There can't be much about the practice of witchcraft, sorcery, and all the rest of it that you don't know,' I said. 'What gave you an interest in it in the first place?'

'Hard to say now . . . It's been so long . . . One looks into a thing idly—and then—one gets gripped! It's a fascinating study. The things people believed—and the damn' fool things they did!'

I laughed.

'That's refreshing. I'm glad you don't believe all you read.'

'You mustn't judge me by poor Sybil. Oh yes, I saw you looking superior! But you were wrong. She's a silly woman in a lot of ways. She takes voodoo, and demonology, and black magic and mixes everything up into a glorious occult pie—but she has the power.'

'The power?'

'I don't know what else you can call it . . . There *are*

people who can become a living bridge between this world and a world of strange uncanny powers. Sybil is one of them. She is a first-class medium. She has never done it for money. But her gift is quite exceptional. When she and I and Bella—'

'Bella?'

'Oh yes. Bella has her own powers. We all have, in our different degrees. As a team—'

She broke off.

'Sorcerers Ltd?' I suggested with a smile.

'One could put it that way.'

I glanced down at the volume I was holding in my hand.

'Nostradamus and all that?'

'Nostradamus and all that.'

I said quietly: 'You *do* believe it, don't you?'

'I don't *believe*. I *know*.'

She spoke triumphantly—I looked at her.

'But how? In what way? For what reason?'

She swept her hand out towards the bookshelves—

'All that! So much of it nonsense! Such grand ridiculous phraseology! But sweep away the superstitions and the prejudices of the times—and the *core* is truth! You only dress it up—it's always been dressed up—to impress people.'

'I'm not sure I follow you?'

'My dear man, *why* have people come throughout the ages to the necromancer—to the sorcerer—to the witch-doctor? Only two reasons really. There are only two things that are wanted badly enough to risk damnation. The love potion or the cup of poison.'

'Ah.'

'So simple, isn't it? Love—and death. The love potion—to win the man you want—the black mass—to keep your lover. A draught to be taken at the full of the moon. Recite the names of devils or of spirits. Draw patterns on the floor or on the wall. All that's window dressing. The truth is the aphrodisiac in the draught!'

'And death?' I asked.

'Death?' She laughed, a queer little laugh that made me uncomfortable. 'Are *you* so interested in death?'

'Who isn't?' I said lightly.

'I wonder.' She shot me a glance, keen, searching. It took me aback.

'Death. There's always been a greater trade in that than there ever has been in love potions. And yet—how childish it all was in the past! The Borgias and their famous secret poisons. Do you know what they *really* used? Ordinary white arsenic! Just the same as any little wife poisoner in the back streets. But we've progressed a long way beyond that nowadays. Science has enlarged our frontiers.'

'With untraceable poisons?' My voice was sceptical.

'Poisons! That's *vieux jeu*. Childish stuff. There are new horizons.'

'Such as?'

'The *mind*. Knowledge of what the mind *is*—what it can *do*—what it can be *made* to do.'

'Please go on. This is most interesting.'

'The principle is well known. Medicine-men have used it in primitive communities for centuries. You don't need to kill your victim. All you need do is—*tell him to die.*'

'Suggestion? But it won't work unless the victim believes in it.'

'It doesn't work on Europeans, you mean,' she corrected me. 'It does sometimes. But that's not the point. We've gone further ahead than the witch-doctor has ever gone. The psychologists have shown the way. The desire for death! It's there—in everyone. Work on that! Work on the death wish.'

'It's an interesting idea.' I spoke with a muted scientific interest. 'Influence your subject to commit suicide? Is that it?'

'You're still lagging behind. You've heard of traumatic illnesses?'

'Of course.'

'People who, because of an unconscious wish to avoid returning to work, develop real ailments. Not malingering— real illnesses with symptoms, with actual pain. It's been a puzzle to doctors for a long time.'

'I'm beginning to get the hang of what you mean,' I said slowly.

'To destroy your subject, power must be exerted on his secret unconscious self. The death wish that exists in all of us must be stimulated, heightened.' Her excitement was growing. 'Don't you see? A *real* illness will be induced, caused by that death-seeking self. You wish to be ill, you wish to die—and so—you do get ill, and die.'

She had flung her head up now, triumphantly. I felt suddenly very cold. All nonsense, of course. This woman was slightly mad . . . And yet—

Thyrza Grey laughed suddenly.

'You don't believe me, do you?'

'It's a fascinating theory, Miss Grey—quite in line with modern thought, I'll admit. But how do you propose to stimulate this death wish that we all possess?'

'That's my secret. The way! The means! There are communications without contact. You've only to think of wireless, radar, television. Experiments in Extra-Sensory Perception haven't gone ahead as people hoped, but that's because they haven't grasped the first simple principle. You *can* accomplish it sometimes by accident—but once you know *how* it works, you could do it every time . . .'

'Can *you* do it?'

She didn't answer at once—then she said, moving away:

'You mustn't ask me, Mr Easterbrook, to give all my secrets away.'

I followed her towards the garden door—

'Why have you told me all this?' I asked.

'You understand my books. One needs sometimes to—to—well—talk to someone. And besides—'

'Yes?'

'I had the idea—Bella has it, too—that you—*may need us.*'

'*Need you?*'

'Bella thinks you came here—to find us. She is seldom at fault.'

'Why should I want to—"find you", as you put it?'

'That,' said Thyrza Grey softly, 'I do not know—yet.'

CHAPTER 7

Mark Easterbrook's Narrative

'So there you are! We wondered where you were.' Rhoda came through the open door, the others behind her. She looked round her. 'This is where you hold your *séances*, isn't it?'

'You're well informed.' Thyrza Grey laughed breezily. 'In a village everyone knows your business better than you do. We've a splendid sinister reputation, so I've heard. A hundred years ago it would have been sink or swim or the funeral pyre. My great-great-aunt—or one or two more greats—was burned as a witch, I believe, in Ireland. Those were the days!'

'I always thought you were Scottish?'

'On my father's side—hence the second sight. Irish on my mother's. Sybil is our pythoness, originally of Greek extraction. Bella represents Old English.'

'A *macabre* human cocktail,' remarked Colonel Despard.

'As you say.'

'Fun!' said Ginger.

Thyrza shot her a quick glance.

'Yes, it is in a way.' She turned to Mrs Oliver. 'You should write one of your books about a murder by black magic. I can give you a lot of dope about it.'

Mrs Oliver blinked and looked embarrassed.

'I only write very plain murders,' she said apologetically.

Her tone was of one who says 'I only do plain cooking.'

'Just about people who want other people out of the way and try to be clever about it,' she added.

'They're usually too clever for me,' said Colonel Despard. He glanced at his watch. 'Rhoda, I think—'

'Oh yes, we must go. It's much later than I thought.'

Thanks and goodbyes were said. We did not go back through the house but round to a side gate.

'You keep a lot of poultry,' remarked Colonel Despard, looking into a wired enclosure.

'I hate hens,' said Ginger. 'They cluck in such an irritating way.'

'Mostly cockerels they be.' It was Bella who spoke. She had come out from a back door.

'White cockerels,' I said.

'Table birds?' asked Despard.

Bella said, 'They'm useful to us.'

Her mouth widened in a long curving line across the pudgy shapelessness of her face. Her eyes had a sly knowing look.

'They're Bella's province,' said Thyrza Grey lightly.

We said goodbye and Sybil Stamfordis appeared from the open front door to join in speeding the parting guests.

'I don't like that woman,' said Mrs Oliver, as we drove off. 'I don't like her *at all*.'

'You mustn't take old Thyrza too seriously,' said Despard indulgently. 'She enjoys spouting all that stuff and seeing what effect it has on you.'

'I didn't mean her. She's an unscrupulous woman, with a keen eye on the main chance. But she's not dangerous like the other one.'

'Bella? She *is* a bit uncanny, I'll admit.'

'I didn't mean her either. I meant the Sybil one. She *seems* just silly. All those beads and draperies and all the stuff about voodoo, and all those fantastic reincarnations she was telling us about. (Why is it that anybody who was a kitchenmaid or an ugly old peasant never seems to get reincarnated? It's always Egyptian Princesses or beautiful Babylonian slaves. Very fishy.) But all the same, though she's stupid, I have a feeling that she could really *do* things—make queer things happen. I always put things badly—but I mean she could be *used*—by something—in a way just because she *is* so silly. I don't suppose anyone understands what I mean,' she finished pathetically.

'I do,' said Ginger. 'And I shouldn't wonder if you weren't right.'

'We really ought to go to one of their *séances*,' said Rhoda wistfully. 'It might be rather fun.'

'No, you don't,' said Despard firmly. 'I'm not having you getting mixed up in anything of that sort.'

They fell into a laughing argument. I roused myself only when I heard Mrs Oliver asking about trains the next morning.

'You can drive back with me,' I said.

Agatha Christie

Mrs Oliver looked doubtful.

'I think I'd better go by train—'

'Oh, come now. You've driven with me before. I'm a most reliable driver.'

'It's not that, Mark. But I've got to go to a funeral tomorrow. So I mustn't be late in getting back to town.' She sighed. 'I do *hate* going to funerals.'

'Must you?'

'I think I must in this case. Mary Delafontaine was a very old friend—and I think she'd *want* me to go. She was that sort of person.'

'Of course,' I exclaimed. 'Delafontaine—of course.'

The others stared at me, surprised.

'Sorry,' I said. 'It's only—that—well, I was wondering where I'd heard the name Delafontaine lately. It was you, wasn't it?' I looked at Mrs Oliver. 'You said something about visiting her—in a nursing home.'

'Did I? Quite likely.'

'What did she die of?'

Mrs Oliver wrinkled her forehead.

'Toxic polyneuritis—something like that.'

Ginger was looking at me curiously. She had a sharp penetrating glance.

As we got out of the car, I said abruptly:

'I think I'll go for a bit of a walk. Such a lot of food. That wonderful lunch and tea on top of it. It's got to be worked off somehow.'

I went off briskly before anyone could offer to accompany me. I wanted badly to get by myself and sort out my ideas.

What was all this business? Let me at least get it clear to myself. It had started, had it not, with that casual but startling remark by Poppy, that if you wanted to 'get rid of someone' the Pale Horse was the place to go.

Following on that, there had been my meeting with Jim Corrigan, and his list of 'names'—as connected with the death of Father Gorman. On that list had been the name of Hesketh-Dubois, and the name of Tuckerton, causing me to hark back to that evening at Luigi's coffee bar. There had been the name of Delafontaine, too, vaguely familiar. It was Mrs Oliver who had mentioned it, in connection with a sick friend. The sick friend was now dead.

After that, I had, for some reason which I couldn't quite identify, gone to beard Poppy in her floral bower. And Poppy had denied vehemently any knowledge of such an institution as the Pale Horse. More significant still, Poppy had been afraid.

Today—there had been Thyrza Grey.

But surely the Pale Horse and its occupants was one thing and that list of names something separate, quite unconnected. Why on earth was I coupling them together in my mind?

Why should I imagine for one moment that there was any connection between them?

Mrs Delafontaine had presumably lived in London. Thomasina Tuckerton's home had been somewhere in Surrey. No one on the list had any connection with the little village of Much Deeping. Unless—

I was just coming abreast of the King's Arms. The

King's Arms was a genuine pub with a superior look about it and a freshly-painted announcement of Lunches, Dinners and Teas.

I pushed its door open and went inside. The bar, not yet open, was on my left, on my right was a minute lounge smelling of stale smoke. By the stairs was a notice: *Office.* The office consisted of a glass window, firmly closed and a printed card. PRESS BELL. The whole place had the deserted air of a pub at this particular time of day. On a shelf by the office window was a battered registration book for visitors. I opened it and flicked through the pages. It was not much patronised. There were five or six entries, perhaps, in a week, mostly for one night only. I flicked back the pages, noting the names.

It was not long before I shut the book. There was still no one about. There were really no questions I wanted to ask at this stage. I went out again into the soft damp afternoon.

Was it only coincidence that someone called Sandford and someone else called Parkinson had stayed at the King's Arms during the last year? Both names were on Corrigan's list. Yes, but they were not particularly uncommon names. But I had noted one other name—the name of Martin Digby. If it was the Martin Digby I knew, he was the great-nephew of the woman I had always called Aunt Min—Lady Hesketh-Dubois.

I strode along, not seeing where I was going. I wanted very badly to talk to someone. To Jim Corrigan. Or to David Ardingly. Or to Hermia with her calm good sense.

I was alone with my chaotic thoughts and I didn't want to be alone. What I wanted, frankly, was someone who would argue me out of the things that I was thinking.

It was after about half an hour of tramping muddy lanes that I finally turned in at the gates of the vicarage, and made my way up a singularly ill-kept drive, to pull a rusty-looking bell at the side of the front door.

'It doesn't ring,' said Mrs Dane Calthrop, appearing at the door with the unexpectedness of a genie.

I had already suspected that fact.

'They've mended it twice,' said Mrs Dane Calthrop. 'But it never lasts. So I have to keep alert. In case it's something important. It's important with you, isn't it?'

'It—well—yes, it is important—to me, I mean.'

'That's what I meant, too . . .' She looked at me thoughtfully. 'Yes, it's quite bad, I can see—Who do you want? The vicar?'

'I—I'm not sure—'

It had been the vicar I came to see—but now, unexpectedly, I was doubtful. I didn't quite know why. But immediately Mrs Dane Calthrop told me.

'My husband's a very good man,' she said. 'Besides being the vicar, I mean. And that makes things difficult sometimes. Good people, you see, don't really understand evil.' She paused and then said with a kind of brisk efficiency, 'I think it had better be *me*.'

A faint smile came to my lips. 'Is evil your department?' I asked.

'Yes, it is. It's important in a parish to know all about the various—well—sins that are going on.'

'Isn't sin your husband's province? His official business, so to speak.'

'The forgiveness of sins,' she corrected me. 'He can give absolution. I can't. But I,' said Mrs Dane Calthrop with the utmost cheerfulness, 'can get sin arranged and classified for him. And if one knows about it one can help to prevent its harming other people. One can't help the people themselves. *I* can't, I mean. Only God can call to repentance, you know—or perhaps you don't know. A lot of people don't nowadays.'

'I can't compete with your expert knowledge,' I said, 'but I would like to prevent people being—harmed.'

She shot me a quick glance.

'It's like that, is it? You'd better come in and we'll be comfortable.'

The vicarage sitting-room was big and shabby. It was much shaded by a gargantuan Victorian shrubbery that no one seemed to have had the energy to curb. But the dimness was not gloomy for some peculiar reason. It was, on the contrary, restful. All the large shabby chairs bore the impress of resting bodies in them over the years. A fat clock on the chimney-piece ticked with a heavy comfortable regularity. Here there would always be time to talk, to say what you wanted to say, to relax from the cares brought about by the bright day outside.

Here, I felt, round-eyed girls who had tearfully discovered themselves to be prospective mothers, had confided their troubles to Mrs Dane Calthrop and received sound, if not always orthodox, advice; here angry relatives had unburdened themselves of their resentment over their in-laws; here mothers had explained that their Bob was *not* a bad boy; just high-spirited, and that to send him away to an approved school was absurd. Husbands and wives had disclosed marital difficulties.

And here was I, Mark Easterbrook, scholar, author, man of the world, confronting a grey-haired weather-beaten woman with fine eyes, prepared to lay my troubles in her lap. Why? I didn't know. I only had that odd surety that she was the right person.

'We've just had tea with Thyrza Grey,' I began.

Explaining things to Mrs Dane Calthrop was never difficult. She leaped to meet you.

'Oh I see. It's upset you? These three are a bit much to take, I agree. I've wondered myself . . . So much boasting. As a rule, in my experience, the really wicked don't boast. They can keep quiet about their wickedness. It's if your sins aren't really bad that you want so much to talk about them. Sin's such a wretched, mean, ignoble little thing. It's terribly necessary to make it seem grand and important. Village witches are usually silly ill-natured old women who like frightening people and getting something for nothing that way. Terribly easy to do, of course. When Mrs Brown's hens die all you have to do is nod your head and say darkly: "Ah, her Billy teased my Pussy last Tuesday week." Bella Webb *might* be only a witch of that kind. But she might, she just *might*, be something more . . . Something that's lasted on from a very early age and which crops up now and then in country places. It's frightening when it does, because there's real malevolence—not just a desire to impress. Sybil Stamfordis is one of the silliest women I've ever met—but she really is a medium—whatever a medium may be. Thyrza—I don't know . . . What did she say to you? It was something that she said that's upset you, I suppose?'

'You have great experience, Mrs Dane Calthrop. Would you say, from all you know and have heard, that a human being could be destroyed from a distance, without visible connection, by another human being?'

Mrs Dane Calthrop's eyes opened a little wider.

'When you say destroyed, you mean, I take it, *killed?* A plain physical fact?'

'Yes.'

'I should say it was nonsense,' said Mrs Dane Calthrop robustly.

'Ah!' I said, relieved.

'But of course I might be wrong,' said Mrs Dane Calthrop. 'My father said that airships were nonsense, and my great-grandfather probably said that railway trains were nonsense. They were both quite right. At that time they both were impossible. But they're not impossible now. What does Thyrza do, activate a death ray or something? Or do they all three draw pentagrams and wish?'

I smiled.

'You're making things come into focus,' I said. 'I must have let that woman hypnotise me.'

'Oh no,' said Mrs Dane Calthrop. 'You wouldn't do that. You're not really the suggestible type. There must have been something else. Something that happened *first*. Before all this.'

'You're quite right.' I told her, then, as simply as I could with an economy of words, of the murder of Father Gorman, and of the casual mention in the night-club of the Pale Horse. Then I took from my pocket the list of names I had copied from the paper Dr Corrigan had shown me.

Mrs Dane Calthrop looked down at it, frowning.

'I see,' she said. 'And these people? What have they all in common?'

'We're not sure. It might be blackmail—or dope—'

'Nonsense,' said Mrs Dane Calthrop. 'That's not what's worrying you. What you really believe is—*that they're all dead?*'

I gave a deep sigh.

'Yes,' I said. 'That's what I believe. But I don't really *know* that that is so. Three of them are dead. Minnie Hesketh-Dubois, Thomasina Tuckerton, Mary Delafontaine. All three died in their beds from natural causes. Which is what Thyrza Grey claims would happen.'

'You mean she claims she *made* it happen?'

'No, no. She wasn't speaking of any actual people. She was expounding what she believes to be a scientific possibility.'

'Which appears on the face of it to be nonsense,' said Mrs Dane Calthrop thoughtfully.

'I know. I would just have been polite about it and laughed to myself, if it hadn't been for that curious mention of the Pale Horse.'

'Yes,' said Mrs Dane Calthrop musingly. 'The Pale Horse. That's suggestive.'

Agatha Christie

She was silent a moment. Then she raised her head.

'It's bad,' she said. 'It's very bad. Whatever is behind it, it's got to be *stopped*. But you know that.'

'Well yes . . . But what can one do?'

'That you'll have to find out. But there's no time to be lost.' Mrs Dane Calthrop rose to her feet, a whirlwind of activity. 'You must get down to it—*at once*.' She considered. 'Haven't you got some friend who could help you?'

I thought. Jim Corrigan? A busy man with little time, and already probably doing all he could. David Ardingly—but would David believe a word? Hermia? Yes, there was Hermia. A clear brain, admirable logic. A tower of strength if she could be persuaded to become an ally. After all, she and I—I did not finish the sentence. Hermia was my steady—Hermia was the person.

'You've thought of someone? Good.'

Mrs Dane Calthrop was brisk and businesslike.

'I'll keep an eye on the Three Witches. I still feel that they are—somehow—not *really* the answer. It's like when the Stamfordis woman dishes out a lot of idiocy about Egyptian mysteries and prophecies from the Pyramid texts. All she says is plain balderdash, but there *are* Pyramids and texts and temple mysteries. I can't help feeling that Thyrza Grey has got hold of something, found out about it, or heard it talked about, and is using it in a kind of wild hotchpotch to boost her own importance and control of occult powers. People are so proud of wickedness. Odd, isn't it, that people who are good are never proud of it? That's where Christian humility comes in, I suppose. They don't even know they are good.'

She was silent for a moment and then said:

'What we really need is a *link* of some kind. A link between one of these names and the Pale Horse. Something tangible.'

CHAPTER 8

Detective Inspector Lejeune heard the well-known tune 'Father O'Flynn' being whistled outside in the passage and raised his head as Dr Corrigan came in.

'Sorry to disoblige everybody,' said Corrigan, 'but the driver of that Jaguar hadn't any alcohol in him at all . . . What P.C. Ellis smelt on his breath must have been Ellis's imagination or halitosis.'

But Lejeune at the moment was uninterested in the daily run of motorists' offences.

'Come and take a look at this,' he said.

Corrigan took the letter handed to him. It was written in a small neat script. The heading was Everest, Glendower Close, Bournemouth.

Dear Inspector Lejeune,
You may remember that you asked me to get in touch with you if I should happen to see the man who was following Father Gorman on the night that he was killed. I kept a good look-out in the neighbourhood of

*my establishment, but never caught a glimpse of him
again.*

*Yesterday, however, I attended a church fête in a
village about twenty miles from here. I was attracted by
the fact that Mrs Oliver, the well-known detective writer,
was going to be there autographing her own books. I am
a great reader of detective stories and I was quite curious
to see the lady.*

*What I did see, to my great surprise, was the man I
described to you as having passed my shop the night
Father Gorman was killed. Since then, it would seem,
he must have met with an accident, as on this occasion
he was propelling himself in a wheeled chair. I made
some discreet inquiries as to who he might be, and it
seems he is a local resident of the name of Venables. His
place of residence is Priors Court, Much Deeping. He is
said to be a man of considerable means.*

*Hoping these details may be of some service to you,
Yours truly,
Zachariah Osborne*

'Well?' said Lejeune.

'Sounds most unlikely,' said Corrigan dampingly.

'On the face of it, perhaps. But I'm not so sure—'

'This Osborne fellow—he couldn't really have seen
anyone's face very clearly on a foggy night like that. I
expect this is just a chance resemblance. You know what
people are. Ring up all over the country to say they've seen
a missing person—and nine times out of ten there's no
resemblance even to the printed description!'

'Osborne's not like that,' said Lejeune.

'What is he like?'

'He's a respectable dapper little chemist, old-fashioned, quite a character, and a great observer of persons. One of the dreams of his life is to be able to come forward and identify a wife poisoner who has purchased arsenic at his shop.'

Corrigan laughed.

'In that case, this is clearly an example of wishful thinking.'

'Perhaps.'

Corrigan looked at him curiously.

'So you think there may be something in it? What are you going to do about it?'

'There will be no harm, in any case, in making a few discreet inquiries about this Mr Venables of—' he referred to the letter—'of Priors Court, Much Deeping.'

CHAPTER 9

Mark Easterbrook's Narrative

'What exciting things happen in the country!' said Hermia lightly.

We had just finished dinner. A pot of black coffee was in front of us—

I looked at her. The words were not quite what I had expected. I had spent the last quarter of an hour telling her my story. She had listened intelligently and with interest. But her response was not at all what I had expected. The tone of her voice was indulgent—she seemed neither shocked nor stirred.

'People who say that the country is dull and the towns full of excitement don't know what they are talking about,' she went on. 'The last of the witches have gone to cover in the tumble-down cottage, black masses are celebrated in remote manor houses by decadent young men. Superstition runs rife in isolated hamlets. Middle-aged spinsters clank their false scarabs and hold *séances* and planchettes run luridly over sheets of blank paper. One could really write a very amusing series of articles on it all. Why don't you try your hand?'

'I don't think you really understand what I've been telling you, Hermia.'

'But I *do*, Mark! I think it's all *tremendously* interesting. It's a page out of history, all the lingering forgotten lore of the Middle Ages.'

'I'm not interested historically,' I said irritably. 'I'm interested in the facts. In a list of names on a sheet of paper. I know what has happened to some of those people. What's going to happen or has happened to the rest?'

'Aren't you letting yourself get rather carried away?'

'No,' I said obstinately. 'I don't think so. I think the menace is real. And I'm not alone in thinking so. The vicar's wife agrees with me.'

'Oh, the vicar's wife!' Hermia's voice was scornful.

'No, not "*the vicar's wife*" like that! She's a very unusual woman. This whole thing is *real*, Hermia.'

Hermia shrugged her shoulders.

'Perhaps.'

'But *you* don't think so?'

'I think your imagination is running away with you a little, Mark. I dare say your middle-aged pussies are quite genuine in believing it all *themselves*. I'm sure they're very nasty old pussies!'

'But not really sinister?'

'Really, Mark, how *can* they be?'

I was silent for a moment. My mind wavered—turning from light to darkness and back again. The darkness of the Pale Horse, the light that Hermia represented. Good everyday sensible light—the electric light bulb firmly fixed in its socket, illuminating all the dark corners. Nothing there—nothing at all—just the everyday objects you always find in a room. But yet—but yet—Hermia's light, clear as it might make things seem, was after all an *artificial* light . . .

My mind swung back, resolutely, obstinately . . .

'I want to look into it all, Hermia. Get to the bottom of what's going on.'

'I agree. I think you should. It might be quite interesting. In fact, really rather fun.'

'Not fun!' I said sharply.

I went on:

'I wanted to ask if you'd help me, Hermia.'

'Help you? How?'

'Help me to investigate. Get right down to what this is all about.'

'But Mark dear, just at present I'm most terribly busy. There's my article for the Journal. And the Byzantium thing. And I've promised two of my students—'

Her voice went on reasonably—sensibly—I hardly listened.

'I see,' I said. 'You've too much on your plate already.'

'That's it.' Hermia was clearly relieved at my acquiescence. She smiled at me. Once again I was struck by her expression of indulgence. Such indulgence as a mother might show over her little son's absorption in his new toy.

Damn it all, I wasn't a little boy. I wasn't looking for a mother—certainly not that kind of a mother. My own mother had been charming and feckless; and everyone in sight, including her son, had adored looking after *her*.

101

I considered Hermia dispassionately across the table.

So handsome, so mature, so intellectual, so well read! And so—how could one put it? So—yes, so damnably *dull*!

The next morning I tried to get hold of Jim Corrigan—without success. I left a message, however, that I'd be in between six and seven, if he could come for a drink. He was a busy man, I knew, and I doubted if he would be able to come at such short notice, but he turned up all right at about ten minutes to seven. While I was getting him a whisky he wandered round looking at my pictures and books. He remarked finally that he wouldn't have minded being a Mogul Emperor himself instead of a hard-pressed over-worked police surgeon.

'Though, I dare say,' he remarked as he settled down in a chair, 'that they suffered a good deal from woman trouble. At least I escape that.'

'You're not married, then?'

'No fear. And no more are you, I should say, from the comfortable mess in which you live. A wife would tidy all that up in next to no time.'

I told him that I didn't think women were as bad as he made out.

I took my drink to the chair opposite him and began:

'You must wonder why I wanted to get hold of you so urgently, but as a matter of fact something has come up that may have a bearing on what we were discussing the last time we met.'

'What was that?—oh, of course. The Father Gorman business.'

'Yes—But first, does the phrase The Pale Horse mean anything to you?'

'The Pale *Horse* . . . The *Pale* Horse—No, I don't think so—why?'

'Because I think it's possible that it might have a connection with that list of names you showed me—I've been down in the country with friends—at a place called Much Deeping, and they took me to an old pub, or what was once a pub, called the Pale Horse.'

'Wait a bit! Much Deeping? Much Deeping . . . Is it anywhere near Bournemouth?'

'It's about fifteen miles or so from Bournemouth.'

'I suppose you didn't come across anyone called Venables down there?'

'Certainly I did.'

'You did?' Corrigan sat up in some excitement. 'You certainly have a knack of going places! What is he like?'

'He's a most remarkable man.'

'He is, is he? Remarkable in what way?'

'Principally in the force of his personality. Although he's completely crippled by polio—'

Corrigan interrupted me sharply—

'*What?*'

'He had polio some years ago. He's paralysed from the waist down.'

Corrigan threw himself back in his chair with a look of disgust.

'That tears it! I thought it was too good to be true.'

103

'I don't understand what you mean.'

Corrigan said, 'You'll have to meet the D.D.I.—Divisional Detective Inspector Lejeune. He'll be interested in what you have to say. When Gorman was killed, Lejeune asked for information from anyone who had seen him in the street that night. Most of the answers were useless, as is usual. But there was a pharmacist, name of Osborne, who has a shop in those parts. He reported having seen Gorman pass his place that night, and he also saw a man who followed close after him—naturally he didn't think anything of it at that time. But he managed to describe this chap pretty closely—seemed quite sure he'd know him again. Well, a couple of days ago Lejeune got a letter from Osborne. He's retired, and living in Bournemouth. He'd been over to some local fête and he said he'd seen the man in question there. He was at the fête in a wheeled chair. Osborne asked who he was and was told his name was Venables.'

He looked at me questioningly. I nodded.

'Quite right,' I said. 'It was Venables. He was at the fête. But he couldn't have been the man who was walking along a street in Paddington following Father Gorman. It's physically impossible. Osborne made a mistake.'

'He described him very meticulously. Height about six feet, a prominent beaked nose, and a noticeable Adam's apple. Correct?'

'Yes. It fits Venables. But all the same—'

'I know. Mr Osborne isn't necessarily as good as he thinks he is at recognising people. Clearly he was misled by the coincidence of a chance resemblance. But it's disturbing to have you come along shooting your mouth off about that very district—talking about some pale horse or other. What is this pale horse? Let's have your story.'

'You won't believe it,' I warned him. 'I don't really believe it myself.'

'Come on. Let's have it.'

I told him of my conversation with Thyrza Grey. His reaction was immediate.

'What unutterable balderdash!'

'It is, isn't it?'

'Of course it is! What's the matter with you, Mark? White cockerels. Sacrifices, I suppose! A medium, the local witch, and a middle-aged country spinster who can send out a death ray guaranteed lethal. It's mad, man—absolutely mad!'

'Yes, it's mad,' I said heavily.

'Oh! stop agreeing with me, Mark. You make me feel there's something in it when you do that. *You* believe there's something in it, don't you?'

'Let me ask you a question first. This stuff about everybody having a secret urge or wish for death. Is there any scientific truth in that?'

Corrigan hesitated for a moment. Then he said:

'I'm not a psychiatrist. Strictly between you and me I think half these fellows are slightly barmy themselves. They're punch drunk on theories. And they go much too far. I can tell you that the police aren't at all fond of the expert medical witness who's always being called in for the defence to explain away a man's having killed some helpless old woman for the money in the till.'

'You prefer your glandular theory?'

He grinned.

'All right. All right. I'm a theorist, too. Admitted. But there's a good physical reason behind my theory—if I can ever get at it. But all this subconscious stuff! Pah!'

'You don't believe in it?'

'Of course I *believe* in it. But these chaps take it much too far. The unconscious "death wish" and all that, there's *something* in it, of course, but not nearly so much as they make out.'

'But there *is* such a thing,' I persisted.

'You'd better go and buy yourself a book on psychology and read all about it.'

'Thyrza Grey claims that she knows all there is to know.'

'Thyrza Grey!' he snorted. 'What does a half-baked spinster in a country village know about mental psychology?'

'She says she knows a lot.'

'As I said before, balderdash!'

'That,' I remarked, 'is what people have always said about any discovery that doesn't accord with recognised ideas. Iron ships? Balderdash! Flying-machines? Balderdash! Frogs twitching their legs on railings—'

He interrupted me.

'So you've swallowed all this, hook, line and sinker?'

'Not at all,' I said. 'I just wanted to know if there is any scientific basis for it.'

Corrigan snorted.

'Scientific basis my foot!'

'All right. I just wanted to know.'

'You'll be saying next she's the Woman with the Box.'

106

'What Woman with a box?'

'Just one of the wild stories that turns up from time to time—by Nostradamus out of Mother Shipton. Some people will swallow anything.'

'You might at least tell me how you are getting on with that list of names.'

'The boys have been hard at work, but these things take time and a lot of routine work. Names without addresses or Christian names aren't easy to trace or identify.'

'Let's take it from a different angle. I'd be willing to bet you one thing. Within a fairly recent period—say a year to a year and a half—*every one of those names has appeared on a death certificate*. Am I right?'

He gave me a queer look.

'You're right—for what it's worth.'

'That's the thing they all have in common—death.'

'Yes, but that mayn't mean as much as it sounds, Mark. Have you any idea how many people die every day in the British Isles? And some of those names are quite common— which doesn't help.'

'Delafontaine,' I said. 'Mary Delafontaine. That's not a very common name, is it? The funeral was last Tuesday, I understand.'

He shot me a quick glance.

'How do you know that? Saw it in the paper, I suppose.'

'I heard it from a friend of hers.'

'There was nothing fishy about her death. I can tell you that. In fact, there's been nothing questionable about any of the deaths the police have been investigating. If they were "accidents" it *might* be suspicious. But the deaths are all perfectly normal deaths. Pneumonia, cerebral haemorrhage, tumour on the brain, gall stones, one case of polio—nothing in the least suspicious.'

I nodded.

'Not accident,' I said. 'Not poisoning. Just plain illnesses leading to death. Just as Thyrza Grey claims.'

'Are you really suggesting that that woman can cause someone she's never seen, miles away, to catch pneumonia and die of it?'

'*I*'m not suggesting such a thing. *She* did. I think it's fantastic and I'd *like* to think it's impossible. But there *are* certain curious factors. There's the casual mention of a Pale Horse—in connection with the removal of unwanted persons. There *is* a place called the Pale Horse—and the woman who lives there practically boasts that such an operation is possible. Living in that neighbourhood is a man who is recognised very positively as the man who was seen following Father Gorman on the night that he was killed—the night when he had been called to a dying woman who was heard to speak of "great wickedness." Rather a lot of coincidences, don't you think?'

'The man couldn't have been Venables, since according to you, he's been paralysed for years.'

'It isn't possible, from the medical point of view, that that paralysis could be faked?'

'Of course not. The limbs would be atrophied.'

'That certainly seems to settle the question,' I admitted. I sighed. 'A pity. If there is a—I don't know quite what to call it—an organisation that specialises in "Removals—Human" Venables is the kind of brain I can see running it.

The things he has in that house of his represent a fantastic amount of money. Where does that money come from?'

I paused—and then said:

'All these people who have died—tidily—in their beds, of this, that and the other—were there people who profited by their deaths?'

'Someone always profits by a death—in greater or lesser degree. There were no notably suspicious circumstances, if that is what you mean.'

'It isn't quite.'

'Lady Hesketh-Dubois, as you probably know, left about fifty thousand net. A niece and a nephew inherit. Nephew lives in Canada. Niece is married and lives in North of England. Both could do with the money. Thomasina Tuckerton was left a very large fortune by her father. If she died unmarried before the age of twenty-one, it reverts to her stepmother. Stepmother seems quite a blameless creature. Then there's your Mrs Delafontaine—money left to a cousin—'

'Ah yes. And the cousin?'

'In Kenya with her husband.'

'All splendidly absent,' I commented.

Corrigan threw me an annoyed glance.

'Of the three Sandfords who've kicked the bucket, one left a wife much younger than himself who has married again—rather quickly. Deceased Sandford was an R.C., and wouldn't have given her a divorce. A fellow called Sidney Harmondsworth who died of cerebral haemorrhage was suspected at the Yard of augmenting his income by discreet blackmail. Several people in high places must be greatly relieved that he is no more.'

'What you're saying in effect is that all these deaths were *convenient* deaths. What about Corrigan?'

Corrigan grinned.

'Corrigan is a common name. Quite a lot of Corrigans have died—but not to the particular advantage of anyone in particular so far as we can learn.'

'That settles it. *You're* the next prospective victim. Take good care of yourself.'

'I will. And don't think that your Witch of Endor is going to strike me down with a duodenal ulcer, or Spanish 'flu. Not a case-hardened doctor!'

'Listen, Jim. I want to investigate this claim of Thyrza Grey's. Will you help me?'

'No, I won't! I can't understand a clever educated fellow like you being taken in by such balderdash.'

I sighed.

'Can't you use another word? I'm tired of that one.'

'Poppycock, if you like it better.'

'I don't much.'

'Obstinate fellow, aren't you, Mark?'

'As I see it,' I said, 'somebody has to be!'

CHAPTER 10

Glendower Close was very very new. It swept round in an uneven semi-circle and at its lower end the builders were still at work. About half-way along its length was a gate inscribed with the name of Everest.

Visible, bent over the garden border, planting bulbs, was a rounded back which Inspector Lejeune recognised without difficulty as that of Mr Zachariah Osborne. He opened the gate and passed inside. Mr Osborne rose from his stooping position and turned to see who had entered his domain. On recognising his visitor, an additional flush of pleasure rose to his already flushed face. Mr Osborne in the country was looking very much the same as Mr Osborne in his shop in London. He wore stout country shoes and was in his shirt sleeves, but even this déshabillé detracted little from the dapper neatness of his appearance. A fine dew of perspiration showed on the shining baldness of his domed head. This he carefully wiped with a pocket handkerchief before advancing to meet his visitor.

'Inspector Lejeune!' he exclaimed pleasurably. 'I take this

as an honour. I do indeed, sir. I received your acknowledge-ment of my letter, but I never hoped to see you in person. Welcome to my little abode. Welcome to Everest. The name surprises you perhaps? I have always been deeply interested in the Himalayas. I followed every detail of the Everest expedition. What a triumph for our country. Sir Edmund Hillary! What a man! What endurance! As one who has never had to suffer any personal discomfort, I do appreciate the courage of those who go forth to scale unconquered mountains or sail through ice-bound seas to discover the secrets of the Pole. But come inside and partake, I beg of you, of some simple refreshment.'

Leading the way, Mr Osborne ushered Lejeune into the small bungalow which was the acme of neatness, though rather sparsely furnished.

'Not quite settled yet,' explained Mr Osborne. 'I attend local sales whenever possible. There is good stuff to be picked up that way, at a quarter of the cost one would have to pay in a shop. Now what can I offer you? A glass of sherry? Beer? A cup of tea? I could have the kettle on in a jiffy?'

Lejeune expressed a preference for beer.

'Here we are, then,' said Mr Osborne, returning a moment later with two brimming pewter tankards. 'We will sit and take our rest. Everest. Ha ha! The name of my house has a double meaning. I am always fond of a little joke.'

Those social amenities satisfied, Mr Osborne leaned forward hopefully.

'My information was of service to you?'

Lejeune softened the blow as much as possible.

'Not as much as we hoped, I am afraid.'

'Ah, I confess I am disappointed. Though, really, there is, I realise, no reason to suppose that a gentleman proceeding in the same direction as Father Gorman should necessarily be his murderer. That was really too much to hope for. And this Mr Venables is well-to-do and much respected locally, I understand, moving in the best social circles.'

'The point is,' said Lejeune, 'that it could not have been Mr Venables that you saw on that particular evening.'

'Oh, but it was. I have absolutely no doubt in my own mind. I am *never* mistaken about a face.'

'I'm afraid you must have been this time,' said Lejeune gently. 'You see, Mr Venables is a victim of polio. For over three years he has been paralysed from the waist down, and is unable to use his legs.'

'Polio!' ejaculated Mr Osborne. 'Oh dear, dear . . . That does seem to settle the matter. And yet—You'll excuse me, Inspector Lejeune. I hope you won't take offence. But that really is so? I mean you have definite medical evidence as to that?'

'Yes, Mr Osborne. We have. Mr Venables is a patient of Sir William Dugdale of Harley Street, a most eminent member of the medical profession.'

'Of course, of course. F.R.C.P. A very well known name! Oh dear, I seem to have fallen down badly. I was so very sure. And to trouble you for nothing.'

'You mustn't take it like that,' said Lejeune quickly. 'Your information is still very valuable. It is clear that the man you saw must bear a very close resemblance to Mr Venables—and since Mr Venables is a man of distinctly unusual appearance, that is extremely valuable knowledge to have. There cannot be many persons answering to that description.'

'True, true.' Mr Osborne cheered up a little. 'A man of the criminal classes resembling Mr Venables in appearance. There certainly cannot be many such. In the files at Scotland Yard—'

He looked hopefully at the inspector.

'It may not be quite so simple as that,' said Lejeune slowly. 'The man may not have a record. And in any case, as you said just now there is as yet no reason to assume that this particular man had anything to do with the attack on Father Gorman.'

Mr Osborne looked depressed again.

'You must forgive me. Wishful thinking, I am afraid, on my part . . . I should so like to have been able to give evidence at a murder trial . . . And they would not have been able to shake me, I assure you of that. Oh no, I should have stuck to my guns!'

Lejeune was silent, considering his host thoughtfully. Mr Osborne responded to the silent scrutiny.

'Yes?'

'Mr Osborne, *why* would you have stuck to your guns, as you put it?'

Mr Osborne looked astonished.

'Because I am so certain—oh—oh yes, I see what you mean. The man was *not* the man. So I have no business to feel certain. And yet I do—'

114

Lejeune leaned forward. 'You may have wondered why I have come to see you today. Having received medical evidence that the man seen by you could not have been Mr Venables, why am I here?'

'Quite. Quite. Well, then, Inspector Lejeune, why did you come?'

'I came,' said Lejeune, 'because the very positiveness of your identification impressed me. I wanted to know on what grounds your certainty was based. It was a foggy night, remember. I have been to your shop. I have stood where you stood in your doorway and looked across the street. On a foggy night it seemed to me that a figure at that distance would be very insubstantial, that it would be almost impossible to distinguish features clearly.'

'Up to a point, of course, you are quite right. Fog *was* setting in. But it came, if you understand me, in patches. It cleared for a short space every now and then. It did so at the moment that I saw Father Gorman walking fast along the opposite pavement. That is why I saw him and the man who followed shortly after him so clearly. Moreover, just when the second man was abreast of me, he flicked on a lighter to relight his cigarette. His profile at that moment was very clear—the nose, the chin, the pronounced Adam's apple. That's a striking-looking man, I thought. I've never seen *him* about before. If he'd ever been into my shop I'd have remembered him, I thought. So, you see—'

Mr Osborne broke off.

'Yes, I see,' said Lejeune thoughtfully.

'A brother,' suggested Mr Osborne hopefully. 'A twin brother, perhaps? Now that *would* be a solution.'

'The identical twin solution?' Lejeune smiled and shook his head. 'So very convenient in fiction. But in real life—' he shook his head. 'It doesn't happen, you know. It really doesn't happen.'

'No . . . No, I suppose not. But possibly an ordinary brother. A close family resemblance—' Mr Osborne looked wistful.

'As far as we can ascertain,' Lejeune spoke carefully, 'Mr Venables has not got a brother.'

'As far as you can ascertain?' Mr Osborne repeated the words.

'Though of British nationality, he was born abroad, his parents only brought him to England when he was eleven years old.'

'You don't know very much about him really, then? About his family, I mean?'

'No,' said Lejeune, thoughtfully. 'It isn't easy to find out very much about Mr Venables—without, that is to say, going and asking him—and we've no grounds for doing that.'

He spoke deliberately. There were ways of finding out things without going and asking, but he had no intention of telling Mr Osborne so.

'So if it wasn't for the medical evidence,' he said, getting to his feet, 'you'd be sure about the identification?'

'Oh yes,' said Mr Osborne, following suit. 'It's quite a hobby of mine, you know, memorising faces.' He chuckled. 'Many a customer I've surprised that way. "How's the asthma?" I'd say to someone—and she'd look quite surprised. "You came in last March," I'd say, "with a prescription. One of Dr Hargreaves's." And wouldn't she look surprised! Did me a lot of good in business. It pleases people to be remembered, though I wasn't as good with names as with faces. I started making a hobby of the thing quite young. If Royalty can do it, I used to say to myself, you can do it, Zachariah Osborne! After a while it becomes automatic. You hardly have to make an effort.'

Lejeune sighed.

'I'd like to have a witness like you in the box,' he said. 'Identification is always a tricky business. Most people can't tell you anything at all. They'll say things like: "Oh, tallish, I think. Fair-haired—well, not very fair, sort of middling. Ordinary sort of face. Eyes blue—or grey—or perhaps brown. Grey mackintosh—or it may have been dark blue."'

Mr Osborne laughed.

'Not much good to you, that sort of thing.'

'Frankly, a witness like you would be a godsend!'

Mr Osborne looked pleased.

'It's a gift,' he said modestly. 'But mind you, I've cultivated my gift. You know the game they play at children's parties—a lot of objects brought in on a tray and a few minutes given to memorise them. I can score a hundred per cent every time. Quite surprises people. How wonderful, they say. It's not wonderful. It's a knack. Comes with practice.' He chuckled. 'I'm not a bad conjurer either. I do a bit to amuse the kiddies at Christmas-time. Excuse me, Mr Lejeune, what *have* you got in your breast pocket?'

He leaned forward and extracted a small ash-tray.

'Tut, tut, sir, and you in the police force!'

He laughed heartily and Lejeune laughed with him. Then Mr Osborne sighed.

'It's a nice little place I've got here, sir. The neighbours seem pleasant and friendly. It's the life I've been looking forward to for years, but I'll admit to you, Mr Lejeune, that I miss the interest of my own business. Always someone coming in and out. Types, you know, lots of types to study. I've looked forward to having my little bit of garden, and I've got quite a lot of interests. Butterflies, as I told you, and a bit of bird watching now and again. I didn't realise that I'd miss what I might call the human element so much.

'I'd looked forward to going abroad in a small way. Well, I've taken one week-end trip to France. Quite nice, I must say—but I felt, very strongly, that England's really good enough for me. I didn't care for the foreign cooking, for one thing. They haven't the least idea, as far as I can see, how to do eggs and bacon.'

He sighed again.

'Just shows you what human nature is. Looked forward no end to retiring, I did. And now—do you know I've actually played with the idea of buying a small share in a pharmaceutical business here in Bournemouth—just enough to give me an interest, no need to be tied to the shop all the time. But I'd feel in the middle of things again. It will be the same with you, I expect. You'll make plans ahead, but when the time comes, you'll miss the excitement of your present life.'

Lejeune smiled.

'A policeman's life is not such a romantically exciting

one as you think, Mr Osborne. You've got the amateur's view of crime. Most of it is dull routine. We're not always chasing down criminals, and following up mysterious clues. It can be quite a dull business, really.'

Mr Osborne looked unconvinced.

'You know best,' he said. 'Goodbye, Mr Lejeune, and I'm sorry indeed that I haven't been able to help you. If there was anything—any time—'

'I'll let you know,' Lejeune promised him.

'That day at the fête, it seemed such a chance,' Osborne murmured sadly.

'I know. A pity the medical evidence is so definite, but one can't get over that sort of thing, can one?'

'Well—' Mr Osborne let the word linger, but Lejeune did not notice it. He strode away briskly. Mr Osborne stood by the gate looking after him.

'Medical evidence,' he said. 'Doctors indeed! If he knew half what I know about doctors—innocents, that's what *they* are! Doctors indeed!'

CHAPTER 11

Mark Easterbrook's Narrative

First Hermia. Now Corrigan.

All right, then, I was making a fool of myself!

I was accepting balderdash as solid truth. I had been hypnotised by that phony woman Thyrza Grey into accepting a farrago of nonsense. I was a credulous, superstitious ass.

I decided to forget the whole damned business. What was it to do with me anyway?

Through the mist of disillusionment, I heard the echoes of Mrs Dane Calthrop's urgent tones.

'*You've got to DO something!*'

All very well—to say things like that.

'*You need someone to help you . . .*'

I had needed Hermia. I had needed Corrigan. But neither of them would play. There was no one else.

Unless—

I sat—considering the idea.

On an impulse I went to the telephone and rang Mrs Oliver.

'Hallo. Mark Easterbrook here.'

120

'Yes?'

'Can you tell me the name of that girl who was staying in the house for the fête?'

'I expect so. Let me see . . . Yes, of course, Ginger. That was her name.'

'I know that. But her other name.'

'What other name?'

'I doubt if she was christened Ginger. And she must have a surname.'

'Well, of course. But I've no idea what it is. One never seems to hear any surnames nowadays. It's the first time I'd ever met her.' There was a slight pause and then Mrs Oliver said, 'You'll have to ring up Rhoda and ask her.'

I didn't like that idea. Somehow I felt shy about it.

'Oh, I can't do that,' I said.

'It's perfectly simple,' said Mrs Oliver encouragingly. 'Just say you've lost her address and can't remember her name and you'd promised to send her one of your books, or the name of a shop that sells cheap caviare, or to return a handkerchief which she lent you when your nose bled one day, or the address of a rich friend who wants a picture restored. Any of those do? I can think of lots more if you'd like.'

'One of those will do beautifully,' I assured her.

I rang off, dialled 100 and presently was speaking to Rhoda.

'Ginger?' said Rhoda. 'Oh, she lives in a Mews. Calgary Place. Forty-five. Wait a minute. I'll give you her telephone number.' She went away and returned a minute later. 'It's Capricorn 35987. Got it?'

'Yes, thanks. But I haven't got her name. I never heard it.'

'Her name? Oh, her *surname*, you mean. Corrigan. Katherine Corrigan. What did you say?'

'Nothing. Thanks, Rhoda.'

It seemed to me an odd coincidence. Corrigan. Two Corrigans. Perhaps it was an omen.

I dialled Capricorn 35987.

Ginger sat opposite me at a table in the White Cockatoo where we had met for a drink. She looked refreshingly the same as she had looked at Much Deeping—a tousled mop of red hair, an engaging freckled face and alert green eyes. She was wearing her London artistic livery of skin-tight pants, a Sloppy Joe jersey and black woollen stockings—but otherwise she was the same Ginger. I liked her very much.

'I've had to do a lot of work to track you down,' I said. 'Your surname and your address and your telephone number—all unknown. I've got a problem.'

'That's what my daily always says. It usually means that I have to buy her a new saucepan scourer or a carpet brush, or something dull.'

'You don't have to buy anything,' I assured her.

Then I told her. It didn't take quite so long as the story I had told to Hermia, because she was already familiar with the Pale Horse and its occupants. I averted my eyes from her as I finished the tale. I didn't want to see her reaction. I didn't want to see indulgent amusement, or stark incredulity. The whole thing sounded more idiotic than ever. No one (except Mrs Dane Calthrop) could possibly feel about it as I felt. I drew patterns on the plastic table top with a stray fork.

Ginger's voice came briskly.

'That's all, is it?'

'That's all,' I admitted.

'What are you going to do about it?'

'You think—I *should* do something about it?'

'Well, of course! *Someone's* got to do something! You can't have an organisation going about bumping people off and not do *anything*.'

'But what *can* I do?'

I could have fallen on her neck and hugged her.

She was sipping *Pernod* and frowning. Warmth spread over me. I was no longer alone.

Presently she said musingly:

'You'll have to find out what it all means.'

'I agree. But how?'

'There seem to be one or two leads. Perhaps I can help.'

'Would you? But there's your job.'

'Plenty could be done out of office hours.' She frowned again as she thought.

'That girl,' she said at last. 'The one at supper after the Old Vic. Poppy or something. She knows about it—she must do—to say what she did.'

'Yes, but she got frightened, and sheered off when I tried to ask her questions. She was scared. She definitely wouldn't talk.'

'That's where I can help,' said Ginger confidently. 'She'd tell me things she wouldn't tell you. Can you arrange for us to meet? Your friend and her and you and me? A show, or dinner or something?' Then she looked doubtful. 'Or is that too expensive?'

I assured her that I could support the expense.

'As for you—' Ginger thought a minute. 'I believe,' she said slowly, 'that your best bet would be the Thomasina Tuckerton angle.'

'But how? She's dead.'

'And somebody wanted her dead, if your ideas are correct! And arranged it with the Pale Horse. There seem two possibilities. The stepmother, or else the girl she had the fight with at Luigi's and whose young man she had pinched. She was going to marry him, perhaps. That wouldn't suit the stepmother's book—or the girl's—if she was crazy enough about the young man. Either of them might have gone to the Pale Horse. We might get a lead there. What was the girl's name, or don't you know?'

'I think it was Lou.'

'Ash blonde lank hair, medium height, rather bosomy?'

I agreed with the description.

'I think I've met her about. Lou Ellis. She's got a bit of money herself—'

'She didn't look like it.'

'They don't—but she has, all right. Anyway, she could afford to pay the Pale Horse's fees. They don't do it for nothing, I suppose.'

'One would hardly imagine so.'

'You'll have to tackle the stepmother. It's more up your street than mine. Go and see her—'

'I don't know where she lives or anything.'

'Luigi knows something about Tommy's home. He'll know what county she lives in, I should imagine. A few books of reference ought to do the rest. But what idiots we are! You saw the notice in *The Times* of her death. You've only got to go and look in their files.'

'I'll have to have a pretext for tackling the stepmother,' I said thoughtfully.

Ginger said that that would be easy.

'You're *someone*, you see,' she pointed out. 'A historian, and you lecture and you've got letters after your name. Mrs Tuckerton will be impressed, and probably tickled to death to see you.'

'And the pretext?'

'Some feature of interest about her house?' suggested Ginger vaguely. 'Sure to have something if it's an old one.'

'Nothing to do with my period,' I objected.

'She won't know that,' said Ginger. 'People always think that anything over a hundred years old must interest a historian or an archaeologist. Or how about a picture? There must be some old pictures of some kind. Anyway, you make an appointment and you arrive and you butter her up and be charming, and then you say you once met her daughter— her stepdaughter—and say how sad etc. . . . And then, bring in, quite suddenly, a reference to the Pale Horse. Be a little sinister if you like.'

'And then?'

'And then you observe the reaction. If you mention the Pale Horse out of the blue, and she has a guilty conscience, I defy anyone not to show *some* sign.'

'And if she does—what next?'

'The important thing is, that we'll know we're on the right track. Once we're *sure*, we can go full steam ahead.'

She added thoughtfully:

'There's something else. Why do you think the Grey woman told you all she did tell you? Why was she so forthcoming?'

'The common-sense answer is because she's potty.'

'I don't mean that. I mean—why *you*? You in particular? I just wondered if there might be some kind of tie-up?'

'Tie-up with what?'

'Wait just a minute—while I get my ideas in order.'

I waited. Ginger nodded twice emphatically and then spoke.

'Supposing—just supposing—it went like this. The Poppy girl knows all about the Pale Horse in a vague kind of way—not through personal knowledge, but by hearing it talked about. She sounds the sort of girl that wouldn't be noticed much by anyone when they were talking—but she'd quite likely take in a lot more than they thought she did. Rather silly people are often like that. Say she was overheard talking to you about it that night, and someone ticks her off. Next day you come and ask her questions, and she's been scared, so she won't talk. But the fact that you've come and asked her also gets around. Now what would be the reason for your asking questions? You're not the police. The *likely* reason would be that you're a possible *client*.'

'But surely—'

'It's logical, I tell you. You've heard rumours of this thing—you want to find out about it—for your own purposes. Presently you appear at the fête in Much Deeping. You are brought to the Pale Horse—presumably because

126

you've asked to be taken there—and what happens? Thyrza Grey goes straight into her sales talk.'

'I suppose it's a possibility.' I considered . . . 'Do you think she can do what she claims to do, Ginger?'

'Personally I'd be inclined to say of course she can't! But odd things *can* happen. Especially with things like hypnotism. Telling someone to go and take a bite out of a candle the next afternoon at four o'clock, and they do it without having any idea *why*. That *sort* of thing. And electric boxes where you put in a drop of blood and it tells you if you're going to have cancer in two years' time. It all sounds rather bogus—but perhaps not entirely bogus. About Thyrza—I don't *think* it's true—but I'm terribly afraid it *might* be!'

'Yes,' I said sombrely, 'that explains it very well.'

'I might put in a bit of work on Lou,' said Ginger thoughtfully. 'I know lots of places where I can run across her. Luigi might know a few things too.

'But the first thing,' she added, 'is to get in touch with Poppy.'

The latter was arranged fairly easily. David was free three nights ahead, we settled on a musical show, and he arrived, with Poppy in tow. We went to the Fantasie for supper and I noticed that Ginger and Poppy after a prolonged retirement to powder their noses, reappeared on excellent terms with each other. No controversial subjects were raised during the party on Ginger's instructions. We finally parted and I drove Ginger home.

'Not much to report,' she said cheerfully. 'I've been on to Lou. The man they quarrelled about was Gene Pleydon, by the way. A nasty bit of goods, if you ask me. Very much on the make. The girls all adore him. He was making quite a play for Lou and then Tommy came along. Lou says he didn't care for her a bit, he was after her money—but she'd probably want to think that. Anyway, he dropped Lou like a hot coal and she was naturally sore about it. According to her, it wasn't much of a row—just a few girlish high spirits.'

'Girlish high spirits! She tugged Tommy's hair out by the roots.'

'I'm just telling you what Lou told me.'

'She seems to have been very forthcoming.'

'Oh, they all like talking about their affairs. They'll talk to anyone who will listen. Anyway, Lou has got another boy friend now—another dud, I'd say, but she's already crazy about him. So it doesn't look to me as though she'd been a client of the Pale Horse. I brought the term up, but it didn't register. I think we can wash her out. Luigi doesn't think there was much in it, either. On the other hand, he thinks Tommy *was* serious about Gene. And Gene was going for her in a big way. What have you done about the stepmother?'

'She was abroad. She comes back tomorrow. I've written her a letter—or rather I got my secretary to write it, asking for an appointment.'

'Good. We're getting things moving. I hope everything doesn't peter out.'

'If it gets us anywhere!'

'Something will,' said Ginger enthusiastically. 'That reminds me. To go back to the beginning of all this, the theory is that Father Gorman was killed after being called out to a dying woman, and that he was murdered because of something she told him or confessed to him. What happened to that woman? Did she die? And who was she? There ought to be some lead there.'

'She died. I don't really know much about her. I think her name was Davis.'

'Well, couldn't you find out more?'

'I'll see what I can do.'

'If we could get at her background, we might find out how she knew what she did know.'

'I see your point.'

I got Jim Corrigan on the telephone early the next morning and put my query to him.

'Let me see now. We did get a bit further, but not much. Davis wasn't her real name, that's why it took a little time to check up on her. Half a moment, I jotted down a few things . . . Oh yes, here we are. Her real name was Archer, and her husband had been a small-time crook. She left him and went back to her maiden name.'

'What sort of a crook was Archer? And where is he now?'

'Oh, very small stuff. Pinched things from department stores. Unconsidered trifles here and there. He had a few convictions. As to where he is now, he's dead.'

'Not much there.'

'No, there isn't. The firm Mrs Davis was working for at the time of her death, the C.R.C. (Customers' Reactions Classified), apparently didn't know anything about her, or her background.'

I thanked him and rang off.

CHAPTER 12

Mark Easterbrook's Narrative

Three days later Ginger rang me up.

'I've got something for you,' she said. 'A name and address. Write it down.'

I took out my notebook.

'Go ahead.'

'Bradley is the name and the address is Seventy-eight Municipal Square Buildings, Birmingham.'

'Well, I'm damned, what is all this?'

'Goodness knows! I don't. I doubt if Poppy does really!'

'Poppy? Is this—'

'Yes. I've been working on Poppy in a big way. I told you I could get something out of her if I tried. Once I got her softened up, it was easy.'

'How did you set about it?' I asked curiously.

Ginger laughed.

'Girls-together stuff. You wouldn't understand. The point is that if a girl tells things to another girl it doesn't really count. She doesn't think it matters.'

'All in the trade union so to speak?'

'You could put it like that. Anyway, we lunched together, and I yapped a bit about my love life—and various obstacles—married man with impossible wife—Catholic— wouldn't divorce him—made his life hell. And how she was an invalid, always in pain, but not likely to die for years. Really much better for her if she *could* die. Said I'd a good mind to try the Pale Horse, but I didn't really know how to set about it—and would it be terribly expensive? And Poppy said yes, she thought it would. She'd heard they charged the earth. And I said "Well, I *have* expectations." Which I have, you know—a great-uncle—a poppet and I'd hate him to die, but the fact came in useful. Perhaps, I said, they'd take something on account? But how did one set about it? And then Poppy came across with that name and address. You had to go to him first, she said, to settle the business side.'

'It's fantastic!' I said.

'It is, rather.'

We were both silent for a moment.

I said incredulously: 'She told you this quite openly? She didn't seem—scared?'

Ginger said impatiently: 'You don't understand. Telling me didn't count. And after all, Mark, if what we think is true the business has to be more or less advertised, hasn't it? I mean they must want new "clients" all the time.'

'We're mad to believe anything of the kind.'

'All right. We're mad. Are you going to Birmingham to see Mr Bradley?'

'Yes,' I said. 'I'm going to see Mr Bradley. If he exists.'

I hardly believed that he did. But I was wrong. Mr Bradley did exist.

Municipal Square Buildings was an enormous honeycomb of offices. Seventy-eight was on the third floor. On the ground-glass door was neatly printed in black: *C. R. Bradley, COMMISSION AGENT*. And below, in smaller letters: *Please enter.*

I entered.

There was a small outer office, empty, and a door marked *PRIVATE*, half ajar. A voice from behind it said:

'Come in, please.'

The inner office was larger. It had a desk, one or two comfortable chairs, a telephone, a stack of box files, and Mr Bradley sitting behind the desk.

He was a small dark man, with shrewd dark eyes. He wore a dark business suit and looked the acme of respectability.

'Just shut the door, will you?' he said pleasantly. 'And sit down. That chair's quite comfortable. Cigarette? No? Well now, what can I do for you?'

I looked at him. I didn't know how to begin. I hadn't the least idea what to say. It was, I think, sheer desperation that led me to attack with the phrase I did. Or it may have been the small beady eyes.

'How much?' I said.

It startled him a little, I was glad to note, but not in the way that he ought to have been startled. He did not assume, as I would have assumed in his place, that someone not quite right in the head had come into his office.

His eyebrows rose.

'Well, well, well,' he said. 'You don't waste much time, do you?'

I held to my line.

'What's the answer?'

He shook his head gently in a slightly reproving manner.

'That's not the way to go about things. We must proceed in the proper manner.'

I shrugged my shoulders.

'As you like. What's the proper manner?'

'We haven't introduced ourselves yet, have we? I don't know your name.'

'At the moment,' I said, 'I don't really think I feel inclined to tell it to you.'

'Cautious.'

'Cautious.'

'An admirable quality—though not always practicable. Now who sent you to me? Who's our mutual friend?'

'Again I can't tell you. A friend of mine has a friend who knows a friend of yours.'

Mr Bradley nodded his head.

'That's the way a lot of my clients come,' he said. 'Some of the problems are rather—delicate. You know my profession, I presume?'

He had no intention of waiting for my reply. He hastened to give me the answer.

'Turf Commission Agent,' he said. 'You're interested, perhaps, in—horses?'

There was just the faintest pause before the last word.

'I'm not a racing man,' I said non-committally.

'There are many aspects of the horse. Racing, hunting,

hacking. It's the sporting aspect that interests me. Betting.' He paused for a moment and then asked casually—almost too casually:

'Any particular horse you had in mind?'

I shrugged my shoulders and burnt my boats.

'A pale horse . . .'

'Ah, very good, excellent. You yourself, if I may say so, seem to be rather a *dark* horse. Ha ha! You mustn't be nervous. There really is no need to be nervous.'

'That's what *you* say,' I said rather rudely.

Mr Bradley's manner became more bland and soothing.

'I can quite understand your feelings. But I can assure you that you needn't have any anxiety. I'm a lawyer myself—disbarred, of course,' he added parenthetically, in what was really almost an engaging way. 'Otherwise I shouldn't be here. But I can assure you that I know my law. Everything I recommend is perfectly legal and above board. It's just a question of a bet. A man can bet on anything he pleases, whether it will rain tomorrow, whether the Russians can send a man to the moon, or whether your wife's going to have twins. You can bet whether Mrs B. will die before Christmas, or whether Mrs C. will live to be a hundred. You back your judgement or your intuition or whatever you like to call it. It's as simple as that.'

I felt exactly as though I were being reasssured by a surgeon before an operation. Mr Bradley's consulting-room manner was perfect.

I said slowly:

'I don't really understand this business of the Pale Horse.'

'And that worries you? Yes, it worries a lot of people.

More things in heaven and earth, Horatio, and so on and so on. Frankly, I don't understand it myself. But it gets results. It gets results in the most marvellous way.'

'If you could tell me more about it—'

I had settled on my role now—cautious, eager—but scared. It was obviously an attitude with which Mr Bradley had frequently had to cope.

'Do you know the place at all?'

I made a quick decision. It would be unwise to lie.

'I—well—yes—I was with some friends. They took me there—'

'Charming old pub. Full of historical interest. And they've done wonders in restoring it. You met her, then. My friend, Miss Grey, I mean?'

'Yes—yes, of course. An extraordinary woman.'

'Isn't she? Yes, isn't she? You've hit it exactly. An extraordinary woman. And with extraordinary powers.'

'The things she claims! Surely—quite—well—impossible?'

'Exactly. That's the whole point. The things she claims to be able to know and *do* are impossible! Everybody would say so. In a court of law, for instance—'

The black beady eyes were boring into mine. Mr Bradley repeated the words with designed emphasis.

'In a court of law, for instance—the whole thing would be ridiculed! If that woman stood up and confessed to murder, murder by remote control or "will power" or whatever nonsensical name she likes to use, that confession couldn't be acted upon! Even if her statement was true (which of course sensible men like you and I don't believe for one moment!) it couldn't be admitted legally. Murder by remote control isn't murder in the eyes of the law. It's just nonsense. That's the whole beauty of the thing—as you'll appreciate if you think for a moment.'

I understood that I was being reassured. Murder committed by occult powers was not murder in an English court of law. If I were to hire a gangster to commit murder with a cosh or a knife, I was committed with him—an accomplice before the fact—I had conspired with him. But if I commissioned Thyrza Grey to use her black arts—those black arts were not admissible. That was what, according to Mr Bradley, was the beauty of the thing.

All my natural scepticism rose up in protest. I burst out heatedly:

'But damn it all, it's fantastic,' I shouted. 'I don't believe it. It's impossible.'

'I agree with you. I really do. Thyrza Grey is an extraordinary woman, and she certainly has some extraordinary powers, but one *can't* believe all the things she claims for herself. As you say, it's too fantastic. In this age, one really can't credit that someone can send out thought-waves or whatever it is, either oneself or through a medium, sitting in a cottage in England and cause someone to sicken and die of a convenient disease out in Capri or somewhere like that.'

'But that *is* what she claims?'

'Oh yes. Of course she *has* powers—she is Scottish and what is called second sight is a peculiarity of that race. It really does exist. What I do believe, and believe without a doubt, is this': he leaned forward, wagging a forefinger impressively, 'Thyrza Grey does know—beforehand—when someone is going to die. It's a gift. And she has it.'

He leaned back, studying me. I waited.

'Let's assume a hypothetical case. Someone, yourself or another, would like very much to know when—let's say Great-Aunt Eliza—is going to die. It's useful, you must admit, to know something like that. Nothing unkind in it, nothing wrong—just a matter of business convenience. What plans to make? Will there be, shall we say, a useful sum of money coming in by next November? If you knew that, definitely, you might take up some valuable option. Death is such a chancy matter. Dear old Eliza might live, pepped up by doctors, for another ten years. You'd be delighted, of course, you're fond of the dear old girl, but how useful it would be to *know*.'

He paused and then leaned a little farther forward.

'Now that's where *I* come in. I'm a betting man. I'll bet on anything—naturally on my own terms. You come to see me. Naturally you wouldn't want to bet on the old girl's passing out. That would be repulsive to your finer feelings. So we put it this way. You bet me a certain sum that Aunt Eliza will be hale and hearty still next Christmas, I bet you that she won't.'

The beady eyes were on me, watching . . .

'Nothing against that, is there? Simple. We have an argument on the subject. I say Aunt E. is lined up for death, you say she isn't. We draw up a contract and sign it. I give you a date. I say that a fortnight either way from that date Auntie E.'s funeral service will be read. You say it won't. If you're right—*I* pay *you*. If you're wrong, you—pay *me!*'

137

I looked at him. I tried to summon up the feelings of a man who wants a rich old lady out of the way. I shifted it to a blackmailer. Easier to throw oneself into that part. Some man had been bleeding me for years. I couldn't bear it any longer. I wanted him dead. I hadn't the nerve to kill him myself, but I'd give anything—yes, anything—

I spoke—my voice was hoarse. I was acting the part with some confidence.

'What terms?'

Mr Bradley's manner underwent a rapid change. It was gay, almost facetious.

'That's where we came in, isn't it? Or rather where you came in, ha ha. "How much?" you said. Really quite startled me. Never heard anyone come to the point so soon.'

'What terms?'

'That depends. It depends on several different factors. Roughly it depends on the amount there is at stake. In some cases it depends on the funds available to the client. An inconvenient husband—or a blackmailer or something of that kind—would depend on how much my client could afford to pay. I don't—let me make that clear—bet with poor clients—except in the kind of case I have just been outlining. In that case it would depend on the amount of Aunt Eliza's estate. Terms are by mutual agreement. We both want something out of it, don't we? The odds, however, work out usually at five hundred to one.'

'Five hundred to one? That's pretty steep.'

'My wager is pretty steep. If Aunt Eliza were pretty well booked for the tomb, you'd know it already, and you wouldn't come to me. To prophesy somebody's death to within two weeks means pretty long odds. Five thousand pounds to one hundred isn't at all out of the way.'

'Supposing you lose?'

Mr Bradley shrugged his shoulders.

'That's just too bad. I pay up.'

'And if I lose, I pay up. Supposing I don't?'

Mr Bradley leaned back in his chair. He half closed his eyes.

'I shouldn't advise that,' he said softly. 'I really shouldn't.'

Despite the soft tone, I felt a faint shiver pass over me. He had uttered no direct menace. But the menace was there.

I got up. I said:

'I—I must think it over.'

Mr Bradley was once more his pleasant and urbane self.

'Certainly think it over. Never rush into anything. If you decide to do business, come back, and we will go into the matter fully. Take your time. No hurry in the world. Take your time.'

I went out with those words echoing in my ears.

'Take your time . . .'

CHAPTER 13

Mark Easterbrook's Narrative

I approached my task of interviewing Mrs Tuckerton with
the utmost reluctance. Goaded to it by Ginger, I was still
far from convinced of its wisdom. To begin with I felt
myself unfitted for the task I had set myself. I was doubtful
of my ability to produce the needed reaction, and I was
acutely conscious of masquerading under false colours.

Ginger, with the almost terrifying efficiency which she
was able to display when it suited her, had briefed me by
telephone.

'It will be quite simple. It's a Nash house. Not the usual
style one associates with him. One of his near-Gothic flights
of fancy.'

'And why should I want to see it?'

'You're considering writing an article or a book on the
influences that cause fluctuation of an architect's style. That
sort of thing.'

'Sounds very bogus to me,' I said.

'Nonsense,' said Ginger robustly. 'When you get on to
learned subjects, or arty ones, the most incredible theories

are propounded and written about, in the utmost seriousness, by the most unlikely people. I could quote you
chapters of tosh.'

'That's why you would really be a much better person
to do this than I am.'

'That's where you are wrong,' Ginger told me. 'Mrs T.
can look you up in *Who's Who* and be properly impressed.
She can't look me up there.'

I remained unconvinced, though temporarily defeated.

On my return from my incredible interview with Mr
Bradley, Ginger and I had put our heads together. It was
less incredible to her than it was to me. It afforded her,
indeed, a distinct satisfaction.

'It puts an end to whether we're imagining things or
not,' she pointed out. 'Now we know that an organisation
does exist for getting unwanted people out of the way.'

'By supernatural means!'

'You're so hidebound in your thinking. It's all that wisp-
iness and the false scarabs that Sybil wears. It puts you off.
And if Mr Bradley had turned out to be a quack practitioner,
or a pseudo-astrologer, you'd still be unconvinced. But since
he turns out to be a nasty down-to-earth little legal crook—
or that's the impression you give me—'

'Near enough,' I said.

'Then that makes the whole thing come into line.
However phony it may sound, those three women at the
Pale Horse have got hold of something that *works*.'

'If you're so convinced, then why Mrs Tuckerton?'

'Extra check,' said Ginger. 'We know what Thyrza Grey
says she can do. We know how the financial side is worked.

We know a little about three of the victims. We want to know more about the client angle.'

'And suppose Mrs Tuckerton shows no signs of having been a client?'

'Then we'll have to investigate elsewhere.'

'Of course, I may boob it,' I said gloomily.

Ginger said that I must think better of myself than that.

So here I was, arriving at the front door of Carraway Park. It certainly did not look like my preconceived idea of a Nash house. In many ways it was a near castle of modest proportions. Ginger had promised to supply me with a recent book on Nash architecture, but it had not arrived in time, so I was here somewhat inadequately briefed.

I rang the bell, and a rather seedy-looking man in an alpaca coat opened the door.

'Mr Easterbrook?' he said. 'Mrs Tuckerton's expecting you.'

He showed me into an elaborately furnished drawing-room. The room made a disagreeable impression upon me. Everything in it was expensive, but chosen without taste. Left to itself, it could have been a room of pleasant proportions. There were one or two good pictures, and a great many bad ones. There was a great deal of yellow brocade. Further cogitations were interrupted by the arrival of Mrs Tuckerton herself. I arose with difficulty from the depths of a bright yellow brocade sofa.

I don't know what I had expected, but I suffered a complete reversal of feeling. There was nothing sinister here; merely a completely ordinary young to middle-aged woman. Not a very interesting woman, and not, I thought, a particularly nice woman. The lips, in spite of a generous application of lipstick, were thin and bad-tempered. The chin receded a little. The eyes were pale blue and gave the impression that she was appraising the price of everything. She was the sort of woman who undertipped porters and cloakroom attendants. There are a lot of women of her type to be met in the world, though mainly less expensively dressed, and not so well made-up.

'Mr Easterbrook?' She was clearly delighted by my visit. She even gushed a little. 'I'm *so* pleased to meet you. Fancy your being interested in this house. Of course I knew it was built by John Nash, my husband told me so, but I never realised that it would be interesting to a person like *you*!'

'Well, you see, Mrs Tuckerton, it's not quite his usual style, and that makes it interesting to—er—'

She saved me the trouble of continuing.

'I'm afraid I'm terribly stupid about that sort of thing—architecture, I mean, and archaeology and all that. But you mustn't mind my ignorance—'

I didn't mind at all. I preferred it.

'Of course all that sort of thing is terribly interesting,' said Mrs Tuckerton.

I said that we specialists, on the contrary, were usually terribly dull and very boring on our own particular subject.

Mrs Tuckerton said she was sure that *that* wasn't true, and would I like to have tea first and see the house afterwards, or see round the house and then have tea.

I hadn't bargained for tea—my appointment had been for three-thirty, but I said that perhaps the house first.

She showed me round, chatting vivaciously most of the time, and thus relieving me of uttering any architectural judgements.

It was lucky, she said, that I'd come now. The house was up for sale—'It's too big for me—since my husband's death'—and she believed there was a purchaser already, though the agents had only had it on their books for just over a week.

'I wouldn't have liked you to see it when it was empty. I think a house needs to be lived in, if one is really to appreciate it, don't you, Mr Easterbrook?'

I would have preferred this house unlived in, and unfurnished, but naturally I could not say so. I asked her if she was going to remain in the neighbourhood.

'Really, I'm not quite sure. I shall travel a little first. Get into the sunshine. I hate this miserable climate. Actually I think I shall winter in Egypt. I was there two years ago. Such a wonderful country, but I expect *you* know all about it.'

I knew nothing about Egypt and said so.

'I expect you're just being modest,' she said gaily and vaguely. 'This is the dining-room. It's octagonal. That's right, isn't it? No corners.'

I said she was quite right and praised the proportions.

Presently, the tour was completed, we returned to the drawing-room and Mrs Tuckerton rang for tea. It was brought in by the seedy-looking manservant. There was a vast Victorian silver teapot which could have done with a clean.

Mrs Tuckerton sighed as he left the room.

'After my husband died, the married couple he had had

for nearly twenty years insisted on leaving. They said they were retiring, but I heard afterwards that they took another post. A very highly-paid one. I think it's absurd, myself, to pay these high wages. When you think what servants' board and lodging costs—to say nothing of their laundry.'

Yes, I thought, mean. The pale eyes, the tight mouth— avarice was there.

There was no difficulty in getting Mrs Tuckerton to talk. She liked talking. She liked, in particular, talking about herself. Presently, by listening with close attention, and uttering an encouraging word now and then, I knew a good deal about Mrs Tuckerton. I knew, too, more than she was conscious of telling me.

I knew that she had married Thomas Tuckerton, a widower, five years ago. She had been 'much, much younger than he was.' She had met him at a big seaside hotel where she had been a bridge hostess. She was not aware that that last fact had slipped out. He had had a daughter at school near there—'so difficult for a man to know what to do with a girl when he takes her out.

'Poor Thomas, he was so lonely . . . His first wife had died some years back and he missed her very much.'

Mrs Tuckerton's picture of herself continued. A gracious kindly woman taking pity on this ageing lonely man. His deteriorating health and her devotion.

'Though, of course, in the last stages of his illness I couldn't really have *any* friends of my own.'

Had there been, I wondered, some men friends whom Thomas Tuckerton had thought undesirable? It might explain the terms of his will.

Ginger had looked up the terms of his will for me at Somerset House.

Bequests to old servants, to a couple of godchildren, and then provision for his wife—sufficient, but not unduly generous. A sum in trust, the income to be enjoyed during her lifetime. The residue of his estate, which ran into a sum of six figures, to his daughter Thomasina Ann, to be hers absolutely at the age of twenty-one, or on her marriage. If she died before twenty-one unmarried, the money was to go to her stepmother. There had been, it seemed, no other members of the family.

The prize, I thought, had been a big one. And Mrs Tuckerton liked money . . . It stuck out all over her. She had never had any money of her own, I was sure, till she married her elderly widower. And then, perhaps, it had gone to her head. Hampered, in her life with an invalid husband, she had looked forward to the time when she would be free, still young, and rich beyond her wildest dreams.

The will, perhaps, had been a disappointment. She had dreamed of something better than a moderate income. She had looked forward to expensive travel, to luxury cruises, to clothes, jewels—or possibly to the sheer pleasure of money itself—mounting up in the bank.

Instead the girl was to have all that money! The girl was to be a wealthy heiress. The girl who, very likely, had disliked her stepmother and shown it with the careless ruthlessness of youth. The girl was to be the rich one—unless . . .

Unless . . . ? Was that enough? Could I really believe that the blonde-haired meretricious creature talking

146

platitudes so glibly was capable of seeking out the Pale Horse, and arranging for a young girl to die?

No, I couldn't believe it . . .

Nevertheless, I must do my stuff. I said, rather abruptly:

'I believe, you know, I met your daughter—stepdaughter—once.'

She looked at me in mild surprise, though without much interest.

'Thomasina? Did you?'

'Yes, in Chelsea.'

'Oh, Chelsea! Yes, it would be . . .' She sighed. 'These girls nowadays. So difficult. One doesn't seem to have *any* control over them. It upset her father very much. *I* couldn't do anything about it, of course. She never listened to anything *I* said.' She sighed again. 'She was nearly grown-up, you know, when we married. A stepmother—' she shook her head.

'Always a difficult position,' I said sympathetically.

'I made allowances—did my best in every way.'

'I'm sure you did.'

'But it was absolutely no use. Of course Tom wouldn't allow her to be actually rude to me, but she sailed as near to the wind as she could. She really made life quite impossible. In a way it was a relief to me when she insisted on leaving home, but I could quite understand how Tom felt about it. She got in with a most undesirable set.'

'I—rather gathered that,' I said.

'Poor Thomasina,' said Mrs Tuckerton. She adjusted a stray lock of blonde hair. Then she looked at me. 'Oh, but perhaps you don't know. She died about a month ago.

Encephalitis—very sudden. It's a disease that attacks young people, I believe—so sad.'

'I did know she was dead,' I said.

I got up.

'Thank you, Mrs Tuckerton, very much indeed for showing me your house.' I shook hands.

Then as I moved away, I turned back.

'By the way,' I said, 'I think you know the Pale Horse, don't you?'

There wasn't any doubt of the reaction. Panic, sheer panic, showed in those pale eyes. Beneath the make-up, her face was suddenly white and afraid.

Her voice came shrill and high:

'Pale Horse? What do you mean by the Pale Horse? I don't know anything about the Pale Horse.'

I let mild surprise show in my eyes.

'Oh—my mistake. There's a very interesting old pub—in Much Deeping. I was down there the other day and was taken to see it. It's been charmingly converted, keeping all the atmosphere. I certainly *thought* your name was mentioned—but perhaps it was your stepdaughter who had been down there—or someone else of the same name.' I paused. 'The place has got—quite a reputation.'

I enjoyed my exit line. In one of the mirrors on the wall I saw Mrs Tuckerton's face reflected. She was staring after me. She was very, very frightened and I saw just how she would look in years to come . . . It was not a pleasant sight.

CHAPTER 14

Mark Easterbrook's Narrative

'So now we're quite sure,' said Ginger.

'We were sure before.'

'Yes—reasonably so. But this does clinch it.'

I was silent for a moment or two. I was visualising Mrs Tuckerton journeying to Birmingham. Entering the Municipal Square Buildings—meeting Mr Bradley. Her nervous apprehension . . . his reassuring bonhomie. His skilful underlining of the lack of risk. (He would have had to underline that very hard with Mrs Tuckerton.) I could see her going away, not committing herself. Letting the idea take root in her mind. Perhaps she went to see her stepdaughter, or her stepdaughter came home for a weekend. There could have been talk, hints of marriage. And all the time the thought of the MONEY—not just a little money, not a miserly pittance—but lots of money, big money, money that enabled you to do everything you had ever wanted! And all going to this degenerate, ill-mannered girl, slouching about in the coffee bars of Chelsea in her jeans and her sloppy jumpers, with her undesirable degenerate friends.

Why should a girl like that, a girl who was no good and would never be any good, have all that beautiful money?

And so—another visit to Birmingham. More caution, more reassurance. Finally, a discussion on terms. I smiled involuntarily. Mr Bradley would not have had it all his own way. She would have been a hard bargainer. But in the end, the terms had been agreed, some document duly signed, and then what?

That was where imagination stopped. That was what we didn't know.

I came out of my meditation to see Ginger watching me. She asked: 'Got it all worked out?'

'How did you know what I was doing?'

'I'm beginning to know the way your mind works. You were working it out, weren't you, following her—to Birmingham and all the rest of it?'

'Yes. But I was brought up short. At the moment when she had settled things in Birmingham—*What happens next?*'

We looked at each other.

'Sooner or later,' said Ginger, '*someone* has got to find out exactly what happens at the Pale Horse.'

'How?'

'I don't know . . . It won't be easy. Nobody who's actually been there, who's actually *done* it, will ever tell. At the same time, they're the only people who *can* tell. It's difficult . . . I wonder . . .'

'We could go to the police?' I suggested.

'Yes. After all, we've got something fairly definite now. Enough to act upon, do you think?'

I shook my head doubtfully.

'Evidence of intent. But is that enough? It's this death wish nonsense. Oh,' I forestalled her interruption, 'it mayn't be nonsense—but it would *sound* like it in court. We've no idea, even, of what the actual procedure is.'

'Well, then, we've got to know. But how?'

'One would have to see—or hear—with one's own eyes and ears. But there's absolutely no place one could hide oneself in that great barn of a room—and I suppose that's where it—whatever "it" is—must take place.'

Ginger sat up very straight, gave her head a kind of toss, rather like an energetic terrier, and said:

'There's only one way to find out what does really happen. You've got to be a genuine *client*.'

I stared at her.

'A genuine client?'

'Yes. You or I, it doesn't matter which, has got to want somebody put out of the way. One of us has got to go to Bradley and fix it up.'

'I don't like it,' I said sharply.

'Why?'

'Well—it opens up dangerous possibilities.'

'For us?'

'Perhaps. But I was really thinking about the—victim. We've got to have a victim—we've got to give him a name. It can't be just invention. They might check up—in fact, they'd almost certainly check up, don't you agree?'

Ginger thought a minute and then nodded.

'Yes. The victim's got to be a real person with a real address.'

'That's what I don't like,' I said.

'And we've got to have a real reason for getting rid of him.'

We were silent for a moment, considering this aspect of the situation.

'The person, whoever it was, would have to agree,' I said slowly. 'It's a lot to ask.'

'The whole set-up has got to be good,' said Ginger, thinking it out. 'But there's one thing, you were absolutely right in what you were saying the other day. The weakness of the whole thing is that they're in a cleft stick. The business has got to be secret—but not too secret. Possible clients have got to be able to hear about it.'

'What puzzles me,' I said, 'is that the police don't seem to have heard about it. After all, they're usually aware of what kind of criminal activities are going on.'

'Yes, but I think that the reason for that is, that this is in every sense of the word, an *amateur* show. It's not professional. No professional criminals are employed or involved. It's not like hiring gangsters to bump people off. It's all—*private*.'

I said that I thought she had something there.

Ginger went on:

'Suppose now that you, or I (we'll examine both possibilities), are desperate to get rid of someone. Now who is there that you and I could want to do away with? There's my dear old Uncle Mervyn—I'll come into a very nice packet when he pops off. I and some cousin in Australia are the only ones left of the family. So there's a motive there. But he's over seventy and more or less ga-ga, so it would really seem more sensible for me to wait for natural causes—unless I was in some terrible hole for money—and

152

that really would be quite difficult to fake. Besides, he's a pet, and I'm very fond of him, and ga-ga or not ga-ga, he quite enjoys life, and I wouldn't want to deprive him of a minute of it—or even risk such a thing! What about you? Have you got any relatives who are going to leave you money?'

I shook my head.

'No one at all.'

'Bother. It could be blackmail, perhaps? That would take a lot of fixing, though. You're not really vulnerable enough. If you were an M.P., or in the Foreign Office, or an up and coming Minister it would be different. The same with me. Fifty years ago it would have been easy. Compromising letters, or photographs in the altogether, but really nowadays, who *cares*? One can be like the Duke of Wellington and say "Publish and be damned!" Well, now, what else is there? Bigamy?' She fixed me with a reproachful stare. 'What a pity it is you've never been married. We could have cooked something up if you had.'

Some expression on my face must have given me away. Ginger was quick.

'I'm sorry,' she said. 'Have I raked up something that hurts?'

'No,' I said. 'It doesn't hurt. It was a long time ago, I rather doubt if there's anyone now who knows about it.'

'You married someone?'

'Yes. Whilst I was at the University. We kept it dark. She wasn't—well, my people would have cut up rough. I wasn't even of age. We lied about our ages.'

I was silent a moment or two, reliving the past.

'It wouldn't have lasted,' I said slowly. 'I know that now. She was pretty and she could be very sweet . . . but . . .'

'What happened?'

'We went to Italy in the long vacation. There was an accident—a car accident. She was killed outright.'

'And you?'

'I wasn't in the car. She was—with a friend.'

Ginger gave me a quick glance. I think she understood the way it had been. The shock of my discovery that the girl I had married was not the kind that makes a faithful wife.

Ginger reverted to practical matters.

'You were married in England?'

'Yes. Registry office in Peterborough.'

'But she died in Italy?'

'Yes.'

'So there will be no record of her death in England?'

'No.'

'Then what more do you want? It's an answer to prayer! Nothing could be simpler! You're desperately in love with someone and you want to marry her—*but* you don't know whether your wife is still alive. You've parted years ago and never heard from her since. Dare you risk it? While you're thinking it out, sudden reappearance of the wife! She turns up out of the blue, refuses to give you a divorce, and threatens to go to your young woman and spill the beans.'

'Who's my young woman?' I asked, slightly confused. 'You?'

Ginger looked shocked.

'Certainly not. I'm quite the wrong type—I'd probably go and live in sin with you. No, you know quite well who

I mean—and she'll be exactly right, I should say. The statuesque brunette you go around with. Very highbrow and serious.'

'Hermia Redcliffe?'

'That's right. Your steady.'

'Who told you about her?'

'Poppy, of course. She's rich, too, isn't she?'

'She's extremely well off. But really—'

'All right, all right. *I'm* not saying you're marrying her for her money. You're not the kind. But nasty minds like Bradley's could easily think so . . . Very well then. Here's the position. You are about to pop the question to Hermia when up turns the unwanted wife from the past. She arrives in London and the fat's in the fire. You urge a divorce—she won't play. She's vindictive. And then—you hear of the Pale Horse. I'll bet anything you like that Thyrza, and that half-witted peasant Bella, thought that that was why you came that day. They took it as a tentative approach, and that's why Thyrza was so forthcoming. It *was* a sales talk they were giving you.'

'It could have been, I suppose.' I went over that day in my mind.

'And your going to Bradley soon after fits in perfectly. You're hooked! You're a prospect—'

She paused triumphantly. There was something in what she said—but I didn't quite see . . .

'I still think,' I said, 'that they'll investigate very carefully.'

'Sure to,' Ginger agreed.

'It's all very well to invent a fictitious wife, resurrected from the past—but they'll want *details*—where she lives—all that. And when I try to hedge—'

'You won't need to hedge. To do the thing properly the wife has got to be there—and she will be there!—

'Brace yourself,' said Ginger. '*I'm your wife!*'

I stared at her. Goggled, I suppose, would be a better term. I wonder, really, that she didn't burst out laughing.

I was just recovering myself when she spoke again.

'There's no need to be so taken aback,' she said. 'It's not a proposal.'

I found my tongue.

'You don't know what you're saying.'

'Of course I do. What I'm suggesting is perfectly feasible—and it has the advantage of not dragging some innocent person into possible danger.'

'It's putting yourself in danger.'

'That's my lookout.'

'No, it isn't. And anyway, it wouldn't hold water for a moment.'

'Oh yes, it would. I've been thinking it out. I arrive at a furnished flat, with a suitcase or two with foreign labels. I take the flat in the name of Mrs Easterbrook—and who on earth is to say I'm not Mrs Easterbrook?'

'Anyone who knows you.'

'Anyone who knows me won't see me. I'm away from my job, ill. A spot of hair dye—what was your wife, by the way, dark or blonde?—not that it really matters.'

'Dark,' I said mechanically.

'Good, I'd hate a bleach. Different clothes and lots of make-up, and my best friend wouldn't look at me twice! And since you haven't had a wife in evidence for the last fifteen years or so—no one's likely to spot that I'm *not* her. Why should anyone in the Pale Horse doubt that I'm who I say I am? If you're prepared to sign papers wagering large sums of money that I'll stay alive, there's not likely to be any doubt as to my being the bona fide article. You're not connected with the police in any way—you're a genuine client. They can verify the marriage by looking up old records in Somerset House. They can check up on your friendship with Hermia and all that—so why should there be any doubts?'

'You don't realise the difficulties—the risk.'

'Risk—Hell!' said Ginger. 'I'd love to help you win a miserly hundred pounds or whatever it is from that shark Bradley.'

I looked at her. I liked her very much . . . Her red hair, her freckles, her gallant spirit. But I couldn't let her take the risks she wanted to take.

'I can't stand for it, Ginger,' I said. 'Suppose—something happened.'

'To me?'

'Yes.'

'Isn't that my affair?'

'No. I got you in on all this.'

She nodded thoughtfully.

'Yes, perhaps you did. But who got there first doesn't matter much. We're both *in* it now—and we've got to do *something*. I'm being serious now, Mark. I'm not pretending this is all just fun. If what we believe to be true is true, it's a sickening beastly thing. And it's got to be *stopped*! You see, it's not hot-blooded murder, from hate or jealousy; it's not even murder from cupidity, the human frailty of murder for gain but taking the risk yourself. It's murder as a *business*—murder that takes no account of who or what the victim may be.

'That is,' she added, 'if the whole thing is true?'

She looked at me in momentary doubt.

'It *is* true,' I said. 'That's why I'm afraid for you.'

Ginger put both elbows on the table, and began to argue.

We thrashed it out, to and fro, ding dong, repeating ourselves whilst the hands of the clock on my mantelpiece moved slowly round.

Finally Ginger summed up.

'It's like this. I'm forewarned and forearmed. I *know* what someone is trying to do to me. And I don't believe for one moment she can do it! If everyone's got a "desire for death" mine isn't well developed! I've good health. And I simply cannot believe that I'll develop gallstones, or meningitis just because old Thyrza draws pentagrams on the floor, or Sybil throws a trance—or whatever it is those women do do.'

'Bella sacrifices a white cock, I should imagine,' I said thoughtfully.

'You must admit it's all terribly bogus!'

'We don't know what actually *does* happen,' I pointed out.

'No. That's why it's important to find out. But do you believe, really believe, that because of what three women can do in the barn of the Pale Horse, I, in a flat in London, will develop some fatal disease? You *can't!*'

'No,' I said. 'I can't believe it.

'But,' I added. 'I do . . .'

We looked at each other.

'Yes,' said Ginger. 'That's our weakness.'

'Look here,' I said. 'Let's make it the other way round. Let me be the one in London. You be the client. We can cook up something—'

But Ginger was vigorously shaking her head.

'No, Mark,' she said. 'It won't work that way. For several reasons. The most important is that I'm known at the Pale Horse already—as my carefree self. They could get all the dope about my life from Rhoda—and there's nothing there. But you are in the ideal position already—you're a nervous client, sniffing around, not able yet to commit yourself. No, it's got to be this way.'

'I don't like it. I don't like to think of you—alone in some place under a false name—with nobody to keep an eye on you. I think, before we embark on this, we ought to go to the police—now—before we try anything else.'

'I'm agreeable to that,' said Ginger slowly. 'In fact I think it's what you ought to do. You've got something to go on. What police? Scotland Yard?'

'No,' I said. 'I think Divisional Detective Inspector Lejeune is the best bet.'

CHAPTER 15

Mark Easterbrook's Narrative

I liked Divisional Detective Inspector Lejeune at first sight.
He had an air of quiet ability. I thought, too, that he was
an imaginative man—the kind of man who would be willing
to consider possibilities that were not orthodox.

He said:

'Dr Corrigan has told me of his meeting with you. He's
taken a great interest in this business from the first. Father
Gorman, of course, was very well known and respected in
the district. Now you say you have some special information for us?'

'It concerns,' I said, 'a place called the Pale Horse.'

'In, I understand, a village called Much Deeping?'

'Yes.'

'Tell me about it.'

I told him of the first mention of the Pale Horse at the
Fantasie. Then I described my visit to Rhoda, and my introduction to the 'three weird sisters'. I related, as accurately
as I could, Thyrza Grey's conversation on that particular
afternoon.

'And you were impressed by what she said?'

I felt embarrassed.

'Well, not really. I mean, I didn't seriously believe—'

'Didn't you, Mr Easterbrook? I rather think you did.'

'I suppose you're right. One just doesn't like admitting how credulous one is.'

Lejeune smiled.

'But you've left something out, haven't you? You were already interested when you came to Much Deeping—why?'

'I think it was the girl looking so scared.'

'The young lady in the flower shop?'

'Yes. She'd thrown out her remark about the Pale Horse so casually. Her being so scared seemed to underline the fact that there was—well, something to be scared about. And then I met Dr Corrigan and he told me about the list of names. Two of them I already knew. Both were dead. A third name seemed familiar. Afterwards I found that she, too, had died.'

'That would be Mrs Delafontaine?'

'Yes.'

'Go on.'

'I made up my mind that I'd got to find out more about this business.'

'And you set about it. How?'

I told him of my call on Mrs Tuckerton. Finally I came to Mr Bradley and the Municipal Square Buildings in Birmingham.

I had his full interest now. He repeated the name.

'Bradley,' he said. 'So Bradley's in this?'

'You know him?'

'Oh yes, we know all about Mr Bradley. He's given us a lot of trouble. He's a smooth dealer, an adept at never doing anything that we can pin on him. He knows every trick and dodge of the legal game. He's always just on the right side of the line. He's the kind of man who could write a book like those old cookery books, "A hundred ways of evading the law." But murder, such a thing as organised murder—I should have said that that was right off his beat. Yes—right off his beat—'

'Now that I've told you about our conversation, could you act upon it?'

Lejeune slowly shook his head.

'No, we couldn't act on it. To begin with, there were no witnesses to your conversation. It was just between the two of you and he could deny the whole thing if he wanted to! Apart from that, he was quite right when he told you that a man can bet on anything. He bets somebody won't die—and he loses. What is there criminal about that? Unless we can connect Bradley in some way with the actual crime in question—and that, I imagine, will not be easy.'

He left it with a shrug of his shoulders. He paused a minute and then said,

'Did you, by any chance, come across a man called Venables when you were down in Much Deeping?'

'Yes,' I said, 'I did. I was taken over to lunch with him one day.'

'Ah! What impression, if I may ask, did he make upon you?'

'A very powerful impression. He's a man of great personality. An invalid.'

'Yes. Crippled by polio.'

'He can only move about in a wheeled chair. But his disability seems to have heightened his determination to live and enjoy living.'

'Tell me all you can about him.'

I described Venables's house, his art treasures, the range and sweep of his interests.

Lejeune said:

'It's a pity.'

'What is a pity?'

He said drily: 'That Venables is a cripple.'

'Excuse me, but you are quite certain he really is a cripple? He couldn't be—well—faking the whole thing?'

'We're as sure of his being a cripple as one can be sure of anything. His doctor is Sir William Dugdale of Harley Street, a man absolutely above suspicion. We have Sir William's assurance that the limbs are atrophied. Our little Mr Osborne may be certain that Venables was the man he saw walking along Barton Street that night. But he's wrong.'

'I see.'

'As I say, it's a pity, because if there is such a thing as an organisation for private murder, Venables is the kind of man who would be capable of planning it.'

'Yes; that's what I thought.'

With his forefinger Lejeune traced interlacing circles on the table in front of him. Then he looked up sharply.

'Let's assemble what we've got; adding to our own knowledge the knowledge you've brought us. It seems reasonably certain that there *is* some agency or organisation that specialises in what one might call the removal of unwanted persons. There's nothing crude about the organisation. It doesn't employ ordinary thugs or gunmen . . . There's nothing to show that the victims haven't died a perfectly natural death. I may say that in addition to the three deaths you've mentioned, we've got a certain amount of rather indefinite information about some of the others—deaths were from natural causes in each instance, but there were those who profited by these deaths. No evidence, mind you.

'It's clever, damnably clever, Mr Easterbrook. Whoever thought it out—and it's been thought out in great detail—has brains. We've only got hold of a few scattered names. Heaven knows how many more of them there are—how widespread the whole thing may be. And we've only got the few names we have got, by the accident of a woman knowing herself to be dying, and wanting to make her peace with heaven.'

He shook his head angrily, and then went on:

'This woman, Thyrza Grey; you say she boasted to you about her powers! Well, she can do so with impunity. Charge her with murder, put her in the dock, let her trumpet to heaven and a jury that she has released people from the toils of this world by will power or weaving spells—or what have you. She wouldn't be guilty according to the law. She's never been near the people who died, we've checked on that, she hasn't sent them poisoned chocolates through the post or anything of that kind. According to her own account, she just sits in a room and employs telepathy! Why, the whole thing would be laughed out of Court!'

I murmured:

'But Lu and Aengus laugh not. Nor any in the high celestial House.'

'What's that?'

'Sorry. A quotation from the "Immortal Hour".'

'Well, it's true enough. The devils in Hell are laughing but not the Host of Heaven. It's an—an *evil* business, Mr Easterbrook.'

'Yes,' I said. 'It's a word that we don't use very much nowadays. But it's the only word applicable here. That's why—'

'Yes?'

Lejeune looked at me inquiringly.

I spoke in a rush. 'I think there's a chance—a possible chance—of getting to know a bit more about all this. I and a friend of mine have worked out a plan. You may think it very silly—'

'I'll be the judge of that.'

'First of all, I take it from what you've said, that you are sure in your mind that there *is* such an organisation as the one we've been discussing, and that it works?'

'It certainly works.'

'But you don't know *how* it works? The first steps are already formulated. The individual I call the client hears vaguely about this organisation, gets to know more about it, is sent to Mr Bradley in Birmingham, and decides that he will go ahead. He enters into some agreement with Bradley, and then is, or so I presume, sent to the Pale Horse. But what happens after *that*, we don't know! What, exactly, *happens* at the Pale Horse? Somebody's got to go and find out.'

'Go on.'

'Because until we *do* know, exactly, what Thyrza Grey actually *does*, we can't get any further—Your police doctor, Jim Corrigan, says the whole idea is poppycock—but is it? Inspector Lejeune, is it?'

Lejeune sighed.

'You know what I'd answer—what any sane person would answer—the answer would be "Yes, of course it is!"—but I'm speaking now unofficially. Very odd things have happened during the last hundred years. Would anyone have believed seventy years ago that a person could hear Big Ben strike twelve on a little box and, after it had finished striking, hear it again with his own ears through the window, from the actual clock itself—and no jiggery pokery. But Big Ben struck *once*—not twice—the sound was brought to the ears of the person by two different kinds of waves! Would you believe you could hear a man speaking in New York in your own drawing-room, without so much as a connecting wire? Would you have believed—? Oh! a dozen other things—things that are now everyday knowledge that a child gabbles off!'

'In other words, anything's possible?'

'That's what I mean. If you ask me if Thyrza Grey can kill someone by rolling her eyes or going into a trance, or projecting her will, I still say "No." But—I'm not sure— How can I be? If she's stumbled on something—'

'Yes,' I said. 'The supernatural seems supernatural. But the science of tomorrow is the supernatural of today.'

'I'm not talking officially, mind,' Lejeune warned me.

'Man, you're talking sense. And the answer is, someone

has got to go and see what actually *happens*. That's what I propose to do—go and see.'

Lejeune stared at me.

'The way's already paved,' I said.

I settled down then, and told him about it. I told him exactly what I and a friend of mine planned to do.

He listened, frowning and pulling at his lower lip.

'Mr Easterbrook, I see your point. Circumstances have, so to speak, given you the entrée. But I don't know whether you fully realise that what you are proposing to do may be dangerous—these are dangerous people. It may be dangerous for you—but it will certainly be dangerous for your friend.'

'I know,' I said, 'I know . . . We've been over it a hundred times. I don't like her playing the part she's going to play. But she's determined—absolutely determined. Damn it all, she wants to!'

Lejeune said unexpectedly:

'She's a red-head, didn't you say?'

'Yes,' I said, startled.

'You can never argue with a red-head,' said Lejeune. 'Don't I know it!'

I wondered if his wife was one.

CHAPTER 16

Mark Easterbrook's Narrative

I felt absolutely no nervousness on my second visit to Bradley. In fact, I enjoyed it.

'Think yourself into the part,' Ginger urged me, before I set off, and that was exactly what I tried to do.

Mr Bradley greeted me with a welcoming smile.

'Very pleased to see you,' he said, advancing a podgy hand. 'So you've been thinking your little problem over, have you? Well, as I said, no hurry. Take your time.'

I said, 'That's just what I can't do. It's—well—it's rather urgent . . .'

Bradley looked me over. He noted my nervous manner, the way I avoided his eyes, the clumsiness of my hands as I dropped my hat.

'Well, well,' he said. 'Let's see what we can do about things. You want to have a little bet on something, is that it? Nothing like a sporting flutter to take one's mind off one's—er—troubles.'

'It's like this—' I said, and came to a dead stop.

I left it to Bradley to do his stuff. He did it.

'I see you're a bit nervous,' he said. 'Cautious. I approve of caution. Never say anything your mother shouldn't hear about! Now, perhaps you have some idea that this office of mine might have a bug in it?'

I didn't understand and my face showed it.

'Slang term for a microphone,' he explained. 'Tape recorders. All that sort of thing. No, I give you my personal word of honour that there's nothing of that sort here. Our conversation will not be recorded in any way. And if you don't believe me,' his candour was quite engaging—'and why should you?—you've a perfect right to name a place of your own, a restaurant, the waiting-room in one of our dear English railway stations; and we'll discuss the matter there instead.'

I said that I was sure it was quite all right here.

'Sensible! That sort of thing wouldn't pay us, I assure you. Neither you nor I is going to say a word that, in legal parlance, could be "used against us". Now let's start this way. There's something worrying you. You find me sympathetic and you feel you'd like to tell me about it. I'm a man of experience and I might be able to advise you. A trouble shared is a trouble halved, as they say. Suppose we put it like that?'

We put it like that, and I stumbled into my story.

Mr Bradley was very adroit. He prompted; eased over difficult words and phrases. So good was he, that I felt no difficulty at all in telling him about my youthful infatuation for Doreen and our secretive marriage.

'Happens so often,' he said, shaking his head. 'So often. Understandable! Young man with ideals. Genuinely pretty girl. And there you are. Man and wife before you can say Jack Robinson. And what comes of it?'

I went on to tell him what came of it.

Here I was purposefully vague over details. The man I was trying to present would not have gone into sordid details. I presented only a picture of disillusionment—a young fool realising that he had been a young fool.

I let it be assumed that there had been a final quarrel. If Bradley took it that my young wife had gone off with another man, or that there had been another man in the offing all along—that was good enough.

'But you know,' I said anxiously, 'although she wasn't—well, wasn't quite what I thought her, she was really a very sweet girl. I'd never have thought that she'd be like this—that she'd behave like this, I mean.'

'What exactly has she been doing to you?'

What my 'wife' had done to me, I explained, was to come back.

'What did you think happened to her?'

'I suppose it seems extraordinary—but I really *didn't* think. Actually, I suppose, I assumed she must be dead.'

Bradley shook his head at me.

'Wishful thinking. Wishful thinking. Why *should* she be dead?'

'She never wrote or anything. I never heard from her.'

'The truth is you wanted to forget all about her.'

He was a psychologist in his way, this beady-eyed little lawyer.

'Yes,' I said gratefully. 'You see, it wasn't as though I wanted to marry someone else.'

170

'But you do now, eh, is that it?'

'Well—' I showed reluctance.

'Come now, tell Papa,' said the odious Bradley.

I admitted, shamefacedly, that, yes, lately, I *had* considered marrying . . .

But I stuck my toes in and refused firmly to give him any details about the girl in question. I wasn't going to have her brought into this. I wasn't going to tell him a thing about her.

Again, I think my reaction here was the correct one. He did not insist. Instead he said:

'Quite natural, my dear sir. You've got over your nasty experience in the past. You've found someone, no doubt, thoroughly suited to you. Able to share your literary tastes and your way of life. A true companion.'

I saw then that he knew about Hermia. It would have been easy. Any inquiries made about me would have revealed the fact that I had only one close woman friend. Bradley, since receiving my letter making the appointment, must have found out all about me, all about Hermia. He was fully briefed.

'What about divorce?' he asked. 'Isn't that the natural solution?'

I said: 'There's no question of divorce. She—my wife—won't hear of it!'

'Dear, dear. What is her attitude towards you, if I may ask?'

'She—er—she wants to come back to me. She—she's utterly unreasonable. She knows there's someone, and—and—'

171

'Acting nasty . . . I see . . . Doesn't look as though there's any way out, unless of course . . . But she's quite young . . .'

'She'll live for years,' I said bitterly.

'Oh, but you never know, Mr Easterbrook. She's been living abroad, you say?'

'So she tells me. I don't know where she's been.'

'May have been out East. Sometimes, you know, you pick up a germ out in those parts—dormant for years! And then you come back home, and suddenly it blows up. I've known two or three cases like that. Might happen in this case. If it will cheer you up,' he paused, 'I'd bet a small amount on it.'

I shook my head.

'She'll live for years.'

'Well, the odds are on your side, I admit . . . But let's have a wager on it. Fifteen hundred to one the lady dies between now and Christmas: how's that?'

'Sooner! It will have to be sooner. I can't wait. There are things—'

I was purposely incoherent. I don't know whether he thought that matters between Hermia and myself had gone so far that I couldn't stall for time—or that my 'wife' threatened to go to Hermia and make trouble. He may have thought that there was another man making a play for Hermia. I didn't mind what he thought. I wanted to stress urgency.

'Alter the odds a bit,' he said. 'We'll say eighteen hundred to one your wife's a goner in under a month. I've got a sort of feeling about it.'

I thought it was time to bargain—and I bargained.

172

Protested that I hadn't got that amount of money. Bradley was skilful. He knew, by some means or other, just what sum I could raise in an emergency. He knew that Hermia had money. His delicate hint that later, when I was married, I wouldn't feel the loss of my bet, was proof of that. Moreover, my urgency put him in a fine position. He wouldn't come down.

When I left him the fantastic wager was laid and accepted.

I signed some form of I.O.U. The phraseology was too full of legal phrases for me to understand. Actually I very much doubted that it had any legal significance whatever.

'Is this legally binding?' I asked him.

'I don't think,' said Mr Bradley, showing his excellent dentures, 'that it will ever be put to the test.' His smile was not a very nice one. 'A bet's a bet. If a man doesn't pay up—'

I looked at him.

'I shouldn't advise it,' he said softly. 'No, I shouldn't advise it. We don't like welshers.'

'I shan't welsh,' I said.

'I'm sure you won't, Mr Easterbrook. Now for the er— arrangements. Mrs Easterbrook, you say, is in London. Where, exactly?'

'Do you have to know?'

'I have to have full details—the next thing to do is to arrange an appointment with Miss Grey—you remember Miss Grey?'

I said of course I remembered Miss Grey.

'An amazing woman. Really an amazing woman. Most

gifted. She'll want something your wife has worn—a glove—handkerchief—anything like that—'

'But why? In the name of—'

'I know, I know. Don't ask *me* why. I've not the least idea. Miss Grey keeps her secrets to herself.'

'But what happens? What does she *do*?'

'You really must believe me, Mr Easterbrook, when I tell you that honestly I haven't the least idea! I don't know—and what is more, *I don't want to know*—let's leave it at that.'

He paused, and then went on in an almost fatherly tone.

'My advice is as follows, Mr Easterbrook. Pay a visit to your wife. Soothe her down, let her think that you're coming round to the idea of a reconciliation. I should suggest that you have to go abroad for a few weeks, but that on your return et cetera, et cetera . . .'

'And then?'

'Having purloined a trifle of daily wear in an unobtrusive manner, you will go down to Much Deeping.' He paused thoughtfully. 'Let me see. I think you mentioned on your previous visit that you had friends—relations—in the neighbourhood?'

'A cousin.'

'That makes it very simple. This cousin will doubtless put you up for a day or so.'

'What do most people do? Stay at the local inn?'

'Sometimes, I believe—or they motor over from Bournemouth. Something of that kind—but I know very little about the matter.'

'What—er—is my cousin likely to think?'

'You express yourself as intrigued by the inhabitants of

the Pale Horse. You want to participate in a *séance* there. Nothing can sound simpler. Miss Grey and her medium friend often indulge in *séances*. You know what spiritualists are. You go protesting that of course it's nonsense, but that it will interest you. That is all, Mr Easterbrook. As you see, nothing can be simpler—'

'And—and, after that?'

He shook his head smiling.

'That's all I can tell you. All, in fact, that I know. Miss Thyrza Grey will then be in charge. Don't forget to take the glove, or handkerchief, or whatever it is with you. Afterwards, I would suggest that you take a little trip abroad. The Italian Riviera is very pleasant at this time of year. Just for a week or two, say.'

I said that I didn't want to go abroad. I said I wanted to stay in England.

'Very well, then, but definitely *not* London. No, I must strongly advise, not London.'

'Why not?'

Mr Bradley looked at me reprovingly.

'Clients are guaranteed complete—er—safety,' he said, '*if* they obey orders.'

'What about Bournemouth? Would Bournemouth do?'

'Yes, Bournemouth would be adequate. Stay at a hotel, make a few acquaintances, be seen in their company. The blameless life—that is what we aim at. You can always go on to Torquay if you get tired of Bournemouth.'

He spoke with the affability of a travel agent.

Once again I had to shake his podgy hand.

CHAPTER 17

Mark Easterbrook's Narrative

'Are you really going to a *séance* at Thyrza's?' Rhoda demanded.

'Why not?'

'I never knew you were interested in that sort of thing, Mark.'

'I'm not really,' I said truthfully. 'But it's such a queer set-up, those three. I'm curious to see what sort of a show they put on.'

I did not find it really easy to put on a light manner. Out of the tail of my eye, I saw Hugh Despard looking at me thoughtfully. He was a shrewd man, with an adventurous life behind him. One of those men who have a kind of sixth sense where danger is concerned. I think he scented its presence now—realised that something more important than idle curiosity was at stake.

'Then I shall come with you,' said Rhoda gleefully. 'I've always wanted to go.'

'You'll do nothing of the sort, Rhoda,' growled Despard.

'But I don't really believe in spirits and all that, Hugh. You know I don't. I just want to go for the fun of it!'

'That sort of business isn't fun,' said Despard. 'There may be something genuine to it, there probably is. But it doesn't have a good effect on people who go out of "idle curiosity".'

'Then you ought to dissuade Mark, too.'

'Mark's not my responsibility,' said Despard.

But again he gave me that quick sidelong look. He knew, I was quite sure, that I had a purpose.

Rhoda was annoyed, but she got over it, and when we chanced to meet Thyrza Grey in the village a little later that morning, Thyrza herself was blunt upon the matter.

'Hallo, Mr Easterbrook, we're expecting you this evening. Hope we can put on a good show for you. Sybil's a wonderful medium, but one never knows beforehand what results one will get. So you mustn't be disappointed. One thing I do ask you. Keep an open mind. An honest inquirer is always welcome—but a frivolous, scoffing approach is bad.'

'I wanted to come too,' said Rhoda. 'But Hugh is so frightfully prejudiced. You know what he's like.'

'I wouldn't have had you, anyway,' said Thyrza. 'One outsider is quite enough.'

She turned to me.

'Suppose you come and have a light meal with us first,' she said. 'We never eat much before a *séance*. About seven o'clock? Good, we'll be expecting you.'

She nodded, smiled, and strode briskly away. I stared after her, so engrossed in my surmises, that I entirely missed what Rhoda was saying to me.

'What did you say? I'm sorry.'

'You've been very odd lately, Mark. Ever since you arrived. Is anything the matter?'

'No, of course not. What should be the matter?'

'Have you got stuck with the book? Something like that?'

'The book?' Just for a moment I couldn't remember anything about the book. Then I said hastily, 'Oh yes, the book. It's getting on more or less all right.'

'I believe you're in love,' said Rhoda accusingly. 'Yes, that's it. Being in love has a very bad effect on men—it seems to addle their wits. Now women are just the opposite—on top of the world, looking radiant and twice as good-looking as usual. Funny, isn't it, that it should suit women, and only make a man look like a sick sheep?'

'Thank you!' I said.

'Oh, don't be cross with me, Mark. I think it's a very good thing really—and I'm delighted. She's really very nice.'

'Who's nice?'

'Hermia Redcliffe, of course. You seem to think I know nothing about *anything*. I've seen it coming on for ages. And she really is just the person for you—good-looking and clever; absolutely suitable.'

'That,' I said, 'is one of the cattiest things you could say about anyone.'

Rhoda looked at me.

'It is rather,' she said.

She turned away and said she had to go and give a pep talk to the butcher. I said that I would go and pay a call at the vicarage.

'But not'—I forestalled any comment—'in order to ask the vicar to put the banns up!'

Coming to the vicarage was like coming home.

The front door was hospitably open, and as I stepped inside I was conscious of a burden slipping from my shoulders.

Mrs Dane Calthrop came through a door at the back of the hall, carrying for some reason unfathomable to me an enormous plastic pail of bright green.

'Hallo, it's you,' she said. 'I thought it would be.'

She handed me the pail. I had no idea what to do with it and stood looking awkward.

'Outside the door, on the step,' said Mrs Calthrop impatiently, as though I ought to have known.

I obeyed. Then I followed her into the same dark shabby room we had sat in before. There was a rather moribund fire there, but Mrs Dane Calthrop poked it into flame and dumped a log on it. Then she motioned me to sit down, plumped down herself, and fixed me with a bright impatient eye.

'Well?' she demanded. 'What have you done?'

From the vigour of her manner we might have had a train to catch.

'You told me to do something. I am doing something.'

'Good. What?'

I told her. I told her everything. In some unspoken way I told her things I did not quite know myself.

'Tonight?' said Mrs Dane Calthrop thoughtfully.

'Yes.'

She was silent for a minute, obviously thinking. Unable to help myself I blurted out,

'I don't like it. My God, I don't like it.'

'Why should you?'

That, of course, was unanswerable.

'I'm so horribly afraid for her.'

She looked at me kindly.

'You don't know,' I said, 'how—how brave she is. If, in some way, they manage to harm her . . .'

Mrs Dane Calthrop said slowly:

'I don't see—I really don't see—*how* they can harm her in the way you mean.'

'But they have harmed—other people.'

'It would seem so, yes . . .' She sounded dissatisfied.

'In any other way, she will be all right. We've taken every imaginable precaution. No *material* harm *can* happen to her.'

'But it's material harm that these people claim to be able to produce,' Mrs Dane Calthrop pointed out. 'They claim to be able to work through the mind on the body. Illness— disease. Very interesting if they *can*. But quite horrible! And it's got to be *stopped*, as we've already agreed.'

'But she's the one who's taking the risk,' I muttered.

'Someone has to,' said Mrs Dane Calthrop calmly. 'It upsets your pride, that it shouldn't be you. You've got to swallow that. Ginger's ideally suited for the part she's playing. She can control her nerves and she's intelligent. She won't let you down.'

'I'm not worrying about *that*!'

'Well, stop worrying at all. It won't do *her* any good.

Don't let's shirk the issue. If she dies as a result of this experiment, then she dies in a good cause.'

'My God, you're brutal!'

'Somebody has to be,' said Mrs Dane Calthrop. 'Always envisage the worst. You've no idea how that steadies the nerves. You begin at once to be sure that it can't be as bad as what you imagine.'

She nodded at me reassuringly.

'You may be right,' I said doubtfully.

Mrs Dane Calthrop said with complete certainty that of course she was right.

I proceeded to details.

'You're on the telephone here?'

'Naturally.'

I explained what I wanted to do.

'After this—this business tonight is over, I may want to keep in close touch with Ginger. Ring her up every day. If I could telephone from here?'

'Of course. Too much coming and going at Rhoda's. You want to be sure of not being overheard.'

'I shall stay on at Rhoda's for a bit. Then perhaps go to Bournemouth. I'm not supposed to—go back to London.'

'No use looking ahead,' Mrs Dane Calthrop said. 'Not beyond tonight.'

'Tonight . . .' I got up. I said a thing that was out of character. 'Pray for me—for us,' I said.

'Naturally,' said Mrs Dane Calthrop, surprised that I should need to ask.

As I went out of the front door a sudden curiosity made me say,

'Why the pail? What's it *for*?'

'The pail? Oh, it's for the schoolchildren, to pick berries and leaves from the hedges—for the church. Hideous, isn't it, but so handy.'

I looked out over the richness of the autumn world. Such soft still beauty . . .

'Angels and Ministers of grace defend us,' I said.

'Amen,' said Mrs Dane Calthrop.

My reception at the Pale Horse was conventional in the extreme. I don't know what particular atmospheric effect I had expected—but it was not this.

Thyrza Grey, wearing a plain dark wool dress, opened the door, said in a businesslike tone: 'Ah, here you are. Good. We'll have supper straight away—'

Nothing could have been more matter-of-fact, more completely ordinary . . .

The table was laid for a simple meal at the end of the panelled hall. We had soup, an omelette, and cheese. Bella waited on us. She wore a black stuff dress and looked more than ever like one of the crowd in an Italian primitive. Sybil struck a more exotic note. She had on a long dress of some woven peacock-coloured fabric, shot with gold. Her beads were absent on this occasion, but she had two heavy gold bracelets clasping her wrists. She ate a minute portion of omelette but nothing else. She spoke little, treating us to a far-away wrapped-up-in-higher-things mood. It ought to have been impressive. Actually it was not. The effect was theatrical and unreal.

Thyrza Grey provided what conversation there was—a brisk chatty commentary on local happenings. She was this evening the British country spinster to the life, pleasant, efficient, uninterested in anything beyond her immediate surroundings.

I thought to myself, I'm mad, completely mad. What is there to fear here? Even Bella seemed tonight only a half-witted old peasant woman—like hundreds of other women of her kind—inbred, untouched by education or a broader outlook.

My conversation with Mrs Dane Calthrop seemed fantastic in retrospect. We had worked ourselves up to imagine goodness knows what. The idea of Ginger—Ginger with her dyed hair and assumed name—being in danger from anything these three very ordinary women could do, was positively ludicrous!

The meal came to an end.

'No coffee,' said Thyrza apologetically. 'One doesn't want to be overstimulated.' She rose. 'Sybil?'

'Yes,' said Sybil, her face taking on what she clearly thought was an ecstatic and other-world expression. 'I must go and PREPARE . . .'

Bella began to clear the table. I wandered over to where the old inn sign hung. Thyrza followed me.

'You can't really see it at all by this light,' she said.

That was quite true. The faint pale image against the dark encrusted grime of the panel could hardly be distinguished as that of a horse. The hall was lit by feeble electric bulbs shielded by thick vellum shades.

'That red-haired girl—what's her name?—Ginger

183

something—who was staying down here—said she'd do a spot of cleaning and restoring on it,' said Thyrza. 'Don't suppose she'll ever remember about it, though.' She added casually, 'She works for some gallery or other in London.'

It gave me a strange feeling to hear Ginger referred to lightly and casually.

I said, staring at the picture:

'It might be interesting.'

'It's not a good painting, of course,' said Thyrza. 'Just a daub. But it goes with the place—and it's certainly well over three hundred years old.'

'Ready.'

We wheeled abruptly.

Bella, emerging out of the gloom, was beckoning.

'Time to get on with things,' said Thyrza, still brisk and matter-of-fact.

I followed her as she led the way out to the converted barn.

As I have said, there was no entrance to it from the house. It was a dark overcast night, no stars. We came out of the dense outer blackness into the long lighted room.

The barn, by night, was transformed. By day it had seemed a pleasant library. Now it had become something more. There were lamps, but these were not turned on. The lighting was indirect and flooded the room with a soft but cold light. In the centre of the floor was a kind of raised bed or divan. It was spread with a purple cloth, embroidered with various cabbalistic signs.

On the far side of the room was what appeared to be

a small brazier, and next to it a big copper basin—an old one by the look of it.

On the other side, set back almost touching the wall, was a heavy oak-backed chair. Thyrza motioned me towards it.

'Sit there,' she said.

I sat obediently. Thyrza's manner had changed. The odd thing was that I could not define exactly in what the change consisted. There was none of Sybil's spurious occultism about it. It was more as though an everyday curtain of normal trivial life had been lifted. Behind it was the real woman, displaying something of the manner of a surgeon approaching the operating table for a difficult and dangerous operation. This impression was heightened when she went to a cupboard in the wall and took from it what appeared to be a kind of long overall. It seemed to be made, when the light caught it, of some metallic woven tissue. She drew on long gauntlets of what looked like a kind of fine mesh rather resembling a 'bullet-proof vest' I had once been shown.

'One has to take precautions,' she said.

The phrase struck me as slightly sinister.

Then she addressed me in an emphatic deep voice.

'I must impress upon you, Mr Easterbrook, the necessity of remaining absolutely still where you are. On no account must you move from that chair. It might not be safe to do so. This is no child's game. I am dealing with forces that are dangerous to those who do not know how to handle them!' She paused and then asked, 'You have brought what you were instructed to bring?'

185

Without a word, I drew from my pocket a brown suède glove and handed it to her.

She took it and moved over to a metal lamp with a gooseneck shade. She switched on the lamp and held the glove under its rays which were of a peculiar sickly colour, turning the glove from its rich brown to a characterless grey.

She switched off the lamp, nodding in approval.

'Most suitable,' she said. 'The physical emanations from its wearer are quite strong.'

She put it down on top of what appeared to be a large radio cabinet at the end of the room. Then she raised her voice a little. 'Bella. Sybil. We are ready.'

Sybil came in first. She wore a long black cloak over her peacock dress. This she flung aside with a dramatic gesture. It slid down, looking like an inky pool on the floor. She came forward.

'I do hope it will be all right,' she said. 'One never knows. Please don't adopt a sceptical frame of mind, Mr Easterbrook. It does so hinder things.'

'Mr Easterbrook has not come here to mock,' said Thyrza.

There was a certain grimness in her tone.

Sybil lay down on the purple divan. Thyrza bent over her, arranging her draperies.

'Quite comfortable?' she asked solicitously.

'Yes, thank you, dear.'

Thyrza switched off some lights. Then she wheeled up what was, in effect, a kind of canopy on wheels. This she placed so that it overshadowed the divan and left Sybil in a deep shadow in the middle of outlying dim twilight.

'Too much light is harmful to a complete trance,' she said.

'Now, I think, we are ready. Bella?'

Bella came out of the shadows. The two women approached me. With her right hand Thyrza took my left. Her left hand took Bella's right. Bella's left hand found my right hand. Thyrza's hand was dry and hard, Bella's was cold and boneless—it felt like a slug in mine and I shivered in revulsion.

Thyrza must have touched a switch somewhere, for music sounded faintly from the ceiling. I recognised it as Mendelssohn's funeral march.

'*Mise en scène*,' I said to myself rather scornfully. 'Meretricious trappings!' I was cool and critical—but nevertheless aware of an undercurrent of some unwanted emotional apprehension.

The music stopped. There was a long wait. There was only the sound of breathing. Bella's slightly wheezy, Sybil's deep and regular.

And then, suddenly, Sybil spoke. Not, however, in her own voice. It was a man's voice, as unlike her own mincing accents as could be. It had a guttural foreign accent.

'I am here,' the voice said.

My hands were released. Bella flitted away into the shadows. Thyrza said: 'Good evening. Is that Macandal?'

'I am Macandal.'

Thyrza went to the divan and drew away the protecting canopy. The soft light flowed down on to Sybil's face. She appeared to be deeply asleep. In this repose her face looked quite different.

The lines were smoothed away. She looked years younger. One could almost say that she looked beautiful.

Thyrza said:

'Are you prepared, Macandal, to submit to my desire and my will?'

The new deep voice said:

'I am.'

'Will you undertake to protect the body of the Dossu that lies here and which you now inhabit, from all physical injury and harm? Will you dedicate its vital force to my purpose, that that purpose may be accomplished through it?'

'I will.'

'Will you so dedicate this body that death may pass through it, obeying such natural laws as may be available in the body of the recipient?'

'The dead must be sent to cause death. It shall be so.'

Thyrza drew back a step. Bella came up and held out what I saw was a crucifix. Thyrza placed it on Sybil's breast in a reversed position. Then Bella brought a small green phial. From this Thyrza poured out a drop or two on to Sybil's forehead, and traced something with her finger. Again I fancied that it was the sign of the cross upside down.

She said to me, briefly, 'Holy water from the Catholic church at Garsington.'

Her voice was quite ordinary, and this, which ought to have broken the spell, did not do so. It made the whole business, somehow, more alarming.

Finally she brought that rather horrible rattle we had seen before. She shook it three times and then clasped Sybil's hand round it.

She stepped back and said:

'All is ready—'

Bella repeated the words:

'All is ready—'

Thyrza addressed me in a low tone:

'I don't suppose you're much impressed, are you, by all the ritual? Some of our visitors are. To you, I dare say, it's all so much mumbo jumbo . . . But don't be too sure. Ritual—a pattern of words and phrases sanctified by time and usage, has an effect on the human spirit. What causes the mass hysteria of crowds? We don't know exactly. But it's a phenomenon that exists. These old-time usages, they have their part—a necessary part, I think.'

Bella had left the room. She came back now, carrying a white cock. It was alive and struggling to be free.

Now with white chalk she knelt down and began to draw signs on the floor round the brazier and the copper bowl. She set down the cock with its beak on the white curving line round the bowl and it stayed there motionless.

She drew more signs, chanting as she did so, in a low guttural voice. The words were incomprehensible to me, but as she knelt and swayed, she was clearly working herself up to some pitch of obscene ecstasy.

Watching me, Thyrza said: 'You don't like it much? It's old, you know, very old. The death spell, according to old recipes handed from mother to daughter.'

I couldn't fathom Thyrza. She did nothing to further the effect on my senses which Bella's rather horrible performances might well have had. She seemed deliberately to take the part of a commentator.

Bella stretched out her hands to the brazier and a flickering flame sprang up. She sprinkled something on the flames and a thick cloying perfume filled the air.

'We are ready,' said Thyrza.

The surgeon, I thought, picks up his scalpel . . .

She went over to what I had taken to be a radio cabinet. It opened up and I saw that it was a large electrical contrivance of some complicated kind.

It moved like a trolley and she wheeled it slowly and carefully to a position near the divan.

She bent over it, adjusted the controls, murmuring to herself:

'Compass, north-north-east . . . degrees . . . that's about right.' She took the glove and adjusted it in a particular position, switching on a small violet light beside it.

Then she spoke to the inert figure on the divan.

'Sybil Diana Helen, you are set free from your mortal sheath which the spirit Macandal guards safely for you. You are free to be at one with the owner of this glove. Like all human beings, her goal in life is towards death. There is no final satisfaction but death. Only death solves all problems. Only death gives true peace. All great ones have known it. Remember Macbeth. "After life's fitful fever he sleeps well." Remember the ecstasy of Tristan and Isolde. Love and death. Love and death. But the greatest of these is death . . .'

The words rang out, echoing, repeating—the big box-like machine had started to emit a low hum, the bulbs in it glowed—I felt dazed, carried away. This, I felt, was no longer something at which I could mock. Thyrza, her power

190

unleashed, was holding that prone figure on the divan completely enslaved. She was using her. Using her for a definite end. I realised vaguely why Mrs Oliver had been frightened, not of Thyrza but of the seemingly silly Sybil. Sybil had a power, a natural gift, nothing to do with mind or intellect; it was a physical power, the power to separate herself from her body. And, so separated, her mind was not hers, but Thyrza's. And Thyrza was using her temporary possession.

Yes, but the box? Where did the box come in?

And suddenly all my fear was transferred to the box! What devilish secret was being practised through its agency? Could there be physically-produced rays of some kind that acted on the cells of the mind? Of a particular mind?

Thyrza's voice went on:

'The weak spot . . . there is always a weak spot . . . deep in the tissues of the flesh . . . Through weakness comes strength—the strength and peace of death . . . Towards death—slowly, naturally, towards death—the true way, the natural way. The tissues of the body obey the mind . . . Command them—command them . . . Towards death . . . Death, the Conqueror . . . Death . . . soon . . . very soon . . . Death . . . Death . . . DEATH!'

Her voice rose in a great swelling cry . . . And another horrible animal cry came from Bella. She rose up, a knife flashed . . . there was a horrible strangled squawk from the cockerel . . . Blood dripped into the copper bowl. Bella came running, the bowl held out . . .

She screamed out:

'Blood . . . the *blood* . . . BLOOD!'

Thyrza whipped out the glove from the machine. Bella took it, dipped it in the blood, returned it to Thyrza who replaced it.

Bella's voice rose again in that high ecstatic call . . .

'*The blood . . . the blood . . . the blood . . .*'

She ran round and round the brazier, then dropped twitching to the floor. The brazier flickered and went out.

I felt horribly sick. Unseeing, clutching the arm of my chair, my head seemed to be whirling in space . . .

I heard a click, the hum the machine ceased.

Then Thyrza's voice rose, clear and composed:

'The old magic and the new. The old knowledge of belief, the new knowledge of science. Together, they will prevail . . .'

CHAPTER 18

Mark Easterbrook's Narrative

'Well, what was it like?' demanded Rhoda eagerly at the breakfast table.

'Oh, the usual stuff,' I said nonchalantly.

I was uneasily conscious of Despard's eye on me. A perceptive man.

'Pentagrams drawn on the floor?'

'Lots of them.'

'Any white cocks?'

'Naturally. That was Bella's part of the fun and games.'

'And trances and things?'

'As you say, trances and things.'

Rhoda looked disappointed.

'You seem to have found it rather dull,' she said in an aggrieved voice.

I said that these things were all much of a muchness. At any rate, I'd satisfied my curiosity.

Later, when Rhoda had departed to the kitchen, Despard said to me:

'Shook you up a bit, didn't it?'

'Well—'

I was anxious to make light of the whole thing, but Despard was not an easy man to deceive.

I said slowly, 'It was—in a way—rather beastly.'

He nodded.

'One doesn't really believe in it,' said Despard. 'Not with one's reasoning mind—but these things have their effect. I've seen a good deal of it in East Africa. The witch-doctors there have a terrific hold on the people, and one has to admit that odd things happen which can't be explained in any rational manner.'

'Deaths?'

'Oh yes. If a man knows he's been marked down to die, he dies.'

'The power of suggestion, I suppose.'

'Presumably.'

'But that doesn't quite satisfy you?'

'No—not quite. There are cases difficult of explanation by any of our glib Western scientific theories. The stuff doesn't usually work on Europeans—(though I have known cases). But if the belief is there in your blood—you've had it!' He left it there.

I said thoughtfully: 'I agree with you that one can't be too didactic. Odd things happen even in this country. I was at a hospital one day in London. A girl had come in— neurotic subject, complaining of terrible pain in bones, arm, etc. Nothing to account for it. They suspected she was a victim of hysteria. Doctor told her cure could be effected by a red-hot rod being drawn down the arm. Would she agree to try it? She did.

'The girl turned her head away and screwed up her eyes. The doctor dipped a glass rod in cold water and drew it down the inside of her arm. The girl screamed with agony. He said, "You'll be all right now." She said, "I expect so, but it was awful. It burnt." The queer thing to me was—not that she believed that she had been burnt, but that her arm actually was burnt. The flesh was actually blistered everywhere the rod had touched it.'

'Was she cured?' Despard asked curiously.

'Oh yes. The neuritis, or whatever it was, never re-appeared. She had to be treated for the burnt arm, though.'

'Extraordinary,' said Despard. 'It goes to show, doesn't it?'

'The doctor was startled himself.'

'I bet he was . . .' He looked at me curiously.

'Why were you really so keen to go to that *séance* last night?'

I shrugged my shoulders.

'Those three women intrigue me. I wanted to see what sort of show they would put up.'

Despard said no more. I don't think he believed me. As I have said, he was a perceptive man.

Presently I went along to the vicarage. The door was open but there seemed to be no one in the house.

I went to the little room where the telephone was, and rang up Ginger.

It seemed an eternity before I heard her voice.

'Hallo!'

'Ginger!'

'Oh, it's *you*. What happened?'

'You're all right?'

'Of course I'm all right. Why shouldn't I be?'

Waves of relief swept over me.

There was nothing wrong with Ginger; the familiar challenge of her manner did me a world of good. How could I ever have believed that a lot of mumbo jumbo could hurt so normal a creature as Ginger?

'I just thought you might have had bad dreams or something,' I said rather lamely.

'Well, I didn't. I expected to have, but all that happened was that I kept waking up and wondering if I felt anything peculiar happening to me. I really felt almost indignant because nothing did happen to me—'

I laughed.

'But go on—tell me,' said Ginger. 'What's it all about?'

'Nothing much out of the ordinary. Sybil lay on a purple couch and went into a trance.'

Ginger gave a spurt of laughter.

'Did she? How wonderful! Was it a velvet one and did she have nothing on?'

'Sybil is no Madame de Montespan. And it wasn't a black mass. Actually Sybil wore quite a lot of clothes, peacock blue, and lots of embroidered symbols.'

'Sounds most appropriate and Sybil-like. What did Bella do?'

'That really was rather beastly. She killed a white cock and then dipped your glove in the blood.'

'Oo—nasty . . . What else?'

'Lots of things,' I said.

I thought that I was doing quite well. I went on:

'Thyrza gave me the whole bag of tricks. Summoned up

a spirit—Macandal was, I think, the name. And there were coloured lights and chanting. The whole thing would have been quite impressive to some people—scared 'em out of their wits.'

'But it didn't scare you?'

'Bella did scare me a bit,' I said. 'She had a very nasty-looking knife, and I thought she might lose her head and add me to the cock as a second victim.'

Ginger persisted:

'Nothing else frightened you?'

'I'm not influenced by that sort of thing.'

'Then why did you sound so thankful to hear I was all right?'

'Well, because—' I stopped.

'All right,' said Ginger obligingly. 'You needn't answer that one. And you needn't go out of your way to play down the whole thing. *Something* about it impressed you.'

'Only, I think, because they—Thyrza, I mean—seemed so calmly confident of the result.'

'Confident that what you've been telling me about could actually *kill* a person?'

Ginger's voice was incredulous.

'It's daft,' I agreed.

'Wasn't Bella confident, too?'

I considered. I said:

'I think Bella was just enjoying herself killing cocks and working herself up into a kind of orgy of ill wishing. To hear her moaning out "The blood . . . the blood" was really something.'

'I wish I'd heard it,' said Ginger regretfully.

'I wish you had,' I said. 'Frankly, the whole thing was quite a performance.'

'You're all right now, aren't you?' said Ginger.

'What do you mean—all right?'

'You weren't when you rang me up, but you are now.'

She was quite correct in her assumption. The sound of her cheerful normal voice had done wonders for me. Secretly, though, I took off my hat to Thyrza Grey. Bogus though the whole business might have been, it had infected my mind with doubt and apprehension. But nothing mattered now. Ginger was all right—she hadn't had so much as a bad dream.

'And what do we do next?' demanded Ginger. 'Have I got to stay put for another week or so?'

'If I want to collect a hundred pounds from Mr Bradley, yes.'

'You'll do that if it's the last thing you ever do . . . Are you staying on with Rhoda?'

'For a bit. Then I'll move on to Bournemouth. You're to ring me every day, mind, or I'll ring you—that's better. I'm ringing from the vicarage now.'

'How's Mrs Dane Calthrop?'

'In great form. I told her all about it, by the way.'

'I thought you would. Well, goodbye for now. Life is going to be very boring for the next week or two. I've brought some work with me to do—and a good many of the books that one always means to read but never has the time to.'

'What does your gallery think?'

'That I'm on a cruise.'

'Don't you wish you were?'

'Not really,' said Ginger . . . Her voice was a little odd.

'No suspicious characters approached you?'

'Only what you might expect. The milkman, the man to read the gas meter, a woman asking me what patent medicines and cosmetics I used, someone asking me to sign a petition to abolish nuclear bombs and a woman who wanted a subscription for the blind. Oh, and the various flat porters, of course. Very helpful. One of them mended a fuse for me.'

'Seems harmless enough,' I commented.

'What were you expecting?'

'I don't really know.'

I had wished, I suppose, for something overt that I could tackle.

But the victims of the Pale Horse died of their own free will . . . No, the word free was *not* the one to use. Seeds of physical weakness in them developed by a process that I did not understand.

Ginger rebuffed a weak suggestion of mine about a false gas meter man.

'He had genuine credentials,' she said. 'I asked for them! He was only the man who gets up on a ladder inside the bathroom and reads off the figures and writes them down. He's far too grand to touch pipes or gas jets. And I can assure you he hasn't arranged an escape of gas in my bedroom.'

No, the Pale Horse did not deal with accidental gas escapes—nothing so concrete!

'Oh! I had one other visitor,' said Ginger. 'Your friend, Dr Corrigan. He's nice.'

'I suppose Lejeune sent him.'

'He seemed to think he ought to rally to a namesake. Up the Corrigans!'

I rang off, much relieved in mind.

I got back to find Rhoda busy on the lawn with one of her dogs. She was anointing it with some unguent.

'The vet's just gone,' she said. 'He says it's ringworm. It's frightfully catching, I believe. I don't want the children getting it—or the other dogs.'

'Or even adult human beings,' I suggested.

'Oh, it's usually children who get it. Thank goodness they're away at school all day—keep quiet, Sheila. Don't wriggle.

'This stuff makes the hair fall out,' she went on. 'It leaves bald spots for a bit but it grows again.'

I nodded, offered to help, was refused, for which I was thankful, and wandered off again.

The curse of the country, I have always thought, is that there are seldom more than three directions in which you can go for a walk. In Much Deeping, you could either take the Garsington road, or the road to Long Cottenham, or you could go up Shadhanger Lane to the main London–Bournemouth road two miles away.

By the following day at lunch-time, I had sampled both the Garsington and the Long Cottenham roads. Shadhanger Lane was the next prospect.

I started off, and on my way was struck by an idea. The entrance to Priors Court opened off Shadhanger Lane. Why should I not go and call on Mr Venables?

The more I considered the idea, the more I liked it. There

would be nothing suspicious about my doing so. When I had been staying down here before, Rhoda had taken me over there. It would be easy and natural to call and ask if I might be shown again some particular object that I had not had time really to look at and enjoy on that occasion.

The recognition of Venables by this chemist—what was his name—Ogden?—Osborne?—was interesting, to say the least of it. Granted that, according to Lejeune, it would have been quite impossible for the man in question to have been Venables owing to the latter's disability, yet it was intriguing that a mistake should have been made about a man living in this particular neighbourhood—and a man, one had to admit, who fitted in so well in character.

There was something mysterious about Venables. I had felt it from the first. He had, I was sure, first-class brains. And there was something about him—what word could I use?—the word vulpine came to me. Predatory—destructive. A man, perhaps, too clever to be a killer himself—but a man who could organise killing very well if he wanted to.

As far as all that went, I could fit Venables into the part perfectly. The master mind behind the scenes. But this chemist, Osborne, had claimed that he had *seen Venables walking along a London street*. Since that was impossible, then the identification was worthless, and the fact that Venables lived in the vicinity of the Pale Horse meant nothing.

All the same, I thought, I would like to have another look at Mr Venables. So in due course I turned in at the gates of Priors Court and walked up the quarter mile of winding drive.

Agatha Christie

The same manservant answered the door, and said that Mr Venables was at home. Excusing himself for leaving me in the hall, 'Mr Venables is not always well enough to see visitors,' he went away, returning a few moments later with the information that Mr Venables would be delighted to see me.

Venables gave me a most cordial welcome, wheeling his chair forward and greeting me quite as an old friend.

'Very nice of you to look me up, my dear fellow. I heard you were down here again, and was going to ring up our dear Rhoda this evening and suggest you all come over for lunch or dinner.'

I apologised for dropping in as I had, but said that it was a sudden impulse. I had gone for a walk, found that I was passing his gate, and decided to gate-crash.

'As a matter of fact,' I said, 'I'd love to have another look at your Mogul miniatures. I hadn't nearly enough time to see them properly the other day.'

'Of course you hadn't. I'm glad you appreciate them. Such exquisite detail.'

Our talk was entirely technical after this. I must admit that I enjoyed enormously having a closer look at some of the really wonderful things he had in his possession.

Tea was brought in and he insisted that I partake of it.

Tea is not one of my favourite meals but I appreciated the smoky China tea, and the delicate cups in which it was served. There was hot buttered anchovy toast, and a plum cake of the luscious old-fashioned kind that took me back to tea-time at my grandmother's house when I was a little boy.

202

'Home-made,' I said approvingly.

'Naturally! A bought cake never comes into *this* house.'

'You have a wonderful cook, I know. Don't you find it difficult to keep a staff in the country, as far away from things as you are here?'

Venables shrugged his shoulders. 'I must have the best. I insist upon it. Naturally—one has to pay! I pay.'

All the natural arrogance of the man showed here. I said dryly: 'If one is fortunate enough to be able to do that, it certainly solves many problems.'

'It all depends, you know, on what one wants out of life. If one's desires are strong enough—that is what matters. So many people make money without a notion of what they want it to do for them! As a result they get entangled in what one might call the money-making machine. They are slaves. They go to their offices early and leave late; they never stop to *enjoy*. And what do they get for it? Larger cars, bigger houses, more expensive mistresses or wives—and, let me say, bigger headaches.'

He leaned forward.

'Just the *getting* of money—that is really the be all and end all for most rich men. Plough it back into bigger enterprises, make more money still. But *why?* Do they ever stop to ask themselves why? They don't know.'

'And you?' I asked.

'I—' he smiled. 'I knew what I wanted. Infinite leisure in which to contemplate the beautiful things of this world, natural and artificial. Since to go and see them in their natural surroundings has of late years been denied me, I have them brought from all over the world to me.'

'But money still has to be got before that can happen.'

'Yes, one must plan one's coups—and that involves quite a lot of planning—but there is no need, really no need nowadays, to serve any sordid apprenticeship.'

'I don't know if I quite understand you.'

'It's a changing world, Easterbrook. It always has been—but now the changes come more rapidly. The tempo has quickened—one must take advantage of that.'

'A changing world,' I said thoughtfully.

'It opens up new vistas.'

I said apologetically:

'I'm afraid, you know, that you're talking to a man whose face is set in the opposite direction—towards the past—not towards the future.'

Venables shrugged his shoulders.

'The future? Who can foresee that? I speak of today—now—the immediate moment! I take no account of anything else. The new techniques are here to use. Already we have machines that can supply us with the answer to questions in seconds—compared to hours or days of human labour.'

'Computers? The electronic brain?'

'Things of that kind.'

'Will machines take the place of men eventually?'

'Of *men*, yes. Men who are only units of manpower—that is. But Man, no. There has to be Man the Controller, Man the Thinker, who works out the questions to ask the machines.'

I shook my head doubtfully.

'Man, the Superman?' I put a faint inflection of ridicule into my voice.

'Why not, Easterbrook? Why not? Remember, we know—or are beginning to know—something about Man the human animal. The practice of what is sometimes, incorrectly, called brain-washing has opened up enormously interesting possibilities in that direction. Not only the body, but the *mind* of man, responds to certain stimuli.'

'A dangerous doctrine,' I said.

'Dangerous?'

'Dangerous to the doctored man.'

Venables shrugged his shoulders.

'All life is dangerous. We forget that, we who have been reared in one of the small pockets of civilisation. For that is all that civilisation really is, Easterbrook. Small pockets of men here and there who have gathered together for mutual protection and who thereby are able to outwit and control Nature. They have beaten the jungle—but that victory is only temporary. At any moment, the jungle will once more take command. Proud cities that were, are now mere mounds of earth, overgrown with rank vegetation, and the poor hovels of men who just manage to keep alive, no more. Life is always dangerous—never forget that. In the end, perhaps, not only great natural forces, but the work of our own hands may destroy it. We are very near to that happening at this moment . . .'

'No one can deny that, certainly. But I'm interested in your theory of power—power over mind.'

'Oh that—' Venables looked suddenly embarrassed. 'Probably I exaggerated.'

I found his embarrassment and partial withdrawal of

his former claim interesting. Venables was a man who lived much alone. A man who is alone develops the need to talk—to someone—anyone. Venables had talked to me—and perhaps not wisely.

'Man the Superman,' I said. 'You've rather sold me on some modern version of the idea, you know.'

'There's nothing new about it, certainly. The formula of the Superman goes back a long way. Whole philosophies have been built on it.'

'Of course. But it seems to me that your Superman is—a Superman with a difference . . . A man who could wield power—and never be *known* to wield power. A man who sits in his chair and pulls the strings.'

I looked at him as I spoke. He smiled.

'Are you casting me for the part, Easterbrook? I wish it were indeed so. One needs something to compensate for— *this!*'

His hand struck down on the rug across his knees, and I heard the sudden sharp bitterness in his voice.

'I won't offer you my sympathy,' I said. 'Sympathy is very little good to a man in your position. But let me say that if we *are* imagining such a character—a man who can turn unforeseen disaster into triumph—you would be, in my opinion, exactly that type of man.'

He laughed easily.

'You're flattering me.'

But he was pleased, I saw that.

'No,' I said. 'I have met enough people in my life to recognise the unusual, the extra gifted man, when I meet him.'

I was afraid of going too far; but can one ever, really,

go too far with flattery? A depressing thought! One must take it to heart and avoid the pitfall oneself.

'I wondered,' he said thoughtfully, 'what actually makes you say that? All this?' He swept a careless hand round the room.

'That is a proof,' I said, 'that you are a rich man who knows how to buy wisely, who has appreciation and taste. But I feel that there is more to it than mere possession. You set out to acquire beautiful and interesting things—and you have practically hinted that they were not acquired through the medium of laborious toil.'

'Quite right, Easterbrook, quite right. As I said, only the fool toils. One must think, plan the campaign in every detail. The secret of all success is something quite simple—but it has to be thought of! Something simple. One thinks of it, one puts it into execution—and there you are!'

I stared at him. Something simple—something as simple as the removal of unwanted persons? Fulfilling a need. An action performed without danger to anybody except the victim. Planned by Mr Venables sitting in his wheeled chair, with his great hooked nose like the beak of a bird of prey, and his prominent Adam's apple moving up and down. Executed by—whom? Thyrza Grey?

I watched him as I said:

'All this talk of remote control reminds me of something that odd Miss Grey said.'

'Ah, our dear Thyrza!' His tone was smooth, indulgent (but had there been a faint flicker of the eyelids?). 'Such nonsense as those two dear ladies talk! And they believe it, you know, they really believe it. Have you been yet—(I'm sure they'll insist on your going)—to one of these ridiculous *séances* of theirs?'

I had a momentary hesitation whilst I decided rapidly what my attitude here ought to be.

'Yes,' I said, 'I—I did go to a *séance*.'

'And you found it great nonsense? Or were you impressed?'

I avoided his eyes and presented to my best ability a man who is ill at ease.

'I—oh well—of course I didn't really believe in any of it. They seem very sincere but—' I looked at my watch. 'I'd no idea it was so late. I must hurry back. My cousin will wonder what I am doing.'

'You have been cheering up an invalid on a dull afternoon. My regards to Rhoda. We must arrange another luncheon party soon. Tomorrow I am going to London. There is an interesting sale at Sotheby's. Medieval French ivories. Exquisite! You will appreciate them, I am sure, if I succeed in acquiring them.'

We parted on this amicable note. Was there an amused and malicious twinkle in his eye as he registered my awkwardness over the *séance*? I thought so, but I could not be sure. I felt it quite likely that I was now imagining things.

CHAPTER 19

Mark Easterbrook's Narrative

I went out into the late afternoon. Darkness had already fallen, and since the sky was overcast, I moved rather uncertainly down the winding drive. I looked back once at the lighted windows of the house. In doing so, I stepped off the gravel on to the grass and collided with someone moving in the opposite direction.

It was a small man, solidly made. We exchanged apologies. His voice was a rich deep bass with a rather fruity and pedantic tone.

'I'm so sorry . . .'

'Not at all. Entirely my fault, I assure you . . .'

'I have never been here before,' I explained, 'so I don't quite know where I'm going. I ought to have brought a torch.'

'Allow me.'

The stranger produced a torch from his pocket, switched it on and handed it to me. By its light I saw that he was a man of middle age, with a round cherubic face, a black moustache and spectacles. He wore a good quality dark raincoat and can only be described as the acme of respectability. All the same, it did just cross my mind to wonder why he was not using his torch himself since he had it with him.

'Ah,' I said rather idiotically. 'I see. I have stepped off the drive.'

I stepped back on it, then offered him back the torch.

'I can find my way now.'

'No, no, pray keep it until you get to the gate.'

'But you—you are going to the house?'

'No, no. I am going the same way that you are. Er—down the drive. And then up to the bus stop. I am catching a bus back to Bournemouth.'

I said, 'I see,' and we fell into step side by side. My companion seemed a little ill at ease. He inquired if I also were going to the bus stop. I replied that I was staying in the neighbourhood.

There was again a pause and I could feel my companion's embarrassment growing. He was the kind of man who does not like feeling in any way in a false position.

'You have been to visit Mr Venables?' he asked, clearing his throat.

I said that that was so, adding, 'I took it that you also were on your way to the house?'

'No,' he said. 'No . . . As a matter of fact—' he paused. 'I live in Bournemouth—or at least near Bournemouth. I have just moved into a small bungalow there.'

I felt a faint stirring in my mind. What had I recently heard about a bungalow at Bournemouth? Whilst I was trying to remember, my companion, becoming even more ill at ease, was finally impelled to speak.

'You must think it very odd—I admit, of course, it *is* odd—to find someone wandering in the grounds of a house when the—er—person in question is not acquainted with the owner of the house. My reasons are a little difficult to explain, though I assure you that I have reasons. But I can only say that although I have only recently settled in Bournemouth, I am quite well known there, and I could bring forward several esteemed residents to vouch for me personally. Actually, I am a pharmacist who has recently sold an old-established business in London, and I have retired to this part of the world which I have always found very pleasant—very pleasant indeed.'

Enlightenment came to me. I thought I knew who the little man was. Meanwhile he was continuing in full spate.

'My name is Osborne, Zachariah Osborne, and as I say I have—had rather—a very nice business in London—Barton Street—Paddington Green. Quite a good neighbourhood in my father's time, but sadly changed now—oh yes, very much changed. Gone down in the world.'

He sighed, and shook his head.

Then he resumed:

'This *is* Mr Venables's house, is it not? I suppose—er—he is a friend of yours?'

I said with deliberation:

'Hardly a friend. I have only met him once before to-day, when I was taken to lunch with him by some friends of mine.'

'Ah yes—I see . . . Yes, precisely.'

We had come now to the entrance gates. We passed

through them. Mr Osborne paused irresolutely. I handed him back his torch.

'Thank you,' I said.

'Not at all. You're welcome. I—' He paused, then words came from him in a rush.

'I shouldn't like you to think . . . I mean, technically, of course, I *was* trespassing. But not, I assure you, from any motive of vulgar curiosity. It must have seemed to you most peculiar—my position—and open to misconstruction. I really would like to explain—to—er—clarify my position.'

I waited. It seemed the best thing to do. My curiosity, vulgar or not, was certainly aroused. I wanted it satisfied.

Mr Osborne was silent for about a minute, then he made up his mind.

'I really would like to explain to you, Mr—er—'

'Easterbrook. Mark Easterbrook.'

'Mr Easterbrook. As I say, I would welcome the chance of explaining my rather odd behaviour. If you have the time—? It is only five minutes' walk up the lane to the main road. There is quite a respectable little café at the petrol station close to the bus stop. My bus is not due for over twenty minutes. If you would allow me to offer you a cup of coffee?'

I accepted. We walked up the lane together. Mr Osborne, his anguished respectability appeased, chatted cosily of the amenities of Bournemouth, its excellent climate, its concerts and the nice class of people who lived there.

We reached the main road. The petrol station was on the corner with the bus stop just beyond it. There was a small clean café, empty except for a young couple in

212

a corner. We entered and Mr Osborne ordered coffee and biscuits for two.

Then he leaned forward across the table and unburdened himself.

'This all stems from a case you may have seen reported in the newspapers some time ago. It was not a very sensational case, so it did not make the headlines—if that is the correct expression. It concerned the Roman Catholic parish priest of the district in London where I have—had—my shop. He was set upon one night and killed. Very distressing. Such happenings are far too frequent nowadays. He was, I believe, a good man—though I myself do not hold with the Roman doctrine. However that may be, I must explain my particular interest. There was a police announcement that they were anxious to interview anyone who had seen Father Gorman on the night in question. By chance I had happened to be standing outside the door of my establishment that evening about eight o'clock and had seen Father Gorman go by. Following him at a short distance was a man whose appearance was unusual enough to attract my attention. At the time, of course, I thought nothing of the matter, but I am an observant man, Mr Easterbrook, and I have the habit of mentally registering what people look like. It is quite a hobby of mine, and several people who have come to my shop have been surprised when I say to them, "Ah yes, I think you came in for this same preparation last March?" It pleases them, you know, to be remembered. Good for business, I have found it. Anyway, I described the man I had seen to the police. They thanked me and that was that.

'Now I come to the rather surprising part of my story. About ten days ago I came over to a church fête in the little village at the bottom of the lane we have just walked up—and what was my surprise to see this same man I have mentioned. He must have had, or so I thought, an accident, since he was propelling himself in a wheeled chair. I inquired about him and was told he was a rich local resident of the name of Venables. After a day or two to debate the matter, I wrote to the police officer to whom I had made my original statement. He came down to Bournemouth— Inspector Lejeune was his name. He seemed sceptical, however, as to whether this was indeed the man I had seen on the night of the murder. He informed me that Mr Venables had been crippled for some years, as a result of polio. I must, he said, have been misled by a chance resemblance.'

Mr Osborne came to an abrupt halt. I stirred the pale fluid in front of me and took a cautious sip. Mr Osborne added three lumps of sugar to his own cup.

'Well, that seems to settle that,' I said.

'Yes,' said Mr Osborne. 'Yes . . .' His voice was markedly dissatisfied. Then he leaned forward again, his round bald head shining under the electric bulb, his eyes quite fanatical behind his spectacles . . .

'I must explain a little more. As a boy, Mr Easterbrook, a friend of my father's, another pharmacist, was called to give evidence in the case of Jean Paul Marigot. You may remember—he poisoned his English wife—an arsenical preparation. My father's friend identified him in court as the man who signed a false name in his poison register.

214

Marigot was convicted and hanged. It made a great impression on me—I was nine years old at the time—an impressionable age. It was my great hope that some day, I, too, might figure in a *cause célèbre* and be the instrument of bringing a murderer to justice! Perhaps it was then that I began to make a study of memorising faces. I will confess to you, Mr Easterbrook, though it may seem to you quite ridiculous, that for many, many years now I have contemplated the possibility that some man, determined to do away with his wife, might enter my shop to purchase what he needed.'

'Or, I suppose, a second Madeleine Smith,' I suggested.

'Exactly. Alas,' Mr Osborne sighed, 'that has never happened. Or, if so, the person in question has never been brought to justice. That occurs, I would say, more frequently than it is quite comfortable to believe. So this identification, though not what I had hoped, opened up at least a *possibility* that I might be a witness in a murder case!'

His face beamed with childish pleasure.

'Very disappointing for you,' I said sympathetically.

'Ye-es.' Again Mr Osborne's voice held that odd note of dissatisfaction.

'I'm an obstinate man, Mr Easterbrook. As the days have passed by I have felt more and more sure that I *was right*. That the man I saw *was* Venables and no other. Oh!' he raised a hand in protest as I was about to speak. 'I know. It was inclined to be foggy. I was some distance away—but what the police have not taken into consideration is that I have made a study of recognition. It was not just the features, the pronounced nose, the Adam's apple; there is the carriage of the head, the angle of the neck on the shoulders. I said to myself "Come, come, admit you were mistaken." But I continued to feel that I had *not* been mistaken. The police said it was impossible. But *was* it impossible? That's what I asked myself.'

'Surely, with a disability of that kind—'

He stopped me by waving an agitated forefinger.

'Yes, yes, but my experiences, under the National Health—Well, really it would surprise you what people are prepared to do—and what they get away with! I wouldn't like to say that the medical profession are credulous—a plain case of malingering they will spot soon enough. But there are ways—ways that a chemist is more likely to appreciate than a doctor. Certain drugs, for instance, other quite harmless-seeming preparations. Fever can be induced—various rashes and skin irritations—dryness of throat, or increase of secretions—'

'But hardly atrophied limbs,' I pointed out.

'Quite, quite. But who says that Mr Venables's limbs *are* atrophied?'

'Well—his doctor, I suppose?'

'Quite. But I have tried to get a little information on that point. Mr Venables's doctor is in London, a Harley Street man—true, he *was* seen by the local doctor here when he first arrived. But that doctor has now retired and gone to live abroad. The present man *has never attended Mr Venables.* Mr Venables goes up once a month to Harley Street.'

I looked at him curiously.

'That still seems to me to present no loophole for er—er—'

'You don't know the things I know,' said Mr Osborne. 'A humble example will suffice. Mrs H.—drawing insurance benefits for over a year. Drew them in three separate places—only in one place she was Mrs C. and in another place Mrs T. . . . Mrs C. and Mrs T. lent her their cards for a consideration, and so she collected the money three times over.'

'I don't see—'

'Suppose—just suppose—' The forefinger was now wiggling excitedly, 'our Mr V. makes contact with a genuine polio case in poor circumstances. He makes a proposition. The man resembles him, let us say, in a general kind of way, no more. Genuine sufferer calling himself Mr V. calls in specialist, and is examined, so that the case history is all correct. Then Mr V. takes house in country. Local G.P. wants to retire soon. Again genuine sufferer calls in doctor, is examined. And there you are! Mr Venables well documented as a polio sufferer with atrophied limbs. He is seen locally (when he is seen) in a wheeled chair, etc.'

'His servants would know, surely,' I objected. 'His valet.'

'But supposing it is a gang—the valet is one of the gang. What could be simpler? Some of the other servants, too, perhaps.'

'But *why*?'

'Ah,' said Mr Osborne. 'That's another question, isn't it? I won't tell you *my* theory—I expect you'd laugh at it. But there you are—a very nice *alibi* set up for a man who might want an alibi. He could be here, there and everywhere, and nobody would know. Seen walking about in Paddington? Impossible! He's a helpless cripple living in the country, etc.' Mr Osborne paused and glanced at his watch. 'My bus is due. I must be quick. I get to brooding about this, you see. Wondered if I could do anything to prove it, as you might say. So I thought I'd come out here (I've time on my hands, these days. I almost miss my business sometimes), go into the grounds and—well, not to put too fine a point upon it, do a bit of spying. Not very nice, you'll say—and I agree. But if it's a case of getting at the truth— of bringing a criminal to book . . . If, for instance, I spotted our Mr Venables having a quiet walk around in the grounds, well, there you are! And then I thought, if they don't pull the curtains too soon—(and you may have noticed people don't when daylight saving first ends—they've got in the habit of expecting it to be dark an hour later)—I might creep up and take a peep. Walking about his library, maybe, never dreaming that anyone would be spying on him? Why should he? No one suspects him as far as he knows!'

'Why are you so sure the man you saw that night was Venables?'

'I *know* it was Venables!'

He shot to his feet.

'My bus is coming. Pleased to have met you, Mr Easterbrook, and it's a weight off my mind to have explained what I was doing there at Priors Court. I dare say it seems a lot of nonsense to *you*.'

'It doesn't altogether,' I said. 'But you haven't told me what you think Mr Venables is up to.'

Mr Osborne looked embarrassed and a little sheepish.

'You'll laugh, I dare say. Everybody says he's rich but nobody seems to know *how he made his money*. I'll tell you what *I* think. I think he's one of those master criminals you read about. You know—plans things, and has a gang that carries them out. It may sound silly to you but I—'

The bus had stopped. Mr Osborne ran for it—

I walked home down the lane very thoughtful . . . It was a fantastic theory that Mr Osborne had outlined, but I had to admit that there might just possibly be something in it.

CHAPTER 20

Mark Easterbrook's Narrative

Ringing up Ginger on the following morning, I told her that I was moving to Bournemouth the next day.

'I've found a nice quiet little hotel called (heaven knows why) the Deer Park. It's got a couple of nice unobtrusive side exits. I *might* sneak up to London and see you.'

'You oughtn't to really, I suppose. But I must say it *would* be rather heaven if you did. The boredom! You've no idea! If you couldn't come here, I could sneak out and meet you somewhere.'

Something suddenly struck me.

'Ginger! Your voice . . . It's different somehow . . .'

'Oh that! It's all right. Don't worry.'

'But your *voice?*'

'I've just got a bit of a sore throat or something, that's all.'

'Ginger!'

'Now look, Mark, anyone can have a sore throat. I'm starting a cold, I expect. Or a touch of 'flu.'

''Flu? Look here, don't evade the point. Are you all right, or aren't you?'

'Don't fuss. I'm all right.'

'Tell me exactly how you're feeling. Do you feel as though you might be starting 'flu?'

'Well—perhaps . . . Aching a bit all over, you know the kind of thing—'

'Temperature?'

'Well, perhaps a bit of a temperature . . .'

I sat there, a horrible cold sort of feeling stealing over me. I was frightened. I knew, too, that however much Ginger might refuse to admit it, Ginger was frightened also.

Her hoarse voice spoke again.

'Mark—don't panic. You *are* panicking—and really there's nothing to panic about.'

'Perhaps not. But we've got to take every precaution. Ring up your doctor and get him to come and see you. At once.'

'All right . . . But—he'll think I'm a terrible fuss-pot.'

'Never mind. *Do* it! Then, when he's been, ring me back.'

After I had rung off, I sat for a long time staring at the black inhuman outline of the telephone. Panic—I mustn't give way to panic . . . There was always 'flu about at this time of year . . . The doctor would be reassuring . . . perhaps it would be only a slight chill . . .

I saw in my mind's eye Sybil in her peacock dress with its scrawled symbols of evil. I heard Thyrza's voice, willing, commanding . . . On the chalked floor, Bella, chanting her evil spells, held up a struggling white cock . . .

Nonsense, all nonsense . . . Of course it was all superstitious nonsense . . .

221

The box—not so easy, somehow, to dismiss the box. The box represented, not human superstition, but a development of scientific possibility . . . But it wasn't possible—it couldn't be possible that—

Mrs Dane Calthrop found me there, sitting staring at the telephone. She said at once:

'What's happened?'

'Ginger,' I said, 'isn't feeling well . . .'

I wanted her to say that it was all nonsense. I wanted her to reassure me. But she didn't reassure me.

'That's bad,' she said. 'Yes, I think that's bad.'

'It's not possible,' I urged. 'It's not possible for a moment that they can do what they say!'

'Isn't it?'

'You don't believe—you can't believe—'

'My dear Mark,' said Mrs Dane Calthrop, 'both you and Ginger have already admitted the possibility of such a thing, or you wouldn't be doing what you are doing.'

'And our believing makes it worse—makes it more likely!'

'You don't go so far as *believing*—you just admit that, with evidence, you might believe.'

'Evidence? What evidence?'

'Ginger's becoming ill is evidence,' said Mrs Dane Calthrop.

I hated her. My voice rose angrily.

'Why must you be so pessimistic? It's just a simple cold—something of that kind. Why must you persist in believing the worst?'

'Because if it's the worst, we've got to face it—not bury our heads in the sand until it's too late.'

'You think that this ridiculous mumbo jumbo *works?* These trances and spells and cock sacrifices and all the bag of tricks?'

'*Something* works,' said Mrs Dane Calthrop. 'That's what we've got to face. A lot of it, most of it, I think, is *trappings*. It's just to create atmosphere—atmosphere is important. But concealed amongst the trappings, there must be the real thing—the thing that *does* work.'

'Something like radio activity at a distance?'

'Something of that kind. You see, people are discovering things all the time—frightening things. Some variation of this new knowledge might be adapted by some unscrupulous person for their own purposes—Thyrza's father was a physicist, you know—'

'But *what? What?* That damned box! If we could get it examined? If the police—'

'Police aren't very keen on getting a search warrant and removing property without a good deal more to go on than we've got.'

'If I went round there and smashed up the damned thing?'

Mrs Dane Calthrop shook her head.

'From what you told me, the damage, if there *has* been damage, was done that night.'

I dropped my head in my hands and groaned.

'I wish we'd never started this damned business.'

Mrs Dane Calthrop said firmly: 'Your motives were excellent. And what's done is done. You'll know more when Ginger rings back after the doctor has been. She'll ring Rhoda's, I suppose—'

I took the hint.

'I'd better get back.'

'I'm being stupid,' said Mrs Dane Calthrop suddenly as I left. 'I know I'm being stupid. *Trappings!* We're letting ourselves be obsessed by trappings. I can't help feeling that we're thinking the way they *want* us to think.'

Perhaps she was right. But I couldn't see any other way of thinking.

Ginger rang me two hours later.

'He's been,' she said. 'He seemed a bit puzzled, but he says it's probably 'flu. There's quite a lot about. He's sent me to bed and is sending along some medicine. My temperature is quite high. But it would be with 'flu, wouldn't it?'

There was a forlorn appeal in her hoarse voice, under its surface bravery.

'You'll be all right,' I said miserably. 'Do you hear? You'll be all right. Do you feel very awful?'

'Well—fever—and aching, and everything hurts, my feet and my skin. I hate anything touching me . . . And I'm so hot.'

'That's the fever, darling. Listen, I'm coming up to you! I'm leaving now—at once. No, don't protest.'

'All right. I'm glad you're coming, Mark. I dare say—I'm not so brave as I thought . . .'

I rang up Lejeune.

'Miss Corrigan's ill,' I said.

'What?'

'You heard me. She's ill. She's called her own doctor. He

says perhaps 'flu. It may be. But it may not. I don't know what *you* can do. The only idea that occurs to me is to get some kind of specialist on to it.'

'What kind of specialist?'

'A psychiatrist—or psychoanalyst, or psychologist. A psycho something. A man who knows about suggestion and hypnotism and brainwashing and all that kind of thing. There *are* people who deal with that kind of thing?'

'Of course there are. Yes. There are one or two Home Office men who specialise in it. I think you're dead right. It may be just 'flu—but it may be some kind of psycho-business about which nothing much is known. Lord, Easterbrook, this may be just what we've been hoping for!'

I slammed down the receiver. We might be learning something about psychological weapons—but all that I cared about was Ginger, gallant and frightened. We hadn't really believed, either of us—or had we? No, of course we hadn't. It had been a game—a cops and robbers game. But it wasn't a game.

The Pale Horse was proving itself a reality.

I dropped my head into my hands and groaned.

CHAPTER 21

Mark Easterbrook's Narrative

I doubt if I shall ever forget the next few days. It appears to me now as a kind of bewildered kaleidoscope without sequence or form. Ginger was removed from the flat to a private nursing home. I was allowed to see her only at visiting hours.

Her own doctor, I gather, was inclined to stand on his high horse about the whole business. He could not understand what the fuss was all about. His own diagnosis was quite clear—broncho-pneumonia following on influenza, though complicated by certain slightly unusual symptoms, but that, as he pointed out, 'happens all the time. No case is ever "typical". And some people don't respond to antibiotics.'

And, of course, all that he said was true. Ginger had broncho-pneumonia. There was nothing mysterious about the disease from which she was suffering. She just had it—and had it badly.

I had one interview with the Home Office psychologist. He was a quaint little cock robin of a man, rising up and down on his toes, with eyes twinkling through very thick lenses.

He asked me innumerable questions, half of which I could see no point in whatever, but there must have been a point, for he nodded sapiently at my answers. He entirely refused to commit himself, wherein he was probably wise. He made occasional pronouncements in what I took to be the jargon of his trade. He tried, I think, various forms of hypnotism on Ginger, but by what seemed to be universal consent, no one would tell me very much. Possibly because there was nothing to tell.

I avoided my own friends and acquaintances, yet the loneliness of my existence was insupportable.

Finally, in an excess of desperation, I rang up Poppy at her flower shop. Would she come out and dine with me? Poppy would love to do so.

I took her to the Fantasie. Poppy prattled happily and I found her company very soothing. But I had not asked her out only for her soothing qualities. Having lulled her into a happy stupor with delicious food and drink, I began a little cautious probing. It seemed to be possible that Poppy might know something without being wholly conscious of what it was she knew. I asked her if she remembered my friend Ginger. Poppy said, 'Of course,' opening her big blue eyes, and asked what Ginger was doing nowadays.

'She's very ill,' I said.

'Poor pet.' Poppy looked as concerned as it was possible for her to look, which was not very much.

'She got herself mixed up with something,' I said. 'I believe she asked your advice about it. Pale Horse stuff. Cost her a terrible lot of money.'

'Oh,' exclaimed Poppy, eyes wider still. 'So it was *you*!'

For a moment or two I didn't understand. Then it dawned upon me that Poppy was identifying me with the 'man' whose invalid wife was the bar to Ginger's happiness. So excited was she by this revelation of our love life that she quite failed to be alarmed by the mention of the Pale Horse.

She breathed excitedly:

'Did it work?'

'It went a bit wrong somehow.' I added, '*The dog it was that died.*'

'What dog?' asked Poppy, at sea.

I saw that words of one syllable would always be needed where Poppy was concerned.

'The—er—business seems to have recoiled upon Ginger. Did you ever hear of that happening before?'

Poppy never had.

'Of course,' I said, 'this stuff they do at the Pale Horse down in Much Deeping—you know about that, don't you?'

'I didn't know where it was. Down in the country some-where.'

'I couldn't quite make out from Ginger what it is they do . . .'

I waited carefully.

'Rays, isn't it?' said Poppy vaguely. 'Something like that. From outer space,' she added helpfully. 'Like the Russians!'

I decided that Poppy was now relying on her limited imagination.

'Something of that kind,' I agreed. 'But it must be quite dangerous. I mean, for Ginger to get ill like this.'

'But it was your wife who was to be ill and die, wasn't it?'

'Yes,' I said, accepting the role Ginger and Poppy had planted on me. 'But it seems to have gone wrong—backfired.'

'You mean—?' Poppy made a terrific mental effort. 'Like when you plug an electric iron in wrong and you get a shock?'

'Exactly,' I said. 'Just like that. Did you ever know that sort of thing happen before?'

'Well, not that way—'

'What way, then?'

'Well, I mean if one didn't pay up—afterwards. A man I knew wouldn't.' Her voice dropped in an awe-stricken fashion. 'He was killed in the tube—fell off the platform in front of a train.'

'It might have been an accident.'

'Oh no,' said Poppy, shocked at the thought. 'It was THEM.'

I poured some more champagne into Poppy's glass. Here, I felt, in front of me was someone who might be helpful if only you could tear out of her the disassociated facts that were flitting about in what she called her brain. She had heard things said, and assimilated about half of them, and got them jumbled up and nobody had been very careful what they said because it was 'only Poppy'.

The maddening thing was that I didn't know what to ask her. If I said the wrong thing she would shut up in alarm like a clam and go dumb on me.

'My wife,' I said, 'is still an invalid, but she doesn't seem any worse.'

'That's too bad,' said Poppy sympathetically, sipping champagne.

'So what do I do next?'

Poppy didn't seem to know.

'You see it was Ginger who—*I* didn't make any of the arrangements. Is there anyone I could get at?'

'There's a place in Birmingham,' said Poppy doubtfully.

'That's closed down,' I said. 'Don't you know anyone else who'd know anything about it?'

'Eileen Brandon *might* know something—but I don't think so.'

The introduction of a totally unexpected Eileen Brandon startled me. I asked who Eileen Brandon was.

'She's terrible really,' said Poppy. 'Very dim. Has her hair very tightly permed, and *never* wears stiletto heels. She's the end.' She added by way of explanation, 'I was at school with her—but she was pretty dim then. She was frightfully good at geography.'

'What's she got to do with the Pale Horse?'

'Nothing really. It was only an idea she got. And so she chucked it up.'

'Chucked what up?' I asked, bewildered.

'Her job with C.R.C.'

'What's C.R.C.?'

'Well, I don't really know exactly. They just say C.R.C. Something about Customers' Reactions or Research. It's quite a small show.'

'And Eileen Brandon worked for them? What did she have to do?'

'Just go round and ask questions—about toothpaste or gas stoves, and what kind of sponges you used. Too too depressing and dull. I mean, who *cares*?'

'Presumably C.R.C.' I felt a slight prickling of excitement.

It was a woman employed by an association of this kind who had been visited by Father Gorman on the fatal night. And—yes—of course, someone of that kind had called on Ginger at the flat . . .

Here was a link of some kind.

'Why did she chuck up her job? Because she got bored?'

'I don't think so. They paid quite well. But she got a sort of idea about it—that it wasn't what it seemed.'

'She thought that it might be connected, in some way, with the Pale Horse? Is that it?'

'Well, I don't know. Something of that kind . . . Anyway, she's working in an Espresso coffee bar off Tottenham Court Road now.'

'Give me her address.'

'She's not a bit your type.'

'I don't want to make sexual advances to her,' I said brutally. 'I want some hints on Customers Research. I'm thinking of buying some shares in one of those things.'

'Oh, I see,' said Poppy, quite satisfied with this explanation.

There was nothing more to be got out of her, so we finished up the champagne, and I took her home and thanked her for a lovely evening.

I tried to ring Lejeune next morning—but failed. However, after some difficulty I managed to get through to Jim Corrigan.

'What about that psychological pipsqueak you brought along to see me, Corrigan? What does he say about Ginger?'

'A lot of long words. But I rather think, Mark, that he's yours truly baffled. And you know, people do *get* pneumonia. There's nothing mysterious or out of the way about that.'

'Yes,' I said. 'And several people we know of, whose names were on a certain list, have died of broncho-pneumonia, gastro-enteritis, bulbar paralysis, tumour on the brain, epilepsy, paratyphoid and other well-authenticated diseases.'

'I know how you feel . . . But what can we do?'

'She's worse, isn't she?' I asked.

'Well—yes . . .'

'Then something's *got* to be done.'

'Such as?'

'I've got one or two ideas. Going down to Much Deeping, getting hold of Thyrza Grey and forcing her, by scaring the living daylights out of her, to reverse the spell or whatever it is—'

'Well—that might work.'

'Or—I might go to Venables—'

Corrigan said sharply:

'Venables? But he's out. How can he possibly have any connection with it? He's a cripple.'

'I wonder. I might go there and snatch off that rug affair and see if this atrophied limbs business is true or false!'

'We've looked into all that—'

'Wait. I ran into that little chemist chap, Osborne, down in Much Deeping. I want to repeat to you what he suggested to me.'

I outlined to him Osborne's theory of impersonation.

'That man's got a bee in his bonnet,' said Corrigan. 'He's the kind of man who has always got to be right.'

'But Corrigan, tell me, *couldn't* it be as he said? It's *possible*, isn't it?'

After a moment or two Corrigan said slowly,

'Yes. I have to admit it's *possible* . . . But several people would have to be in the know—and would have to be paid very heavily for holding their tongues.'

'What of that? He's rolling in money, isn't he? Has Lejeune found out yet how he's made all that money?'

'No. Not exactly . . . I'll admit this to you. There's something wrong about the fellow. He's got a past of some kind. The money's all very cleverly accounted for, in a lot of ways. It isn't possible to check up on it all without an investigation which might take years. The police have had to do that before—when they've been up against a financial crook who has covered his traces by a web of infinite complexity. I believe the Inland Revenue has been smelling around Venables for some time. But he's clever. What do you see him as—the head of the show?'

'Yes. I do. I think he's the man who plans it all.'

'Perhaps. He sounds as though he'd have the kind of brains for that, I agree. But surely he wouldn't have done anything so crude as killing Father Gorman himself!'

'He might have if there was sufficient urgency. Father Gorman might have had to be silenced before he could pass on what he had learnt from that woman about the activities of the Pale Horse. Besides—'

I stopped short.

'Hallo—you still there?'

233

'Yes, I was thinking . . . Just an idea that occurred to me . . .'

'What was it?'

'I've not got it clear yet . . . Just that real safety could only be achieved one way. I haven't worked it out yet . . . Anyway, I must go now. I've got a rendezvous at a coffee bar.'

'Didn't know you were in the Chelsea coffee bar set!'

'I'm not. My coffee bar is in Tottenham Court Road, as a matter of fact.'

I rang off and glanced at the clock.

I started for the door when the telephone rang.

I hesitated. Ten to one, it was Jim Corrigan again, ringing back to know more about my idea.

I didn't want to talk to Jim Corrigan just now.

I moved towards the door whilst the telephone rang on persistently, naggingly.

Of course, it might be the hospital—Ginger—

I couldn't risk that. I strode across impatiently and jerked the receiver off its hook.

'Hallo?'

'Is that you, Mark?'

'Yes, who is it?'

'It's me, of course,' said the voice reproachfully. 'Listen, I want to tell you something.'

'Oh, it's you.' I recognised the voice of Mrs Oliver. 'Look here, I'm in a great hurry, got to go out. I'll ring you back later.'

'That won't do at all,' said Mrs Oliver, firmly. 'You've got to listen to me now. It's important.'

'Well, you'll have to be quick. I've got an appointment.'

'Pooh,' said Mrs Oliver. 'You can always be late for an appointment. Everybody is. They'll think all the more of you.'

'No, really, I've got to—'

'Listen, Mark. This is important. I'm sure it is. It *must* be!'

I curbed my impatience as best I could, glancing at the clock.

'Well?'

'My Milly had tonsilitis. She was quite bad and she's gone to the country—to her sister—'

I gritted my teeth.

'I'm frightfully sorry about that, but really—'

'Listen. I've not begun yet. Where was I? Oh yes. Milly had to go to the country and so I rang up the agency I always go to—the Regency—such a silly name I always think—like a cinema—'

'I really must—'

'And said what could they send? And they said it was very difficult just now—which they always say as a matter of fact—but they'd do what they could—'

Never had I found my friend Ariadne Oliver so maddening.

'—and so, this morning a woman came along, and who do you think she turned out to be?'

'I can't imagine. Look—'

'A woman called Edith Binns—comic name, isn't it?—and *you* actually know her.'

'No, I don't. I never heard of a woman called Edith Binns.'

'But you do know her and you saw her not very long ago. She had been with that godmother of yours for years. Lady Hesketh-Dubois.'

'Oh, with her!'

'Yes. She saw you the day you came to collect some pictures.'

'Well, that's all very nice and I expect you're very lucky to find her. I believe she's most trustworthy and reliable and all that. Aunt Min said so. But really—now—'

'*Wait*, can't you? I haven't got to the point. She sat and talked a great deal about Lady Hesketh-Dubois and her last illness, and all that sort of thing, because they do love illnesses and death and then she said it.'

'Said what?'

'The thing that caught my attention. She said something like: "Poor dear lady, suffering like she did. That nasty thing on her brain, a growth, they say, and she in quite good health up to just before. And pitiful it was to see her in the nursing home and all her hair, nice thick white hair it was, and always blued regularly once a fortnight, to see it coming out all over the pillow. Coming out in handfuls. And then, Mark, I thought of Mary Delafontaine, that friend of mine. *Her hair came out.* And I remembered what you told me about some girl you'd seen in a Chelsea coffee place fighting with another girl, and getting her hair all pulled out in handfuls. Hair doesn't come out as easily as that, Mark. You try—just try to pull your own hair, just a little bit of it, out by the roots! Just *try* it! You'll see. It's not natural, Mark, for all those people to have hair that comes out by the roots. It's not natural. It

236

must be some special kind of new illness—it must *mean* something.'

I clutched the receiver and my head swam. Things, half-remembered scraps of knowledge, drew together. Rhoda and her dogs on the lawn—an article I had read in a medical journal in New York—Of course . . . Of course!

I was suddenly aware that Mrs Oliver was still quacking happily.

'Bless you,' I said. 'You're wonderful!'

I slammed back the receiver, then took it off again. I dialled a number and was lucky enough this time to get Lejeune straight away.

'Listen,' I said, 'is Ginger's hair coming out by the roots in handfuls?'

'Well—as a matter of fact I believe it is. High fever, I suppose.'

'Fever my foot,' I said. 'What Ginger's suffering from, what they've all suffered from, is thallium poisoning. Please God, we may be in time . . .'

CHAPTER 22

Mark Easterbrook's Narrative

'Are we in time? Will she live?'

I wandered up and down. I couldn't sit still.

Lejeune sat watching me. He was patient and kind.

'You can be sure that everything possible is being done.'

It was the same old answer. It did nothing to comfort me.

'Do they know how to treat thallium poisoning?'

'You don't often get a case of it. But everything possible will be tried. If you ask me, I think she'll pull through.'

I looked at him. How could I tell if he really believed what he was saying? Was he just trying to soothe me?

'At any rate, they've verified that it *was* thallium.'

'Yes, they've verified that.'

'So that's the simple truth behind the Pale Horse. Poison. No witchcraft, no hypnotism, no scientific death rays. Plain poisoning! And she flung that at me, damn her. Flung it in my face. Laughing in her cheek all the while, I expect.'

'Who are you talking about?'

'Thyrza Grey. That first afternoon when I went to tea

there. Talked about the Borgias and all the build up of "rare and untraceable poisons" the poisoned gloves and all the rest of it. "Common white arsenic," she said, "and nothing else." This was just as simple. All that hooey! The trance and the white cocks and the brazier and the pentagrams and the voodoo and the reversed crucifix—all that was for the crudely superstitious. And the famous "box" was another bit of hooey for the contemporary-minded. We don't believe in spirits and witches and spells nowadays, but we're a gullible lot when it comes to "rays" and "waves" and psychological phenomena. That box, I bet, is nothing but a nice little assembly of electrical show-off, coloured bulbs and humming valves. Because we live in daily fear of radio fall out and strontium 90 and all the rest of it, we're amenable to suggestion along the line of scientific talk. The whole set-up at the Pale Horse was bogus! The Pale Horse was a stalking horse, neither more nor less. Attention was to be focused on that, so that we'd never suspect what might be going on in another direction. The beauty of it was that it was quite safe for them. Thyrza Grey could boast out loud about what occult powers she had or could command. She could never be brought into court and tried for murder on that issue. Her box could have been examined and proved to be harmless. Any court would have ruled that the whole thing was nonsense and impossible! And, of course, that's exactly what it *was*.'

'Do you think they're all three in it?' asked Lejeune.

'I shouldn't think so. Bella's belief in witchcraft is genuine, I should say. She believes in her own powers and rejoices in them. The same with Sybil. She's got a genuine gift of mediumship. She goes into a trance and she doesn't know what happens. She believes everything that Thyrza tells her.'

'So Thyrza is the ruling spirit?'

I said slowly:

'As far as the Pale Horse is concerned, yes. But she's not the real *brains* of the show. The real brain works behind the scenes. He plans and organises. It's all beautifully dovetailed, you know. Everyone has his or her job, and no one has anything on anyone else. Bradley runs the financial and legal side. Apart from that, he doesn't know what happens elsewhere. He's handsomely paid, of course; so is Thyrza Grey.'

'You seem to have got it all taped to your satisfaction,' said Lejeune drily.

'I haven't. Not yet. But we know the basic necessary fact. It's the same as it has been through the ages. Crude and simple. Just plain poison. The dear old death potion.'

'What put thallium into your head?'

'Several things suddenly came together. The beginning of the whole business was the thing I saw that night in Chelsea. A girl whose hair was being pulled out by the roots by another girl. And she said: "*It didn't really hurt.*" It wasn't bravery, as I thought; it was simple fact. It didn't hurt.

'I read an article on thallium poisoning when I was in America. A lot of workers in a factory died one after the other. Their deaths were put down to astonishingly varied causes. Amongst them, if I remember rightly, were paratyphoid, apoplexy, alcoholic neuritis, bulbar paralysis, epilepsy, gastro-enteritis, and so on. Then there was a woman who poisoned seven people. Diagnoses included brain tumour, encephalitis, and lobar pneumonia. The symptoms vary a good deal, I understand. They may start with diarrhoea and vomiting, or there may be a stage of intoxication, again it may begin with pain in the limbs, and be put down as polyneuritis or rheumatic fever or polio—one patient was put in an iron lung. Sometimes there's pigmentation of the skin.'

'You talk like a medical dictionary!'

'Naturally. I've been looking it up. But one thing always happens sooner or later. *The hair falls out.* Thallium used to be used for depilation at one time—particularly for children with ringworm. Then it was found to be dangerous. But it's occasionally given internally, but with very careful dosage going by the weight of the patient. It's mainly used nowadays for rats, I believe. It's tasteless, soluble, and easy to buy. There's only one thing, poisoning mustn't be suspected.'

Lejeune nodded.

'Exactly,' he said. 'Hence the insistence by the Pale Horse that the murderer must stay away from his intended victim. No suspicion of foul play ever arises. Why should it? There's no interested party who *could* have had access to food or drink. No purchase of thallium or any other poison is ever made by him or her. That's the beauty of it. The real work is done by someone who has no connection whatever with the victim. Someone, I think, who appears once and once only.'

He paused.

'Any ideas on that?'

'Only one. A common factor appears to be that on every occasion some pleasant harmless-seeming woman calls with a questionnaire on behalf of a domestic research unit.'

'You think that that woman is the one who plants the poison? As a sample? Something like that?'

'I don't think it's quite as simple as that,' I said slowly. 'I have an idea that the women are quite genuine. But they come into it somehow. I think we may be able to find out something if we talk to a woman called Eileen Brandon, who works in an Espresso off Tottenham Court Road.'

Eileen Brandon had been fairly accurately described by Poppy—allowing, that is to say, for Poppy's own particular point of view. Her hair was neither like a chrysanthemum, nor an unruly birds' nest. It was waved back close to her head, she wore the minimum of make-up and her feet were encased in what is called, I believe, sensible shoes. Her husband had been killed in a motor accident, she told us, and left her with two small children. Before her present employment, she had been employed by a firm called Customers' Reactions Classified for over a year. She had left of her own accord as she had not cared for the type of work.

'Why didn't you care for it, Mrs Brandon?'

Lejeune asked the question. She looked at him.

'You're a detective inspector of police? Is that right?'

'Quite right, Mrs Brandon.'

'You think there's something wrong about that firm?'

'It's a matter I'm inquiring into. Did you suspect something of that kind? Is that why you left?'

'I've nothing definite to go upon. Nothing definite that I could tell you.'

'Naturally. We understand that. This is a confidential inquiry.'

'I see. But there is really very little I could say.'

'You can say why you wanted to leave.'

'I had a feeling that there were things going on that I didn't know about.'

'You mean you didn't think it was a genuine concern?'

'Something of the kind. It didn't seem to me to be run in a business-like way. I suspected that there must be some ulterior object behind it. But what that object was I still don't know.'

Lejeune asked more questions as to exactly what work she had been asked to do. Lists of names in a certain neighbourhood had been handed out. Her job was to visit those people, ask certain questions, and note down the answers.

'And what struck you as wrong about that?'

'The questions did not seem to me to follow up any particular line of research. They seemed desultory, almost haphazard. As though—how can I put it?—they were a cloak for something else.'

'Have you any idea what the something else might have been?'

'No. That's what puzzled me.'

She paused a moment and then said doubtfully:

'I did wonder, at one time, whether the whole thing

could have been organised with a view perhaps to burglaries, a spying out of the land, so to speak. But that couldn't be it, because I was never asked for any description of the rooms, fastenings, etc, or when the occupants of the flat or house were likely to be out or away.'

'What articles did you deal with in the questions?'

'It varied. Sometimes it was foodstuffs. Cereals, cake mixes, or it might be soap flakes and detergents. Sometimes cosmetics, face powders, lipsticks, creams, etc. Sometimes patent medicines or remedies, brands of aspirin, cough pastilles, sleeping pills, pep pills, gargles, mouth-washes, indigestion remedies and so on.'

'You were not asked,' Lejeune spoke casually, 'to supply samples of any particular goods?'

'No. Nothing of that kind.'

'You merely asked questions and noted down the answers?'

'Yes.'

'What was supposed to be the object of these inquiries?'

'That was what seemed so odd. We were never told exactly. It was supposed to be done in order to supply information to certain manufacturing firms—but it was an extraordinarily amateurish way of going about it. Not systematic at all.'

'Would it be possible, do you think, that amongst the questions you were told to ask, there was just one question or one group of questions, that was the object of the enterprise, and that the others might have been camouflage?'

She considered the point, frowning a little, then she nodded.

'Yes,' she said. 'That would account for the haphazard choice—but I haven't the least idea *what* question or questions were the important ones.'

Lejeune looked at her keenly.

'There must be more to it than what you've told us,' he said gently.

'That's the point, there isn't really. I just felt there was something wrong about the whole set-up. And then I talked to another woman, a Mrs Davis—'

'You talked to a Mrs Davis—yes?'

Lejeune's voice remained quite unchanged.

'She wasn't happy about things, either.'

'And why wasn't she happy?'

'She'd overheard something.'

'What had she overheard?'

'I told you I couldn't be definite. She didn't tell me in so many words. Only that from what she had overheard, the whole set-up was a racket of some kind. "It's not what it seems to be." That is what she said. Then she said: "Oh well, it doesn't affect us. The money's very good and we're not asked to do anything that's against the law—so I don't see that we need bother our heads about it".'

'That was all?'

'There was one other thing she said. I don't know what she meant by it. She said: "Sometimes I feel like Typhoid Mary." At the time I didn't know what she meant.'

Lejeune took a paper from his pocket and handed it to her.

'Do any of the names on that list mean anything to you? Did you call upon any of them that you can remember?'

245

'I wouldn't remember.' She took the paper. 'I saw so many . . .' She paused as her eye went down the list. She said:

'Ormerod.'

'You remember an Ormerod?'

'No. But Mrs Davis mentioned him once. He died very suddenly, didn't he? Cerebral haemorrhage. It upset her. She said, "He was on my list a fortnight ago. Looked like a man in the pink of condition." It was after that that she made the remark about Typhoid Mary. She said, "Some of the people I call on seem to curl up their toes and pass out just from having one look at me." She laughed about it and said it was a coincidence. But I don't think she liked it much. However, she said she wasn't going to worry.'

'And that was all?'

'Well—'

'Tell me.'

'It was some time later. I hadn't seen her for a while. But we met one day in a restaurant in Soho. I told her that I'd left the C.R.C. and got another job. She asked me why, and I told her I'd felt uneasy, not knowing what was going on. She said: "Perhaps you've been wise. But it's good money and short hours. And after all, we've all got to take our chance in this life! I've not had much luck in *my* life and why should I care what happens to other people?" I said: "I don't understand what you're talking about. What exactly *is* wrong with that show?" She said: "I can't be sure, but I'll tell you I recognised someone the other day. Coming out of a house where he'd no business to be and carrying a bag of tools. What was he doing with those I'd like to know?" She asked me, too, if I'd ever come across a woman who ran a pub called the Pale Horse somewhere. I asked her what the Pale Horse had to do with it.'

'And what did she say?'

'She laughed and said "Read your Bible".'

Mrs Brandon added: 'I don't know what she meant. That was the last time I saw her. I don't know where she is now, whether she's still with C.R.C. or whether she's left.'

'Mrs Davis is dead,' said Lejeune.

Eileen Brandon looked startled.

'Dead! But—how?'

'Pneumonia, two months ago.'

'Oh, I see. I'm sorry.'

'Is there anything else you can tell us, Mrs Brandon?'

'I'm afraid not. I have heard other people mention that phrase—the Pale Horse, but if you ask them about it, they shut up at once. They look afraid, too.'

She looked uneasy.

'I—I don't want to be mixed up in anything dangerous, Inspector Lejeune. I've got two small children. Honestly, I don't know anything more than I've told you.'

He looked at her keenly—then he nodded his head and let her go.

'That takes us a little further,' said Lejeune when Eileen Brandon had gone. 'Mrs Davis got to know too much. She tried to shut her eyes to the meaning of what was going on, but she must have had a very shrewd suspicion of what it was. Then she was suddenly taken ill, and when she was dying, she sent for a priest and told him what she knew and suspected. The question is, how much *did* she know?

That list of people, I should say, is a list of people she had
called on in the course of her job, and who had subsequently
died. Hence the remark about Typhoid Mary. The real
question is, who was it she "recognised" coming out of a
house where he had no business to be, and pretending to
be a workman of some kind? That must have been the
knowledge that made her dangerous. If she recognised him,
he may have recognised her—and he may have realised
that she *had* recognised him. If she'd passed on that particular item to Father Gorman, then it was vital that Father
Gorman should be silenced at once before he could pass
it on.'

He looked at me.

'You agree, don't you? That must have been the way of
it.'

'Oh yes,' I said. 'I agree.'

'And you've an idea, perhaps, who the man is?'

'I've an idea, but—'

'I know. We haven't a particle of evidence.'

He was silent a moment. Then he got up.

'But we'll get him,' he said. 'Make no mistake. Once we
know definitely who it is, there are always ways. We'll try
every damned one of them!'

CHAPTER 23

Mark Easterbrook's Narrative

It was some three weeks later that a car drove up to the front door of Priors Court.

Four men got out. I was one of them. There was also Detective Inspector Lejeune and Detective-Sergeant Lee. The fourth man was Mr Osborne, who could hardly contain his delight and excitement at being allowed to be one of the party.

'You must hold your tongue, you know,' Lejeune admonished him.

'Yes, indeed, Inspector. You can count on me absolutely. I won't utter a word.'

'Mind you don't.'

'I feel it's a privilege. A great privilege, though I don't quite understand—'

But nobody was entering into explanations at this moment.

Lejeune rang the bell and asked for Mr Venables.

Looking rather like a deputation, the four of us were ushered in.

If Venables was surprised at our visit, he did not show

249

it. His manner was courteous in the extreme. I thought
again, as he wheeled his chair a little back so as to widen
the circle round him, what a very distinctive appearance
the man had. The Adam's apple moving up and down
between the wings of his old-fashioned collar, the haggard
profile with its curved nose like a bird of prey.

'Nice to see you again, Easterbrook. You seem to spend
a lot of time down in this part of the world nowadays.'

There was a faint malice in his tone, I thought. He
resumed:

'And—Detective Inspector Lejeune, is it? That rouses my
curiosity, I must admit. So peaceful in these parts, so free
from crime. And yet, a detective inspector calls! What can
I do for you, Detective Inspector?'

Lejeune was very quiet, very suave.

'There is a matter on which we think you might be able
to assist us, Mr Venables.'

'That has a rather familiar ring, does it not? In what
way do you think I can assist you?'

'On October seventh—a parish priest of the name of
Father Gorman was murdered in West Street, Paddington.
I have been given to understand that you were in the
neighbourhood at that time—between 7.45 and 8.15 in
the evening, and you may have seen something that may
have a bearing on the matter?'

'Was I really in the neighbourhood at that time? Do
you know, I doubt it, I very much doubt it. As far as I
can recall I have never been in that particular district of
London. Speaking from memory, I do not even think I was
in London at all just then. I go to London occasionally for

an interesting day in the sale room, and now and then for a medical check up.'

'With Sir William Dugdale of Harley Street, I believe.'

Mr Venables stared at him coldly.

'You are very well informed, Inspector.'

'Not quite so well as I should like to be. However, I'm disappointed that you can't assist me in the way that I hoped. I think I owe it to you to explain the facts connected with the death of Father Gorman.'

'Certainly, if you like. It is a name I have never heard until now.'

'Father Gorman had been called out on that particular foggy evening to the death-bed of a woman nearby. She had become entangled with a criminal organisation, at first almost unwittingly, but later certain things made her suspect the seriousness of the matter. It was an organisation which specialised in the removal of unwanted persons—for a substantial fee, naturally.'

'Hardly a new idea,' murmured Venables. 'In America—'

'Ah, but there were some novel features about this particular organisation. To begin with, the removals were ostensibly brought about by what might perhaps be called psychological means. What is referred to as a "death wish", said to be present in everyone, is stimulated—'

'So that the person in question obligingly commits suicide? It sounds, if I may say so, Inspector, too good to be true.'

'Not suicide, Mr Venables. The person in question dies a perfectly natural death.'

'Come now. Come now. Do you really believe that? How very unlike our hard-headed police force!'

'The headquarters of this organisation are said to be a place called the Pale Horse.'

'Ah, *now* I begin to understand. So that is what brings you to our pleasant rural neighbourhood; my friend Thyrza Grey, and her nonsense! Whether she believes it herself or not, I've never been able to make out. But nonsense it is! She has a silly mediumistic friend, and the local witch cooks her dinners (quite brave to eat them—hemlock in the soup any moment!). And the three old dears have worked up quite a local reputation. Very naughty, of course, but don't tell me Scotland Yard, or wherever you come from, take it all seriously?'

'We take it very seriously indeed, Mr Venables.'

'You really believe that Thyrza spouts some highfalutin' nonsense, Sybil throws a trance, and Bella does black magic, and as a result somebody dies?'

'Oh no, Mr Venables—the cause of death is simpler than that—' He paused a moment.

'The cause is thallium poisoning.'

There was a momentary pause—

'*What* did you say?'

'Poisoning—by thallium salts. Quite plain and straightforward. Only it had to be covered up—and what better method of covering up than a pseudo-scientific, psychological set-up—full of modern jargon and reinforced by old superstitions. Calculated to distract attention from the plain fact of administration of poison.'

'Thallium,' Mr Venables frowned. 'I don't think I've ever heard of it.'

'No? Used extensively as rat poison, occasionally as a

depilatory for children with ringworm. Can be obtained quite easily. Incidentally there's a packet of it tucked away in a corner of your potting shed.'

'In *my* potting shed? It sounds most unlikely.'

'It's there all right. We've examined some of it for testing purposes—'

Venables became slightly excited.

'Someone must have put it there. I know nothing about it! Nothing at all.'

'Is that so? You're a man of some wealth, aren't you, Mr Venables?'

'What has that got to do with what we are talking about?'

'The Inland Revenue have been asking some awkward questions lately, I believe? As to source of income, that is.'

'The curse of living in England is undoubtedly our system of taxation. I have thought very seriously of late of going to live in Bermuda.'

'I don't think you'll be going to Bermuda just yet awhile, Mr Venables.'

'Is that a threat, Inspector? Because if so—'

'No, no, Mr Venables. Just an expression of opinion. Would you like to hear just how this little racket was worked?'

'You are certainly determined to tell me.'

'It's very well organised. Financial details are arranged by a debarred solicitor called Mr Bradley. Mr Bradley has an office in Birmingham. Prospective clients visit him there, and do business. This is to say, there is a bet on whether someone will die within a stated period . . . Mr Bradley, who is fond of a wager, is usually pessimistic in his prognostications. The client is usually more hopeful. When Mr Bradley wins his bet, the money has to be paid over promptly—or else some-thing unpleasant is liable to happen. That is all Mr Bradley has to do—make a bet. Simple, isn't it?

'The client next visits the Pale Horse. A show is put on by Miss Thyrza Grey and her friends, which usually impresses him in the way it is meant to do.

'Now for the simple facts behind the scenes.

'Certain women, *bona-fide* employees of one of the many consumer research concerns, are detailed to canvass a particular neighbourhood with a questionnaire. "What bread do you prefer? What toilet articles and cosmetics? What laxative, tonics, sedatives, indigestion mixtures, etc.?" People nowadays are conditioned to answering quizzes. They seldom object.

'And so to—the last step. Simple, bold, successful! The only action performed by the originator of the scheme in person. He may be wearing a mansion flat porter's uniform, he may be a man calling to read the gas or the electric meter. He may be a plumber, or an electrician, or a workman of some kind. Whatever he is, he will have what appear to be the proper credentials with him if anyone asks to see them. Most people don't. Whatever role he is playing, his real object is simple—the substitution of a preparation he brings with him for a similar article which he knows (by reason of the C.R.C. questionnaires) that his victim uses. He may tap pipes, or examine meters, or test water pres-sure—but that is his real object. Having accomplished it, he leaves, and is not seen in that neighbourhood again.

'And for a few days perhaps nothing happens. But sooner or later, the victim displays symptoms of illness. A doctor is called in, but has no reason to suspect anything out of the ordinary. He may question what food and drink, etc., the patient has taken, but he is unlikely to suspect the ordinary proprietary article that the patient has taken for years.

'And you see the beauty of the scheme, Mr Venables? The only person who knows *what the head of the organisation actually does*—is the head of the organisation himself. *There is no one to give him away.*'

'So how do *you* know so much?' demanded Mr Venables pleasantly.

'When we have suspicions of a certain person, there are ways of making sure.'

'Indeed? Such as?'

'We needn't go into all of them. But there's the camera, for instance. All kinds of ingenious devices are possible nowadays. A man can be snapped without his suspecting the fact. We've got some excellent pictures, for instance, of a uniformed flat porter, and a gas man and so on. There are such things as false moustaches, different dentures, etc., but our man has been recognised, quite easily—first by Mrs Mark Easterbrook, alias Miss Katherine Corrigan, and also by a woman called Edith Binns. Recognition is an interesting thing, Mr Venables. For instance, this gentleman here, Mr Osborne, is willing to swear he saw you following Father Gorman in Barton Street on the night of the seventh of October about eight o'clock.'

'And I *did* see you!' Mr Osborne leaned forward, twitching with excitement. 'I described you exactly!'

'Rather too exactly, perhaps,' said Lejeune. 'Because you *didn't* see Mr Venables that night when you were standing outside the doorway of your shop. *You weren't standing there at all.* You were across the street *yourself*—following Father Gorman until he turned into West Street, and you came up with him *and killed him . . .*'

Mr Zachariah Osborne said:

'*What?*'

It might have been ludicrous. It *was* ludicrous! The dropped jaw, the staring eyes . . .

'Let me introduce you, Mr Venables, to Mr Zachariah Osborne, pharmacist, late of Barton Street, Paddington. You'll feel a personal interest in him when I tell you that Mr Osborne, who has been under observation for some time, was unwise enough to plant a packet of thallium salts in your potting shed. Not knowing of your disability, he'd amused himself by casting you as the villain of the piece; and being a very obstinate, as well as a very stupid man, he refused to admit he'd made a bloomer.'

'Stupid? You dare to call *me* stupid? If you knew—if you'd any idea what I've done—what I can do—I—'

Osborne shook and spluttered with rage.

Lejeune summed him up carefully. I was reminded of a man playing a fish.

'You shouldn't have tried to be so clever, you know,' he said reprovingly. 'Why, if you'd just sat back in that shop of yours, and let well alone, I shouldn't be here now, warning you, as it's my duty to do, that anything you say will be taken down and—'

It was then that Mr Osborne began to scream.

CHAPTER 24

Mark Easterbrook's Narrative

'Look here, Lejeune, there are lots of things I want to know.'

The formalities over, I had got Lejeune to myself. We were sitting together with two large tankards of beer opposite us.

'Yes, Mr Easterbrook? I gather it was a surprise to you.'

'It certainly was. My mind was set on Venables. You never gave me the least hint.'

'I couldn't afford to give hints, Mr Easterbrook. You have to play these things close to your chest. They're tricky. The truth is we hadn't a lot to go on. That's why we had to stage the show in the way we did with Venables's co-operation. We had to lead Osborne right up the garden path and then turn on him suddenly and hope to break him down. And it worked.'

'Is he mad?' I asked.

'I'd say he's gone over the edge now. He wasn't to begin with, of course, but it does something to you, you know. Killing people. It makes you feel powerful and larger than

Agatha Christie

life. It makes you feel you're God Almighty. But you're not. You're only a nasty bit of goods that's been found out. And when that fact's presented to you suddenly your ego just can't stand it. You scream and you rant and you boast of what you've done and how clever you are. Well, you saw him.'

I nodded. 'So Venables was in on the performance you put up,' I said. 'Did he like the idea of cooperating?'

'It amused him, I think,' said Lejeune. 'Besides, he was impertinent enough to say that one good turn deserves another.'

'And what did he mean by that cryptic remark?'

'Well, I shouldn't be telling you this,' said Lejeune, 'this is off the record. There was a big outbreak of bank robberies about eight years ago. The same technique every time. *And* they got away with it! The raids were cleverly planned by someone who took no part in the actual operation. That man got away with a lot of money. We may have had our suspicions who it was, but we couldn't prove it. He was too clever for us. Especially on the financial angle. And he's had the sense never to try and repeat his success. I'm not saying more. He was a clever crook but he wasn't a murderer. No lives were lost.'

My mind went back to Zachariah Osborne. 'Did you always suspect Osborne?' I asked. 'Right from the beginning?'

'Well, he would draw attention to himself,' said Lejeune. 'As I told him, if he'd only sat back and done nothing, we'd never have dreamed that the respectable pharmacist, Mr Zachariah Osborne, had anything to do with the business. But it's a funny thing, that's just what murderers can't do. There they are, sitting pretty, safe as houses. But they can't let well alone. I'm sure I don't know why.'

'The desire for death,' I suggested. 'A variant of Thyrza Grey's theme.'

'The sooner you forget all about Miss Thyrza Grey and the things she told you, the better,' said Lejeune severely. 'No,' he said thoughtfully, 'I think really it's loneliness. The knowledge that you're such a clever chap, but that there's nobody you can talk to about it.'

'You haven't told me when you started to suspect him,' I said.

'Well, straight away he started telling lies. We asked for anyone who'd seen Father Gorman that night to communicate with us. Mr Osborne communicated and the statement he made was a palpable lie. He'd seen a man following Father Gorman and he described the features of that man, but he couldn't possibly have seen him across the street on a foggy night. An aquiline nose in profile he might have seen, but not an Adam's apple. That was going too far. Of course, that lie might have been innocent enough. Mr Osborne might just want to make himself important. Lots of people *are* like that. But it made me focus my attention on Mr Osborne and he was really rather a curious person. At once he started to tell me a lot about himself. Very unwise of him. He gave me a picture of someone who had always wanted to be more important than he was. He'd not been content to go into his father's old-fashioned business. He'd gone off and tried his fortunes on the stage, but he obviously hadn't been a success.

Probably, I should say, because he couldn't take production. Nobody was going to dictate to *him* the way he should play a part! He was probably genuine enough when he told of his ambition to be a witness in a murder trial, successfully identifying a man who had come in to buy poison. His mind ran on those lines a good deal, I should think. Of course we don't know at what point, and when, the idea occurred to him that he might become a really big criminal, a man so clever that he could never be brought to justice.

'But that's all surmise. To go back. Osborne's description of the man he had seen that night was interesting. It was so obviously a description of a real person whom he had at one time seen. It's extraordinarily difficult, you know, to make up a description of anybody. Eyes, nose, chin, ears, bearing, all the rest of it. If you try it you'll find yourself unconsciously describing somebody that you've noticed somewhere—in a tram or a train or an omnibus. Osborne was obviously describing a man with somewhat unusual characteristics. I'd say that he noticed Venables sitting in his car one day in Bournemouth and was struck by his appearance—if he'd seen him that way, he wouldn't realise the man was a cripple.

'Another reason that kept me interested in Osborne was that he was a pharmacist. I thought it just possible that that list we had might tie up with the narcotic trade somewhere. Actually that wasn't so, and I might, therefore, have forgotten all about Mr Osborne if Mr Osborne himself hadn't been determined to keep in the picture. He wanted, you see, to know just what we were doing, and so he writes to say that he's seen the man in question at a church fête in Much Deeping. He still didn't know that Mr Venables was a paralysis case. When he did find that out he hadn't the sense to shut up. That was his vanity. Typical criminal's vanity. He wasn't going to admit for one moment that he'd been wrong. Like a fool, he stuck to his guns and put forward all sorts of preposterous theories. I had a very interesting visit to him at his bungalow in Bournemouth. The name of it ought to have given the show away. Everest. That's what he called it. And he'd hung up a picture of Mount Everest in the hall. Told me how interested he was in Himalayan exploration. But that was the kind of cheap joke that he enjoyed. Ever rest. That was his trade—his profession. He did give people eternal rest on payment of a suitable fee. It was a wonderful idea, one's got to hand him that. The whole set-up was clever. Bradley in Birmingham, Thyrza Grey holding her *séances* in Much Deeping. And who was to suspect Mr Osborne who had no connection with Thyrza Grey, no connection with Bradley and Birmingham, no connection with the victim? The actual mechanics of the thing was child's play to a pharmacist. As I say, if only Mr Osborne had had the sense to keep quiet.'

'But what did he do with the money?' I asked. 'After all, he did it for money presumably?'

'Oh, yes, he did it for the money. Had grand visions, no doubt, of himself travelling, entertaining, being a rich and important person. But of course he wasn't the person he imagined himself to be. I think his sense of power was exhilarated by the actual performance of murder. To get away with murder again and again intoxicated him, and what's more, he'll enjoy himself in the dock. You see if he doesn't. The central figure with all eyes upon him.'

'But what did he *do* with the money?' I demanded.

'Oh, that's very simple,' said Lejeune, 'though I don't know that I should have thought of it unless I'd noticed the way he'd furnished the bungalow. He was a miser, of course. He loved money and he wanted money, but not for spending. That bungalow was sparsely furnished and all with stuff that he'd bought cheap at sales. He didn't like spending money, he just wanted to *have* it.'

'Do you mean he banked it all?'

'Oh no,' said Lejeune. 'I'd say we'll find it somewhere under the floor in that bungalow of his.'

Both Lejeune and I were silent for some minutes while I contemplated the strange creature that was Zachariah Osborne.

'Corrigan,' said Lejeune dreamily, 'would say it was all due to some gland in his spleen or his sweetbread or something either over-functioning or under-producing—I never can remember which. I'm a simple man—I think he's just a wrong 'un—What beats me—it always does—is how a man can be so clever and yet be such a perfect fool.'

'One imagines a master mind,' I said, 'as some grand and sinister figure of evil.'

Lejeune shook his head. 'It's not like that at all,' he said. 'Evil is not something superhuman, it's something *less* than human. Your criminal is someone who wants to be important, but who never will be important, because he'll always be less than a man.'

CHAPTER 25

Mark Easterbrook's Narrative

At Much Deeping everything was refreshingly normal.

Rhoda was busy doctoring dogs. This time, I think, it was deworming. She looked up as I came in and asked me if I would like to assist. I refused and asked where Ginger was.

'She's gone over to the Pale Horse.'

'*What?*'

'She said she had something to do there.'

'But the house is empty.'

'I know.'

'She'll overtire herself. She's not fit yet—'

'How you fuss, Mark. Ginger's all right. Have you seen Mrs Oliver's new book? It's called *The White Cockatoo*. It's over on the table there.'

'God bless Mrs Oliver. And Edith Binns, too.'

'Who on earth is Edith Binns?'

'A woman who has identified a photograph. Also faithful retainer to my late godmother.'

'Nothing you say seems to make sense. What's the matter with you?'

I did not reply, but set out for the Pale Horse.

Just before I got there, I met Mrs Dane Calthrop.

She greeted me enthusiastically.

'All along I knew I was being stupid,' she said. 'But I didn't see how. Taken in by trappings.'

She waved an arm towards the inn, empty and peaceful in the late autumn sunshine.

'The wickedness was never there—not in the sense it was supposed to be. No fantastic trafficking with the Devil, no black and evil splendour. Just parlour tricks done for money—and human life of no account. That's real wickedness. Nothing grand or big—just petty and contemptible.'

'You and Inspector Lejeune would seem to agree about things.'

'I like that man,' said Mrs Dane Calthrop. 'Let's go into the Pale Horse and find Ginger.'

'What's she doing there?'

'Cleaning up something.'

We went in through the low doorway. There was a strong smell of turpentine. Ginger was busy with rags and bottles. She looked up as we entered. She was still very pale and thin, a scarf wound round her head where the hair had not yet grown, a ghost of her former self.

'*She's* all right,' said Mrs Dane Calthrop, reading my thoughts as usual.

'Look!' said Ginger triumphantly.

She indicated the old inn sign on which she was working.

The grime of years removed, the figure of the rider on the horse was plainly discernible; a grinning skeleton with gleaming bones.

Mrs Dane Calthrop's voice, deep and sonorous, spoke behind me:

'Revelation, Chapter Six, Verse Eight. *And I looked, and behold a pale horse: and his name that sat on him was Death, and Hell followed with him . . .*'

We were silent for a moment or two, and then Mrs Dane Calthrop, who was not one to be afraid of anti-climax, said,

'So that's that,' in the tone of one who puts something in the wastepaper basket.

'I must go now,' she added. 'Mothers' Meeting.'

She paused in the doorway, nodded at Ginger, and said unexpectedly:

'You'll make a good mother.'

For some reason Ginger blushed crimson . . .

'Ginger,' I said, 'will you?'

'Will I what? Make a good mother?'

'You know what I mean.'

'Perhaps . . . But I'd prefer a firm offer.'

I made her a firm offer . . .

After an interlude, Ginger demanded:

'Are you quite sure you don't want to marry that Hermia creature?'

'Good lord!' I said. 'I quite forgot.'

I took a letter from my pocket.

'This came three days ago, asking me if I'd come to the Old Vic with her to see *Love's Labour's Lost*.'

Ginger took the letter out of my hand and tore it up.

'If you want to go to the Old Vic in future,' she said firmly, 'you'll go with me.'